THE 100

HOMECOMING

KASS MORGAN

HODDER

First published in the United States of America in 2015
by Little, Brown and Company

First published in Great Britain in 2015
by Hodder & Stoughton
An Hachette UK company

3

A CIP catalogue record for this title is available from the British Library

Paperback ISBN 978 1 473 61079 8
eBook ISBN 978 1 473 61080 4

Produced by Alloy Entertainment
1700 Broadway
New York, NY 10019
www.alloyentertainment.com

Printed and bound by CPI Group (UK) Ltd, Croydon CR0 4YY

Hodder & Stoughton policy is to use papers that are natural,
renewable and recyclable products and made from wood grown in
sustainable forests. The logging and manufacturing processes are expected
to conform to the environmental regulations of the country of origin.

Hodder & Stoughton Ltd
338 Euston Road
London NW1 3BH

www.hodder.co.uk

Praise for *The 100* series:

'Fantastic teen romance . . . packed with powerful and empowered characters'   *Starburst* magazine

'Fast-paced and engaging . . . there are multiple fascinating issues that appear to have arisen in this post-apocalyptic society'
The Book Bag

'An adventurous page-turner . . . dramatic, open, fast and accessible'
Adventures with Words

'It's incomparable to any other book alike, but for fans of *Divergent* and the classic *The Hunger Games*, you will adore this'
Pretty Little Memoirs

'I was practically glued to the pages'   City of Books

'An ingenious double-twist on the jeopardy-driven "lifeboat" scenario'
Evening Standard

'Both books are riveting. The story is exciting and powerful . . . a great read for young and old alike. It's pure excitement from page one to the end'   *Seattle P-I*

'If you haven't tried these series yet, I highly recommend it!'
I'd So Rather Be Reading

Kass Morgan received a BA from Brown University and a Master's degree from Oxford University. She currently works as an editor and lives in Brooklyn, New York.

Also by Kass Morgan and available from Hodder:

The 100

Day 21

*For Joelle Hobeika, whose imagination brings stories to life
and makes crazy dreams come true.
And for Annie Stone, editor extraordinaire.*

CHAPTER 1

Glass

Glass's hands were sticky with her mother's blood. The realization came to her slowly, as if through a thick haze—as if the hands belonged to someone else, and the blood was part of a nightmare. But they were her hands, and the blood was real.

Glass could feel her right palm sticking to the arm of her seat in the first row of the dropship. And she could feel someone squeezing her left hand, hard. It was Luke. He hadn't let go ever since he'd pulled Glass away from her mother's body and carried her to her seat. His fingers were grasping hers so tightly he might've been trying to siphon the pulsing pain out of her body and store it in his.

Glass tried to stay focused on the warmth of his hand on

hers. She concentrated on the strength of his grip, how he showed no signs of loosening his hold even when the dropship began shaking and dipping on its violent trajectory toward Earth.

Not more than a few minutes ago, Glass had been sitting in a seat next to her mother, ready to face the new world together. But now her mother was dead, shot by a deranged guard desperate for a spot on the last shuttle to escape the dying Colony. Glass squeezed her eyes shut, trying to stop the scene from playing out again in her mind: Her mother falling, silently, to the ground. Glass dropping onto the floor next to her mother as she gasped and moaned, unable to do anything to stop the bleeding. Glass, pulling her mother's head onto her lap and battling sobs to say how much she loved her. Watching the dark stain on her mother's dress spread as the life faded from her. Watching her face go slack, just after hearing those final words: *I'm so proud of you.*

There was no stopping the images, just as there was no changing the truth. Her mother was dead, and Glass and Luke were hurtling through space on a ship that would crash into Earth at any moment.

The dropship rattled loudly and jerked from side to side. Glass hardly noticed. She had the vague sensation of a harness digging into her ribs as her body followed the ship's movements, but the pain of her mother's death gouged deeper than the metal buckle.

She'd always imagined grief as a weight—that is, when she'd thought about it at all. The old Glass hadn't spent a great deal of time dwelling on other people's anguish. That changed after her best friend's mother died, and she'd watched Wells slump around the ship as if carrying an enormous, invisible burden. But Glass felt different—carved out, hollow, as if all emotion had been scraped out of her. The only thing reminding her that she was still alive was Luke's reassuring hand on hers.

People pressed against Glass from all sides. Every seat was filled, and men, women, and children stood in every spare inch of the cabin. They held on to each other for balance, though no one could fall down—they were packed too tightly, an undulating mass of flesh and quiet tears. Some whispered the names of people they'd left behind, while others jerked their heads wildly, refusing to accept that they'd said good-bye to loved ones for the last time.

The only person who didn't look panicked was the man sitting immediately to Glass's right, Vice Chancellor Rhodes. He was staring straight ahead, either oblivious or impervious to the distraught faces around him. A flash of indignation momentarily masked her pain. Wells's father, the Chancellor, would've been doing everything in his power to comfort those around him. Not that he would've accepted a spot on the final dropship in the first place. But Glass was hardly in a position to judge. The only reason she'd made it onto the dropship was because Rhodes had brought Glass and her mother with him when he forced his way on board.

A violent jolt threw Glass back against her seat as the dropship lurched sideways, then tilted almost forty-five degrees before righting itself with a stomach-turning swoop. A child's wail cut through the collective gasp. Several people shrieked as the metal frame of the dropship began buckling, as if caught in the grasp of a giant fist. A high-pitched, mechanical whine screeched through the cabin, threatening to burst their eardrums, drowning out the cries and terrified sobs.

Glass gripped the arm of her seat and clutched Luke's hand, waiting for the surge of fear. But it never came. She knew she should be afraid, but the events of the past few days had left her numb. It was hard enough watching her home fall apart as the Colony ran out of oxygen. Hard enough risking an insane, unauthorized spacewalk to make it from Walden to Phoenix, where there was still breathable air. Everything she'd gone through had seemed worth it, though, when Glass, her mother, and Luke had made it onto the dropship. But at this moment, Glass didn't care if she never got to see Earth. Better to end it all now than have to wake up every morning and remember that her mother was gone.

She glanced to the side and saw Luke staring straight ahead, his face a stony mask of resolve. Was he trying to be brave for her? Or had his extensive guard training taught him how to remain calm under pressure? He deserved better than this. After everything Glass had put him through, was this how it was going to end? Had they escaped certain death on the Colony only to hurtle headlong into a different horrific fate? Humans weren't scheduled to return to Earth for at least another century, when scientists were sure the radiation left after the Cataclysm would have subsided. This was a premature homecoming, a desperate exodus promising nothing but uncertainty.

Glass looked over at the row of small windows lining the vessel. Hazy gray clouds filled each portal. It was oddly beautiful, she thought, just as the windows suddenly popped and shattered, spraying shards of hot glass and metal throughout the cabin. Flames shot through the broken panes. The people closest to the windows frantically tried to duck and move away, but there was nowhere to go. They leaned backward, falling onto the people behind them. The tang of scorched metal burned Glass's nostrils, while the scent of something else made her gag. . . . With rising fear, Glass realized it was the smell of burned flesh.

Pushing hard against the force of the ship's velocity, she turned her head to look at Luke. For a moment, Glass couldn't hear the sounds of whimpering and crying or the crunch of metal. She couldn't feel her mother's last breath. She could only see the side of Luke's face, the perfect profile and strong jaw that she'd traced in her mind night after night during those terrible months in Confinement, when she'd been sentenced to die on her eighteenth birthday.

Glass was brought back to reality by the sound of metal ripping from metal. It vibrated through her eardrums and down into her jaw, through her bones and into her gut. She ground her teeth together. She watched in helpless horror as the roof peeled off and flew away, as if it were nothing more than a scrap of fabric.

She forced herself to turn back to Luke, who'd closed his eyes but was now gripping her hand with renewed intensity.

"I love you," she said, but her words were swallowed up by the screams all around them. Suddenly, with a bone-shaking crack, the dropship slammed into Earth, and everything went black.

———

In the distance, Glass heard a low, guttural moaning, a sound full of more anguish than anything she'd ever heard. She tried to open her eyes, but the slightest effort sent her head into a sickening spin. She gave up and allowed herself to sink back into the darkness. A few moments passed. Or was it a few hours? Again, she struggled against the comforting quiet, fighting her way toward consciousness. For a sweet, groggy millisecond, she had no idea where she was. All she could focus on was the barrage of strange smells. Glass hadn't known it was possible to smell so many things at once: There was something she sort of recognized from the solar fields—her favorite spot to meet Luke—but amplified a thousand times over. There was something sweet, but not like sugar or perfume. Deeper, richer. Every breath she took sent her brain into overdrive as it struggled to identify the swirling scents. Something spicy. Metallic. Then a familiar scent jolted her brain to attention. Blood.

Glass's eyes fluttered open. She was in a space so large she couldn't see the walls, and the transparent, star-filled ceiling looked like it was miles away. Slowly, her awareness clicked into place, and her confusion gave way to awe. She was looking up at the sky—the real sky, on Earth—and she was alive. But her wonder lasted only a few moments before an urgent thought ripped through her brain, and panic shot through her body. *Where was Luke?* She snapped into alertness and pushed herself into an upright position, ignoring the nausea and pain that tried to force her back to the ground.

"Luke!" she cried out, jerking her head from side to side, praying to see his familiar outline among the mass of unfamiliar shadows. *"Luke!"* The growing chorus of screams and wails swallowed her cries. *Why won't someone turn on the lights?* she thought groggily, before remembering that she was on the ground. The stars gave off nothing more than a dull glimmer, and the moon offered just enough light for Glass to tell that the moaning, flailing black shapes were her fellow passengers. This had to be a nightmare. This wasn't what Earth was supposed to be like. This wasn't a place worth dying for. She called for Luke again, but there was no response.

She needed to stand, but her body felt strangely heavy, as if invisible weights were tugging on her limbs. Gravity here felt different, harsher—or was she injured? Glass placed her hand on her shin and gasped. Her legs were wet. Was she bleeding? She glanced down, afraid of what she might find. Her pant legs were torn, and the skin underneath was badly scratched, but there were no visible wounds. She placed her hands on the floor, no, *ground*, and gasped. She was sitting in water—water that stretched out far in front of her across an impossibly vast distance, with only the faintest shadow of trees at its far edge. Glass blinked, waiting for her eyes to recalibrate and reveal something that made more sense, but the image didn't change. *Lake*. The word slid smoothly into her mind. She was sitting on the edge, on the *shore*, of a lake on Earth—a fact that felt as surreal to her as the devastation surrounding her on every side. When she turned to look, she saw only horror: Bodies lying limp and broken on the ground. Wounded people crying and begging for help. The mangled, smoking shells of several dropships that had all landed within a few meters of each other, their frames cracked open and splintered. People running into the still smoldering wreckage, then clambering back out with heavy, still figures draped over their shoulders.

Who had carried her out? If it was Luke, where was he?

Glass struggled to her feet, her legs shaky beneath her. She locked her knees to prevent them from giving way and swung her arms out to regain her balance. She stood in the icy water, cold creeping up her legs. She took a deep breath and felt her head clear slightly, although her legs continued to tremble. She took a few wobbly steps forward and knocked her foot against a few rocks below the surface.

Glass looked down and inhaled sharply. There was just enough moonlight to tell that the water was tinged a deep pink. Did the pollution and radiation of the Cataclysm cause lakes to change color? Or was there an area of Earth where water was naturally pink? She'd never paid much attention in her Earth geography tutorials—a fact she was starting to regret more and more by the second. But a desperate cry from a crumpled figure on the ground nearby brought the painful answer to her mind: This wasn't a long-lasting side effect of radiation—the water was colored with blood.

She shuddered, then walked toward the woman who had

called out. She was slumped on the shore, the bottom half of her body in the rapidly reddening water. Glass stooped down and took her hand. "Don't worry, you're going to be fine," she said, hoping she sounded more certain than she felt. The woman's eyes were wide with fear and pain. "Have you seen Thomas?" she wheezed.

"Thomas?" Glass repeated, scanning the shadow landscape of bodies and wreckage. She needed to find Luke. The only thing more terrifying than being on Earth was the thought of Luke lying somewhere out there, injured and alone.

"My son, Thomas," the woman said, tightening her grip on Glass's hand. "We were on different dropships. My neighbor—" She cut herself off with an anguished gasp. "She promised she'd take care of him."

"We'll find him," Glass said, wincing as the woman's fingernails dug into her skin. She hoped that the first sentence she'd spoken on Earth didn't turn out to be a lie. She thought back to the chaotic scene she'd barely escaped back on the ship: The crush of wheezing people filling the launch deck, desperate for one of the remaining seats off the dying Colony. The frantic parents who'd become separated from their children. The blue-lipped, shell-shocked kids searching for the family members they'd probably never lay eyes on again.

Glass only managed to escape when the woman cried out in pain and let her hand fall back to the water. "I'll look for him," Glass said shakily as she started to inch away. "We'll find him."

The guilt building in her stomach was almost enough to stop Glass in her tracks, but she knew she had to keep moving. There was nothing she could do to ease this woman's suffering. She wasn't a doctor like Wells's girlfriend, Clarke. She wasn't even a people person, like Wells or Luke, who both always knew the right thing to say at the right time. There was only one person on the planet she had any power to help, and she had to find him before it was too late.

"I'm sorry," Glass whispered, turning back to face the woman, whose face was contorted in pain. "I'll come back for you. I need to go find my—someone."

The woman nodded through a clenched jaw and squeezed her eyes shut, tears sneaking from behind her eyelids.

Glass wrenched her gaze away and kept walking. She squinted, trying to make sense of the scene in front of her. The combination of the darkness, the dizziness, the smoke, and the shock of being on Earth seemed to make everything a blur. The dropships had landed on the edge of a lake, leaving piles of smoldering wreckage everywhere she looked. In the distance, she could just make out the faint outline of trees, but she was too distraught to give them more than a fleeting glance. What good were trees or even flowers if Luke wasn't there to see any of it with her?

Her eyes darted from one dazed and battered survivor to another. An old man sat on a large piece of metal torn from the dropship, his head in his hands. A young boy with a bloody face stood alone, just a few meters away from a tangle of sizzling, sparking wires. Oblivious to the danger, he stood staring blankly up at the sky, as if searching for a way to get back home.

All around lay the broken bodies of the dead. People with the ghosts of heart-wrenching good-byes still on their lips, people who'd never even gotten a glimpse of the blue sky they'd sacrificed everything to see. They would've been better off staying behind, taking their last breaths surrounded by their friends and families instead of being left here, all alone.

Still a little unsteady on her feet, Glass staggered toward the nearest figures on the ground, praying with all her might that none of the lifeless faces had Luke's strong chin, narrow nose, or curly blond hair. She sighed with bittersweet relief as she looked down at the first person. Not Luke. With equal parts dread and hope, she moved to the next body. And the next. She held her breath as she rolled people onto their backs or pushed heavy chunks of wreckage off them. With each bloody, battered stranger, she exhaled and allowed herself to believe that Luke might still be alive.

"Are you okay?"

Startled, Glass jerked her head to the side to follow the voice. A man with a large gash above his left eye was looking at her quizzically.

"Yes, I'm fine," she said automatically.

"You sure? Shock can do crazy things to the body."

"I'm okay. I'm just looking . . ." She trailed off, unable to shape the mass of panic and hope in her chest into words.

The man nodded. "Good. I already checked this area, but if you find any survivors I missed, just shout. We're gathering the injured over there." He pointed a finger into the darkness where, in the distance, Glass could just make out the shapes of bent figures hovering over still forms on the ground.

"There's a woman, over by the water. I think she's hurt."

"Okay, we'll go get her."

He signaled to someone Glass couldn't see, then broke into a lurching jog. She felt a strange urge to call out, to tell him that it was better to look for the missing Thomas first. Glass felt sure that the woman would rather bleed out in the water than face a lifetime on Earth without the only person who made her life worth living. But the man was already gone.

Glass took a deep breath and willed herself to keep moving, but her feet no longer seemed connected to her brain. If Luke were unharmed, wouldn't he have found her by now? The fact that she hadn't heard his deep voice calling her name through the din meant that, at best, he was lying somewhere, too hurt to move. And at worst . . .

Glass tried to resist the grim thoughts, but it was like attempting to shove a shadow. Nothing could keep the darkness out of her mind. It would be unimaginably cruel to lose Luke mere hours after their reunion. She couldn't go through it again, not after what happened to her mother. No. Choking back a sob, she rose onto the balls of her feet and looked around. There was more light now. Some of the survivors had used the burning pieces of dropship to create makeshift torches, but the jagged, flashing light was hardly comforting. Everywhere she looked, Glass saw glimpses of mangled bodies and panicked faces emerging from the shadows.

The trees were closer now. She could see the bark, the twisted branches, the canopy of leaves. After spending her whole life staring at one solitary tree, it was startling to see so many all together, like turning a corner and facing a dozen clones of your best friend.

Glass turned to glance at one particularly large tree and gasped. A boy with curly hair was slumped against the trunk.

A boy in a guard's uniform.

"Luke!" Glass shouted, breaking into a jerky run. As she got closer, she saw that his eyes were closed. Was he unconscious or . . .

"*Luke!*" she cried again before the thought could gain traction.

Glass's limbs felt both clumsy and electrified, like a reanimated corpse. She tried to speed up, but the ground seemed to be pulling her down. Even from a dozen meters away, she could tell: It was Luke. His eyes were closed, his body slack, but he was breathing. *He was alive.*

Glass fell to her knees by his side and fought the urge to throw herself across him. She didn't want to hurt him any further. "Luke," she whispered. "Can you hear me?"

He was pale, and over his eye there was a deep cut, which oozed blood down the bridge of his nose. Glass pulled her sleeve down over her hand and pressed it against the cut. Luke moaned slightly but didn't move. She pressed a little harder, hoping to staunch the bleeding, and looked down to survey the rest of him. His left wrist was purple and swollen, but apart from that, he looked okay. Tears of relief and gratitude sprang to her eyes, and she let them slide down her cheeks. After a few minutes, she took her sleeve away and examined the wound again. It looked like the bleeding had stopped.

Glass put a hand on his chest. "Luke," she said gently. She ran her fingers lightly over his collarbone. "Luke. It's me. Wake up."

Luke stirred at the sound of her voice, and Glass let out a mangled sound that was part laugh, part sob. He groaned, his eyelids fluttering open and sinking closed again. "Luke, wake up," Glass repeated, then brought her mouth to his ear, just like she used to do on mornings when he was in danger of missing check-in at work. "You're going to be late," she said with a small smile.

His eyes opened again, slowly, and fixed on her. He tried to speak, but no sound came out. Instead he smiled back.

"Hey there," Glass said, feeling her fear and sorrow melt away for a moment. "It's okay. You're okay. We're here, Luke. We made it. Welcome to Earth."

CHAPTER 2

Wells

"You look exhausted," Sasha said, tilting her head to the side so her long black hair spilled across her shoulder. "Why don't you go to bed?"

"I'd rather be here with you." Wells suppressed a yawn by turning it into a grin. It wasn't hard. Every time he looked at Sasha, he noticed something that made him smile. The way her green eyes glowed in the flickering light of the campfire. How the smattering of freckles on her sharp cheekbones could be as fascinating to him as the nighttime constellations were to her. She was staring at them now, her chin pointed upward as she gazed in wonder at the sky.

"I can't believe you *lived* up there," she said quietly before lowering her eyes to meet Wells's. "Don't you miss it? Being surrounded by stars?"

"It's even more beautiful down here." He raised his hand, placed a finger on Sasha's cheek, then gently traced a path from one freckle to another. "I could stare at your face all night. I couldn't do that with the Big Dipper."

"I'd be surprised if you lasted five more minutes. You can barely keep your eyes open."

"It's been a long day."

Sasha raised an eyebrow, and Wells smiled. They both knew that was a bit of an understatement. Over the past few hours, Wells had been kicked out of the camp for helping Sasha—the hundred's former prisoner—escape. That was before he ran into Clarke and Bellamy, who had just rescued Bellamy's sister, Octavia, thereby proving that Sasha's people, the Earthborns, weren't the enemy they'd once appeared to be. That alone would've been a lot to explain to the rest of the camp members, most of whom were still a little uneasy around Sasha, but it was only the beginning. Just that evening, Bellamy and Wells had made a shocking discovery. Although Wells, the son of the Chancellor, had grown up privileged on Phoenix, while Bellamy, an orphan, had scraped by on Walden, they were in fact half brothers.

It was all too much to process. And while Wells was mostly happy, the shock and confusion kept the full weight of the news from sinking in. That, and the fact that he hadn't had a good night's sleep in ages. Over the past few weeks, he'd become the de facto leader of the camp. It wasn't a position he'd necessarily sought, but his officer training combined with his lifelong fascination with Earth had given him a certain set of skills. Yet, while he was glad to be able to help, and grateful for the group's trust, the position came with an enormous amount of responsibility.

"Maybe I'll rest for a minute," he said, lowering his elbows to the ground, then lying back so he could rest his head in Sasha's lap. Although he and Sasha were sitting apart from the rest of the group gathered around the campfire, the crackle of the flames didn't fully mask the sound of the typical evening arguments. It was just a matter of time before someone came rushing over to complain that someone else had taken her cot, or to get Wells to settle a dispute about water duty, or to ask what they were meant to do with the scraps from that day's hunt.

Wells sighed as Sasha ran her fingers through his hair, and for a moment, he forgot about everything except the warmth of her skin as he let his head sink against her. He forgot about the terrible week they'd just had, the violence they had witnessed. He forgot about finding the body of his friend Priya. He forgot that his father had been shot in front of his eyes during a scuffle with Bellamy, who'd been desperate to get onto the dropship with his sister. He forgot about the fire that had destroyed their original camp and killed Clarke's friend, Thalia—a tragedy that had severed the last remaining bonds of his and Clarke's romance.

Maybe he and Sasha could spend the whole night out in the clearing. It was the only way they'd get any privacy. He smiled at the idea and felt himself sinking deeper toward sleep.

"What the hell?" Sasha's hand stopped suddenly, and there was a note of anxiety in her voice.

"What's wrong?" Wells asked as his eyes snapped open. "Is everything okay?"

He sat up and took a quick survey of the clearing. Most of the hundred were still huddled in clumps around the fire, speaking in low murmurs that blended into a soothing hum. But then his gaze fell on Clarke, and although she was curled up next to Bellamy, he could tell she was focused on something else entirely. Although his intense, all-consuming feelings for her had evolved into something akin to real friendship, he could still read her like a tablet. He knew her every expression: the way she pursed her lips in concentration when studying a medical procedure, or how her eyes practically sparkled when talking about one of her weird interests, like biological classification or theoretical physics. Right now, her brows were knitted together in concern as she threw her head back, assessing and calculating something in the sky. Bellamy's head was tilted up too, his expression stony. He turned and whispered something in Clarke's ear, an intimate gesture that would've once made Wells's stomach roil, but now only filled him with apprehension.

Wells looked up but didn't see anything unusual. Just stars. Sasha was still staring at the sky. "What is it?" Wells asked, placing his hand on her back.

"There." Sasha's voice tightened as she pointed straight up into the night, high above the infirmary cabin and the trees that ringed the clearing. She knew this sky as well as he knew the stars up close. An Earthborn, she'd been looking up her whole life, while he'd been looking down. Wells followed her finger and saw it: a swiftly moving bright light, arcing toward Earth. Toward them. Just behind it was another, then two more. Together they looked like a star shower, raining down on the peaceful gathering around the fire.

Wells inhaled sharply as his entire body went rigid.

"The dropships," he said quietly. "They're coming down. All of them." He felt Sasha's body tense next to his. He wrapped his arm around her shoulders and pulled her close as they watched the descending ships in silence for a moment, their breath falling into the same rhythm.

"Do you . . . do you think your father's on one of them?" Sasha asked, clearly trying to sound more hopeful than she felt. While the Earthborns had come to terms with sharing the planet with a hundred juvenile delinquents in exile, Wells sensed that facing the entire population of the Colony was an entirely different matter.

Wells fell silent as hope and dread battled for supremacy in his already overtaxed brain. There was a chance that his father's injury hadn't been as serious as it'd appeared, that he'd made a full recovery and was making his way down to Earth. Then again, there was also a chance that the Chancellor was still clinging to life in the medical center—or worse, already floating still and silent among the stars. What would he do if his father didn't disembark from one of those dropships? How could Wells go on knowing that he'd never get to win the Chancellor's forgiveness for the terrible crimes Wells committed back on the Colony?

Wells tore his eyes away and twisted around to look across the fire. Clarke had turned to look at him, and they locked eyes, which filled Wells with a flood of sudden gratitude. They didn't have to exchange a single word. She understood his mixture of relief and dread. She knew how much he stood to gain or lose when those doors opened.

"He's going to be so proud of you," Sasha said, squeezing Wells's hand.

Despite his anxiety, Wells felt his face soften into a smile. Sasha understood too. Even though she'd never met Wells's father, even though she'd never witnessed their complicated relationship, she also knew what it was like to grow up with a parent responsible for the well-being of an entire community. Or in Wells's case, a parent responsible for all known survivors of the human race. Sasha's father was the leader of the Earthborns, just as Wells's father was leader of the Colony. She knew what it meant to bear the weight of that duty. Sasha understood that being a leader was as much a sacrifice as it was an honor.

Wells looked around the fire at the gaunt, exhausted faces of the nearly one hundred teenagers who'd survived the traumatic first few weeks on Earth. Normally, the sight filled him with various degrees of worry as he fretted about food stores and other rapidly dwindling supplies, but this time, all he felt was relief. Relief and pride. They'd done it. Despite the odds, they'd *survived*, and now help was on its way. Even if his father wasn't on one of those dropships, there would be huge amounts of rations, tools, medicine— everything they needed to make it through the upcoming winter and beyond.

He couldn't wait to see the look on the new arrivals' faces when they saw how much the hundred had accomplished. They had certainly made some mistakes along the way, and there had been horrible losses—Asher and Priya, almost Octavia—but there had been triumphs too.

Wells turned his head and saw Sasha staring at him in concern. He grinned, and before she had time to react, he tangled his fingers in her glossy hair and brought his lips to hers. She seemed surprised at first, but soon relaxed into him and kissed him back. He rested his forehead against hers for a moment, gathering his thoughts, then stood. It was time to tell the others.

He shot a quick glance at Clarke, silently asking for her consent. She pressed her lips together and turned briefly to Bellamy before meeting Wells's eyes and nodding.

Wells cleared his throat, which caught a few people's attention, but not many. "Can everyone hear me?" he asked, raising his voice to be heard over the buzz of conversation and the crackle of flames.

A few meters away, Graham exchanged a sneer with one of his Arcadian friends. When they'd first landed on Earth, he'd led the charge against Wells, trying to convince the others that the Chancellor's son had been sent as a spy. And while most of the hundred had grown loyal to Wells, Graham hadn't lost all his power—there was still a considerable portion of the camp who feared Graham more than they trusted Wells.

Lila, a pretty Waldenite who fawned over Graham, whispered something to him, then giggled loudly at whatever he whispered back.

"Will you shut up?" Octavia snapped, shooting them a dark look. "Wells is trying to talk."

Lila glared at Octavia and muttered something under her breath, but Graham looked mildly amused. Maybe it was because Octavia had spent less time in camp than the others, but she was one of the few who wasn't intimidated by Graham, and she was willing to stand up to him.

"What's going on, Wells?" Eric asked. The tall, serious-faced Arcadian was holding the hand of his boyfriend, Felix, who'd recently recovered from a mysterious illness. Though naturally undemonstrative, Eric's relief had temporarily overpowered his reserve. Wells hadn't seen him let go of Felix's hand all day.

Wells smiled. Soon, they wouldn't have to worry about battling strange diseases. There would be fully trained doctors on those dropships. Doctors with more medicine than there had been on Earth in centuries.

"We did it," Wells said, unable to contain his excitement. "We lasted long enough to prove that Earth is survivable, and the others are on their way." He pointed up at the sky with a grin.

Dozens of heads snapped up, the flickering flames reflecting on their faces. A chorus of whoops and cries—and a few curses—rang out in the clearing as everyone jumped to their feet. The ships were low in the sky now, descending rapidly, picking up speed as they approached Earth.

"My mom is coming!" a young girl named Molly said, bouncing from side to side. "She promised me she'd be on the first ship."

Two Walden girls clutched each other and began squealing, while Antonio, a normally cheerful Waldenite who'd grown quiet in recent days, started muttering to himself. "We did it . . . we did it . . ."

"Remember what my father told us," Wells said, shouting over the noise. "About our crimes being forgiven. From this point on, we're regular citizens again." He paused, then grinned. "Actually, that's not entirely true. You're not regular citizens—you're heroes."

There was a smattering of applause, but it was quickly drowned out by a piercing screech that suddenly filled the air. It seemed to emanate from the sky itself and grew to a deafening volume, forcing everyone in the clearing to cover their ears.

"They're about to land," Felix shouted.

"Where?" a girl asked in response.

It was impossible to say, but it was clear that the ships were coming in fast and hard, with no detectable control over their approach. Wells watched in helpless shock as the first vessel passed directly overhead, just a few kilometers above them, so low that showers of burning debris singed the tops of the tallest trees.

Wells cursed under his breath. If the trees caught on fire, it wouldn't matter who was on those dropships—they'd all be dead before morning.

"Great," Bellamy said, loud enough to be heard over the din. "We risk our lives to prove that Earth is safe, just so they can come down and set it on fire." His voice had its usual careless, mocking tone, but Wells could tell Bellamy was scared. Unlike the others, he'd forced his way onto the dropship—and gotten the Chancellor shot in the process. There was no way of knowing whether Bellamy would be forgiven for his crimes, or whether the guards had orders to shoot him on sight.

As the dropship moved past the clearing, Wells caught a glimpse of the letters on the side—Trillion Galactic, the company that built the ships generations ago. His stomach twisted as he realized that one was flying on its side, at a full forty-five-degree angle to Earth. What could that mean for everyone inside the cabin? It passed over the clearing, disappearing behind the tops of the tallest trees, continuing its descent out of their line of vision.

Wells held his breath, waiting. After a tortured moment, a flash of light and fire exploded far out beyond the trees. It was at least a few kilometers from their camp, but seemed as bright as a solar flare. A millisecond later came the delayed sound of the crash, a deep thundering that drowned out all other noise. Before anyone could process what they'd just seen, the second ship passed directly over their heads and landed in the same catastrophic fashion, sending up more light and noise. A third ship followed.

Each crash shook the ground, sending violent vibrations up through Wells's feet and into his stomach. Was this what happened when their ship crashed? Their landing had also been terrible—a few people had even been killed. The frightening noises stopped abruptly. As Earth grew quiet again, flames shot into the sky, coloring the darkness, and smoke began to curl upward. Wells turned away from the trees and back to the others. Their faces, illuminated in the orange light from above, asked the same question that was repeating on a loop in his own head: *Could anyone have survived that?*

"We have to go to them," Eric said firmly, raising his voice to be heard over the chorus of gasps and nervous murmurs.

"How will we find them?" Molly asked, trembling. Wells knew she hated being in the woods, especially at night.

"It looks like they might've landed near the lake," Wells replied, rubbing his fingers in circles against his temples. "But they could be much farther." *If anyone even survived*, he thought. He didn't need to say it out loud. They were all thinking the same thing. Wells turned back toward the crash. The flames rising above the trees were subsiding, shrinking down into the woods. "We better start moving. Once that fire goes out, there's no way we'll be able to find them in the dark."

"Wells," Sasha murmured, placing a hand on his shoulder, "maybe you should wait until morning. It's not safe out there."

Wells hesitated. Sasha was right about the danger. There was a violent faction of Earthborns who'd rebelled against her father and were now roaming the woods in between Mount Weather and the hundred's camp. They were the ones who'd kidnapped Octavia, who'd killed Asher and Priya. But he couldn't bear the thought of the injured and scared Colonists waiting for their help.

"We won't all go," Wells said to the group. "I just need a few volunteers to take emergency supplies and lead everyone back to camp." He looked around the clearing they'd worked so hard to turn into a home and felt a surge of pride.

Octavia took a few steps toward Wells so she was standing in the center of the circle. She was only fourteen, but unlike the other younger members of the group, she wasn't shy about speaking up. "I say we let them find their own way," she said, raising her chin defiantly. "Or better yet, they can just stay where they are. They pretty much sentenced us to die when they sent us down here. Why should we risk our lives going to rescue them?" A murmur of assent rippled around the crowd. Octavia shot a quick glance at her brother, maybe seeking his support, but when Wells looked at Bellamy, his face was strangely inscrutable.

"Are you *kidding*?" Felix asked, looking at Octavia with dismay. His voice was still weak from his illness, but his anxiety was clear. "If there's even the slightest chance that my parents are out there, then I have to try to find them. Tonight." He stepped closer to Eric, who put an arm around Felix's shoulders and squeezed him tight.

"And I'm going with him," Eric said.

Wells scanned the group for Clarke and Bellamy. They met his eye, then Clarke took Bellamy's hand and hurried along the outer edge of the circle to where Wells was standing.

"I should go too," Clarke said quietly. "There are probably injured people who need my help."

Wells glanced over at Bellamy, waiting for him to object to the risk. But he'd gone tense and quiet, staring into the darkness beyond Wells. Perhaps he knew it was futile to argue with Clarke when she had her mind set on something.

"Okay," Wells said. "Let's get ready. Most of you should stay here and prepare the camp for new arrivals."

Clarke ran to the infirmary cabin for the medical supplies, while Wells assigned other people to carry drinking water and blankets. "Eric, can you find some food—anything we've got."

As his team scurried off to prepare, Wells turned back to Sasha, who was still standing next to him, her lips pressed together in concentration. "We should bring something to use as a stretcher," she said, casting an appraising glance around the cleáring. "There might be people who can't walk back." She started toward the supply tent without waiting for Wells to reply.

He broke into a jog after her. "Smart thinking," he said, matching her quick strides. "But I don't think it's a good idea for you to come with us."

She stopped abruptly. "What are you talking about? None of you know the terrain as well as I do. If anyone can get you there and back safely, it's me."

Wells sighed. She was right, of course, but the thought of Sasha facing hundreds of Colonists—and, most likely, many armed guards—who had no idea Earthborns even existed sent a jolt of fear through him. He remembered the shock and disorientation he'd felt when he first laid eyes on her—it was as if his entire understanding of the universe had been flipped on its head. He certainly hadn't trusted her at first, and it had taken the rest of his group even longer to believe that she was telling the truth about belonging to a peaceful community of people living on Earth.

Wells shifted his weight from side to side as he stared into Sasha's almond-shaped eyes, which were already burning with defiance. She was beautiful, and she was anything but fragile. She had proven how well she could take care of herself, and she didn't need him to protect her. But all the strength and intelligence in the world wouldn't be able to stop the bullet of a panicked guard.

"I just don't want you to get hurt," he said, grabbing her hand. "They all think the planet is empty. Now's probably not the right time for them to learn about Earthborns. Not when they're disoriented and scared. The guards could do something stupid."

"But I'll be *helping* them," Sasha said, her voice a mix of patience and confusion. "It'll be pretty clear that I'm not the enemy."

Wells fell silent, thinking about all the patrols he'd gone on during officer training. The people he'd seen arrested for crimes as minor as breaking curfew by five minutes or accidentally entering a restricted area. He knew that strict order was absolutely necessary on the ship, but it'd be hard for the guards to abandon their mantra of shoot first, ask questions later.

"The thing you have to understand about my people—"

She cut him off by placing her hands on his shoulders, rising onto her toes, and silencing him with a kiss. "Your people *are* my people now."

"I hope they get that quote right in the history books," he said with a smile.

"I thought *you* wanted to write that book." She put on what he assumed was the Earthborn version of a snooty voice. "*A firsthand account of man's return to Earth.* Sounds like a great read, except for the fact that, you know, some people never left."

"You better watch it, or else I'll take some artistic liberties with your description."

"What? You'll say I was horribly ugly? See if I care."

Wells reached out to tuck a strand of long hair behind her ear. "I'll say that you were so beautiful, you made me do ridiculous, reckless things."

She smiled, and for a moment, every thought drained from Wells's brain except for how much he wanted to kiss her again. Then their reverie was broken by voices calling out through the darkness. "Wells? We're ready." The bitter smell of smoke from the crash site had begun wafting through the trees, filling their noses.

"Okay," he said to Sasha, his voice firm. "Let's go."

CHAPTER 3

Clarke

Clarke stared at the crash scene, eyes straining in the dark, waiting for the inevitable moment when her training would kick in, when her instincts would anesthetize her panic. But hovering at the edge of the wide expanse of debris, absorbing the destruction, all she felt was horror.

It was far worse than when the hundred had landed. From what she could see, three dropships had slammed into the ground just a few dozen meters apart. It was amazing that they hadn't crashed on top of each other. Their jagged metal carcasses protruded from the earth around the water's edge, looming high above the surface of the lake. Motionless bodies were scattered everywhere. The fires had mostly gone out, but the stench of burning metal lay heavy on the air.

Even worse than the sight of so many bodies was the growing number of wounded. By Clarke's quick estimation, there were three hundred and fifty or so survivors in various states of distress.

"Holy . . ." Wells's voice trailed off next to her. But within moments, his expression hardened into resolve. "Okay," he said, taking a deep breath. "Where do we start?"

Clarke's brain kicked into gear, and a familiar calmness stole over her as she began to mentally triage the people in her sightline—sorting the ones with mangled limbs from the ones who sat up on their own, beginning with the children and moving upward in age.

They could do this. She could do this. Each of the dropships had to be stocked with medical supplies. She had a lot more to work with this time around, and she'd learned a massive amount over the past few weeks. Besides, there had to be at least one or two fully qualified doctors among the passengers. She could only hope that they were among the survivors. She winced as a pang of regret radiated through her chest. She needed her parents more than ever, but was no closer to finding them than she had been when she left the camp days ago.

"Start separating them into groups," she said to Wells, Sasha, and the other members of the rescue party. "Leave the worst injuries where they are and lead anyone who can walk back to the clearing."

"What about the people in between?" Eric asked. "Should we let them rest here or get them moving?"

"Everyone needs to get moving, as fast as possible," Wells said before Clarke could answer. "The dropships could blow at any moment. We'll break into two teams. One half starts from the left, one from the right."

Clarke nodded, distributed the bandages and other basic medical supplies, then headed into the center of the fray. She stepped over piles of twisted metal and shards of fiberglass, and knelt down next to a little boy whose dark skin was caked with gray ash. He was sitting with his knees pulled to his chest as he stared straight ahead, wide-eyed and whimpering.

"Hey," Clarke said, placing her hand on his shoulder. "I'm Clarke. What's your name?"

He didn't answer. There was no sign that he'd even heard Clarke or felt the pressure of her touch.

"I know you're scared. But everything's going to be okay. You're going to love it here, I promise."

She stood up and beckoned to Eric, who ran over.

"He's fine. Just in shock. Can you find someone to look after him?"

Eric nodded, scooped the little boy into his arms, and hurried away.

Off to the left, Clarke could see Wells reassuring a middle-aged woman. He helped her to her feet and walked her over to Sasha, who was getting ready to bring the first group of survivors back to the camp. An icy chill ran down Clarke's spine when she saw a young man in a guard uniform standing among them. Bellamy had promised to stay out of sight for the time being, but it wouldn't take much to draw him into a confrontation. What if something happened to him while she was gone?

"Clarke!" She turned to see Felix signaling for her. "We need your help over here."

She hurried over and found him kneeling next to a young girl with long, tangled, strawberry-blond hair. Felix had tried to bandage her arm, but it was already soaked through with blood. "It won't stop," he whispered, his face pale. "You need to do something."

"I got it," Clarke said. "You keep moving."

She unwrapped the bandaged and surveyed the wound. "Am I going to die?" the girl whispered hoarsely.

Clarke shook her head and smiled. "Nope. No way I'm going to let that happen. Not before you get the chance to explore Earth!" She reached into her kit and pulled out the antiseptic, praying that she'd find some more at the crash site. She was almost out. "Guess what I saw the other day?" she said, trying to distract the girl as she prepared to stitch the deep gash in her arm. "A real live rabbit."

"Really?" The girl turned her head to the side, as if expecting to see one hop out from behind a pile of wreckage.

Ten minutes later, the girl was being led away by Wells, freeing Clarke to deal with the more seriously injured. It was distressing to see so many people in pain, but the intense focus it required provided a welcome relief from her thoughts.

Clarke had spent the past few days in a haze, each new development or revelation proving more bewildering than the last. She had gotten back together with Bellamy, who had somehow found a way to forgive her for what she had done to Lilly. Then they had rescued Octavia from Sasha's faction of Earthborns—who in turn had rescued Octavia from the violent splinter group.

But the thing that made Clarke's head spin most of all was the discovery that her parents were alive. And on Earth. She kept thinking she was dreaming and that the joy and relief bubbling in her chest would suddenly sharpen into aching sorrow all over again. But the parents she had mourned for a year hadn't been executed and floated into space. They had somehow made their way to Earth and even lived with Sasha's family before heading off on their own. Now she just had to figure out how to track them, which seemed impossible in a thousand ways. But sitting still and doing nothing wasn't an option either. As soon as she'd done all she could for these survivors, she'd be making her plans to leave.

"This one's not breathing," Eric said with a grimace as Clarke approached.

She crouched down and brought her hand to the man's neck. His skin was still warm, but there wasn't even the faintest whisper of a pulse. Clarke pressed her lips together, then lowered her ear to the man's chest, praying for a heartbeat. But there was nothing but silence. "There's nothing we can do for him," Clarke said, trying not to meet Eric's eyes. She didn't want to see the horror in his face. And she didn't want him to see the helplessness in hers.

She looked down at the man again, seeing his face properly for the first time. Clarke gasped as an invisible hand punched through her sternum and wrapped its fingers around her heart. It was her old biology tutor, Mr. Peters, the one who gave Clarke access to the ship's restricted archive center when she was only ten so she could look at photos of elephants.

"You okay?" Eric asked.

Clarke nodded, trying to blink away the tears threatening to blur her vision. Had Mr. Peters lasted long enough for a glimpse at the night sky? Had he been able to see the moon reflecting off the water, or catch the scent of trees in the wind? Or had he died without ever setting eyes on the planet he'd spent his whole life revering from afar?

"We should leave the bodies here for now," she said,

turning away. "It's more important to deal with the injured."
Clarke left Eric and carefully stepped over a pile of twisted,
red-hot metal in order to make her way toward a man lying on
his side. He wore a coat that had once been white but was now
covered with dust, soot . . . and a slowly expanding patch of
blood. His eyes were shut, and his mouth twisted in defiance
of his pain. Clarke let out a low gasp as she took in his tall,
lanky frame and shoulder-length gray hair. It was Dr. Lahiri,
her former mentor and one of her father's oldest friends. The
last time she'd seen him was when he'd come to her cell, and
she'd accused him of betraying her parents. He called her a
traitor in response, and before she could think better of it,
she'd actually socked him in the face.

The rage that had consumed her that day felt strangely distant now. Although her parents had certainly been betrayed,
they were alive. And Clarke knew there were people far more
accountable than Dr. Lahiri—like Vice Chancellor Rhodes,
the man who'd ordered her parents to perform the monstrous
radiation trials in the first place.

Clarke crouched down and placed her hand near his elbow.
"Dr. Lahiri," she said in what she hoped was a confidence-
inspiring tone. "Can you hear me? It's Clarke."

His eyes sputtered open, and he stared at her for a long
moment, as though unable to tell if she were real or a halluci-
nation. When he finally spoke, it was through a clenched jaw,

as if any extraneous movement would push him past the limit of bearable pain. "Clarke . . . you're alive."

"Yes, despite your best efforts," she said, smiling so he'd know she was mostly joking. "Let me see what's going on here, okay?"

He nodded slightly, then shut his eyes and winced. Clarke gently opened his coat, palpating his abdomen, ribs, and chest. He grimaced when she reached his collarbone. She carefully opened his eyes and checked his pupils, and ran her hands over his scalp to check for any contusions she'd missed.

"I think it's just my shoulder and clavicle," Dr. Lahiri said through gritted teeth.

"And a concussion," Clarke added, trying to keep her voice neutral. "I think the bones are broken. I can set them and make you a sling, but I'm afraid we don't really have much here for the pain. Did you bring any supplies with you?"

"I don't know what's on the dropships," Dr. Lahiri said, causing Clarke's stomach to plummet with disappointment. "It all happened so quickly. There wasn't time to prepare."

"We'll make do. I'm going to help you sit up. Are you ready?" She kneeled behind him and placed one hand under his good arm and the other behind his shoulder blade. "On my count. One, two, three." She raised him to a sitting position, and he let out a pained cry as she helped him lean against a wall of debris. The color began returning to his face. "Just stay as still as possible until my friends come to get you." She waved a hand in the air, gesturing for Wells and his team. "They'll help you get somewhere safe."

"Clarke," Dr. Lahiri muttered, his voice growing hoarse. She reached for her water container and lifted it to his lips. He took a small sip and continued. "I'm sorry about what I said last time. Your parents would be so proud of you. *I'm* so proud of you."

"Thank you," Clarke said slowly, wondering whether Dr. Lahiri really believed that her parents were dead or whether he was still too afraid to tell her the truth. "I'm sorry for . . . for losing my temper."

Despite the pain, he smiled. "I just wish I could take as much credit for your left hook as I can your surgical skills."

———

The next few hours passed in a blur. Clarke hardly noticed the dawn breaking, except for the fact that it made suturing easier. By the time the sun was high in the sky, all the uninjured Colonists had been led to camp, and a good portion of the injured had been carried away as well. Throughout the morning, a few more members of the hundred came down to the lake to help and to search for their parents among the new arrivals. But the relatively small number of happy reunions had been disheartening. Apparently, the families of the hundred hadn't been given priority on the dropships, never mind that their kids had been sent on an impossibly dangerous mission to Earth.

Clarke finished fashioning a splint for an elderly woman's leg and then stood up to stretch quickly before moving on to her next patient. She noticed that the guards who'd been standing in a circle around their captain a few minutes earlier had dispersed to help carry the wounded up to the camp. She could only hope they remained more focused on helping their fellow Colonists than on hunting down the boy who had gotten the Chancellor shot.

Her eyes settled on a guard who looked uncomfortably familiar. Clarke stared at him for a long moment, trying to figure out why she felt suddenly queasy. He was standing at the center of a slow-moving scrum of people, directing them with one good arm and cradling an injured hand to his chest.

Clarke turned away quickly so he wouldn't see her, stalling for time by taking inventory of her bandages while she racked her mind for the guard's name.

Scott.

Scott had often been assigned to medical center patrol during her apprenticeship, and Clarke had come to dread their frequent encounters. Although the guards typically didn't interact with the doctors and apprentices unless there was a security issue, Scott had been an expert at making his presence known. He wasn't much older than she was, and there was something snide and officious about him. He never looked at the patients when he was in the room—only at the doctors or other guards, like he was too good for anyone else. But what had really bothered Clarke was the way he acted when he was alone with her, and the lengths to which he seemed willing to go to make that happen.

Clarke had to force herself not to break into a jog as she walked swiftly down the corridor toward the medical center. She was nearly twenty minutes late for her rounds shadowing Dr. Lahiri, but the punishment for "hazardous behavior" was even harsher than that for tardiness. Being late meant that she was in trouble with her supervisor. Breaking one of the ship's rules meant facing the Council. It was rare for guards to write someone up for *running*, but the boy who'd been patrolling the medical center recently had quickly gained a reputation for being a power-tripping bully.

Clarke turned the corner and groaned. She'd hoped to slip into the medical center unnoticed, but Scott was standing in front of the checkpoint. His back was to her, but she recognized his broad shoulders and slightly greasy blond hair that always looked to be longer than was typically allowed by guard regulations.

Clarke could tell he was in the middle of some kind of confrontation, but only as she drew closer did she realize he was holding a woman by her wrists. He had them pinched together behind her back. She was a sanitation worker from Arcadia, and based on the loud scolding Scott was doling out for everyone to hear, she had simply forgotten her pass. Most guards would have let her off with a warning, but not Scott, who was making a big show of slapping restraints on her wrists. The poor woman had tears in her eyes and could barely raise her head when Clarke slipped past.

Indignation and disgust curdled in Clarke's stomach, but she didn't dare look back. She stood to gain nothing by intervening. If she tried to get in the middle, Scott would probably threaten the woman with even more severe repercussions, just to prove his power to Clarke.

By the time Clarke started seeing patients, she'd pushed the incident out of her mind. That was one of the things she loved about being a medical apprentice, the way her mind could be one hundred percent focused on the task at hand, leaving no room to worry about anything else in her life. Not about her parents, or Lilly, or the terrible secret she was keeping from Wells.

However, later that day, while she was busy cleaning a five-year-old girl's cut knee, there was no avoiding Scott when he strode unannounced into Clarke's exam room.

"What do you want?" Clarke asked, not bothering to hide her irritation. It was one thing for him to strut down the halls like he was Chancellor of the corridors. It was another for him to barge into her exam room when she was with a patient.

He waved a bruised and swollen finger in front of Clarke's face and smirked. "You won't believe it, but that bitch actually *bit* me when I was cuffing her."

"Watch your language, please," Clarke hissed, shooting a glance at the little girl staring at Scott wide-eyed from the exam table.

He laughed unpleasantly. "I'm sure she's heard worse. She looks like a Waldenite."

Clarke narrowed her eyes. "Aren't *you* a Waldenite?" she asked, doing her best impression of Glass and her snooty friends.

He ignored the jab and took a step closer. "I'm in need of your services, Doctor," he said in a voice that somehow managed to be both mocking and vaguely threatening.

"If you'll just take a seat outside, I can look at that for you after I'm done with Cressida here."

"Well I'm sure little *Cressida*"—he tilted his head in the girl's direction—"would understand that a member of the guard suffered a painful injury while subduing a threat to the Gaia Doctrine this morning. And that I am in a hurry to get back to my work protecting this ship."

Clarke fought the urge to roll her eyes. She just managed to keep her expression neutral while she sprayed a skin regenerator on Cressida's knee, gently affixed a bandage over it, and patted the girl on the leg. "You're all set. Just keep it clean and dry until tomorrow, okay?"

Cressida nodded and hopped down from the table, running out the door to her mom, who waited just outside.

Clarke turned to Scott and held out her hand. He placed his wrist in her palm and winced as she uncurled his swollen finger. "You're going to need to see the actual doctor for this," she said, releasing her hold and stepping back.

He raised his eyebrows and gave her a humorless smile. "Who? The old guy you follow around all day? No thank you."

"Dr. Lahiri is the most respected doctor on the ship."

"Yeah, well, he's not who I want checking out my *other* injury."

"What are you talking about?"

"That piece of Arcadian trash also tried to kick me. I knocked her down, but she managed to knee me in a rather sensitive area, if you know what I mean."

Clarke sighed. "Is there bruising?"

"I haven't had time to look," Scott said with a smirk. "Don't you want to do the honors?" He reached for his belt buckle as he stepped toward Clarke.

"I should call a nurse," Clarke said, moving toward the intercom.

"Now, just hold on a second." Scott grabbed Clarke's arm with his good hand and pulled her back. "I don't need a nurse. I just need you to do your job . . . *Doctor*."

Before he could utter another word, the door behind him banged open, and Wells strode in, looking even taller than usual in his officer's uniform. Scott snapped to attention, his gaze locking on the floor. Clarke couldn't help but smile at Wells over Scott's shoulder.

"I'm sure you're not preventing this medical apprentice from getting her work done, are you?" Wells asked, his voice stern, but his eyes playful.

"No, sir," Scott said stiffly.

"Glad to hear it, Guard. Carry on with your rounds."

"Yes, sir."

Clarke stifled a grin until the door clicked shut behind Scott, then stepped over to Wells and wrapped her arms around him. He tilted her chin up and kissed her softly on the lips.

"Thank you, Officer Jaha."

"You're welcome, Medical Apprentice Griffin."

Clarke was exhausted. She hadn't eaten anything since the previous evening, and all the food they'd taken to the crash site had gone to the survivors. The team had taken turns leading the survivors back to camp, and there were only a few injured left to deal with. She had put it off as long as she possibly could, but there was no way to avoid treating Scott. He sat on a log at the edge of the clearing, looking up at her as she approached.

"I thought you'd never get to me," he said, his lips pressed together into something resembling a grin.

"I'm sorry about the wait," Clarke said, hoping that maybe he wouldn't recognize her after all the months she'd spent in Confinement and her weeks down on Earth.

"It's okay, Doc. It took me this long to come to Earth just so you could finally show me your bandaging skills. I believe we were interrupted last time."

Clarke's heart sank. Scott knew exactly who she was, and he hadn't grown any more charming since she'd last seen him.

"Let's see what's going on here." She gestured for him to show her his wrist. He held out his hand to her, and she took it, her stomach churning in protest as she made contact with his clammy skin. She turned his hand over, moving it gently back and forth and from side to side.

"So you're a real doctor finally?" Scott said. "I guess that means you can't afford to get all squeamish during examinations now."

"Not exactly," Clarke replied without looking up. "I never finished my training, but I'm the closest thing we've got down here."

"Well, doctor or no doctor, you'd better do a good job." He wiggled his fingers in her palm. "That's my shooting hand after all."

Clarke pulled a bandage from her supply bag and began

winding it around his wrist and hand. "It's not broken," she said matter-of-factly, hoping to get out of the conversation as quickly as possible. "But you'll need to limit your use of this hand for a few days to allow the swelling to go down." She inhaled deeply and looked him directly in the eye. "Which shouldn't be a problem, since we hunt with spears and arrows here, not guns."

Scott met her gaze with a glint in his eye. The skin on Clarke's arms rippled with goose bumps. "I wasn't talking about shooting *animals*," he pronounced coolly. Before Clarke could ask him what he meant, he cocked his head to the side and surveyed her with the same expression that used to make her want to shower as quickly as possible. "So, why didn't you finish your training?"

"I was Confined before I completed it," Clarke said flatly, not meeting his eyes.

"Confined? *You?*" He paused for a moment, then snickered. "Little Miss Perfect, *Confined*. You know what, though? I don't mind being treated by a convict. I kinda like knowing that, all that time, there was a bad girl hiding under those scrubs." He lowered his voice as a woman in an officer's uniform strode past, talking urgently with a man Clarke vaguely recognized. "I hope you brought those scrubs to Earth. I always liked the way that they made your—"

"You're all set," Clarke said with exaggerated cheer as she secured the bandage and gave him an extrahard pat on the wrist, ignoring his grimace of pain. "I'll see you around."

Without giving Scott another look, Clarke hurried away, shuddering as if to throw off the weight of his heavy, lingering gaze.

CHAPTER 4

Wells

Wells winced as he trudged up the slope toward the lake for the eighth time that day. He'd walked nearly twenty miles trekking back and forth, leading survivors to the camp and then heading back for another group.

There were more adults than kids in the clearing, a sight that seemed almost as a strange as the two-headed deer they'd spotted their first week on Earth. Their presence was made all the more conspicuous by the fact that they could do nothing more than stare in wonder and shock at their surroundings while, all around them, teens who'd been rotting away in a detention center just a few short weeks ago were barking out directions.

Wells had also been struck by the lack of happy reunions. He'd only witnessed two of them finding any relatives, and they were both Phoenicians. None of the Waldenites or Arcadians had any loved ones on the ships.

"I can't believe I made it." A young woman panted as she gratefully accepted Wells's assistance climbing the steep slope.

"You had a pretty rough landing there," he said, shortening his stride so it'd be easier for her to keep up. Although it'd been only a few weeks since his own arrival, he'd forgotten how unsteady he'd felt at first.

"Not the landing," she said, stopping to look up at him. "On Phoenix. It was . . . terrifying." She turned to glance up at the sky, then sighed and shook her head. "They don't have much time left."

Her words were like a fist to Wells's gut. Before he could ask what she meant, though, Eric stepped in to lead the young woman through the woods to the camp, freeing Wells to return to the lake.

A hot coil of guilt tightened around Wells's stomach. He didn't need to know the details to understand that he had probably been responsible for whatever grim fate lay ahead for the people still on the Colony. He may have become a leader down here on Earth, but he was still a coldhearted murderer back on the ship. Wells could almost feel the cool metal of the airlock at his fingertips as he opened it, just a little, allowing precious oxygen to leak out of the ship. He had only been trying to speed up the inevitable so Clarke could travel to Earth before her eighteenth birthday—before her certain execution. But, he knew now, he had also hastened the demise of thousands of innocent people still trapped on the Colony.

As he got closer to the lake, he wrinkled his nose at the now-familiar smell of the crash site. Under the acrid scent of smoke and the metallic tang of blood and sweat, he sensed something else. It took him a moment to place it, but as soon as he did, his heart began to pound: It was fuel. The smashed dropships were leaking it into the grass, dirt, and water all around them. Most of the flames had started to die out, but all it would take was one spark in the wrong place to turn the whole place into an inferno.

Then, like a scene out of a nightmare, Wells saw it happen. About a hundred meters away, an enormous flame shot out the top of one of the charred dropships, hurtling chunks of flaming wreckage into the air. "Watch out!" Wells shouted, breaking into a run. "Everybody, *move*."

Luckily, the injured had all been triaged in another area, but there was too much smoke in the air to confirm that the others had moved to safety. Wheezing, Wells ran forward, coughing and wiping his eyes with his sleeves as he called out for anyone who needed help.

There was a faint buzzing sound, like something flying through the air. Wells looked up but couldn't see anything but dark gray smoke. It grew louder, but before Wells could react, he felt himself flying through the air, landing on the ground with a hard thud. He tried to roll over, but something—or someone—was on top of him. After a moment, the weight moved, and Wells looked up with a groan. Just a few meters from his head was an enormous piece of smoldering fuselage. If he hadn't been knocked to the ground, it would've crushed his skull.

He turned to the other side and saw a slim figure standing over him, a girl wearing the Colony's standard-issue thin gray pants and T-shirt. She reached for his hand and pulled him to his feet. "Thank you," Wells said, blinking rapidly as he waited for his vision to clear. When the world came back into focus, the first thing he saw sent a wave of joy through him.

It was Glass.

They locked eyes at the same moment, and their faces lit up into matching giant grins. Wells closed the space between them in an instant and wrapped his arms around his childhood best friend, pulling her into a tight hug. A million images flashed rapid-fire through his brain—years of happy memories crashing together and replaying in a steady stream. He had been so focused on following Clarke to Earth that he hadn't had much time to worry about Glass after she bolted from the dropship just before the hundred launched. The familiar smell of her hair—that particular blend of Glass and the synthetically scented shampoo back on the Colony— filled him with comfort, and for a brief moment, Wells was transported back to simpler times.

Growing up, she'd been the only one able to forget the fact that he was the Chancellor's son, the only one who made him feel like he wasn't on display. Around Glass, he could be immature, or playful, or sometimes even mischievous—like the time he said he was taking her to the archives to watch a video of some boring royal wedding when his real plan was to watch a great white shark attack an orca. And in turn, Glass wasn't afraid to show him her goofy side. While the rest of the ship saw Glass as this perfectly polished, well-mannered Phoenician girl, Wells knew that she liked to make up silly dances and that she burst into laughter anytime someone mentioned Uranus.

"I can't believe you're here," Wells said, pulling away so he could look at her. "Are you okay? I was so worried about you."

"Are you kidding? Think about how worried I was about *you*," she said. "No one knew if you guys made it. Are *you* okay? What's it like here?"

It made his head spin just thinking about how much he had to tell her. So much had happened since the last time they'd seen each other. He'd set the Eden Tree on fire to get himself arrested, been Confined, faced off with his father, rode with the rest of the hundred on the dropship Glass had escaped from, and spent the last few weeks fighting for his life on Earth.

"The weird thing is—" he started.

"Are there actually—" she said at the same time.

"You go first," they both said together, then laughed. They pulled away from each other, the smiles fading on their lips as the scent of smoke and charred metal reminded them of where they were, and why. Wells struggled with the question that bubbled up in his throat, and the way Glass's face grew serious told him she knew what he was thinking. He swallowed hard and found the courage to ask.

"Do you know anything about my father?"

Glass pressed her lips together, and her eyes filled with sympathy, a look Wells recognized from the terrible weeks after his mother's death. Wells braced himself for whatever she was about to tell him, just grateful that if he had to hear agonizing news, it would be from her.

"They haven't told anyone much," she began, her voice soft but steady. Wells held his breath, waiting for her to continue. "But the last we heard, he was still in a coma." Glass paused, waiting for him to absorb the information.

Wells nodded, his mind swirling with images of his

father lying alone in the medical center, his tall, broad frame looking frail under a thin sheet. He focused his efforts on keeping his expression neutral as Glass's words sank down into his chest, lodging themselves in the deepest part of his heart. "Okay," he said with a long sigh. "Thanks for telling me."

Glass stepped toward him. "Wells," was all she said before wrapping her arms around him again, this time in a comforting embrace. Glass knew him far too well to let him get away with his stoic act. The best part of their friendship was that he didn't mind.

After a long moment, they pulled away from each other. There was something Wells needed to tell Glass before she got to camp.

"Glass," he started, "things are a little . . . *different* here on Earth than we expected."

Concern flashed across her face. "What is it?"

He tried to choose his words carefully, but there was no way to sugarcoat the shocking, disorienting information. "We're not alone. Here. On Earth." He said it quietly so no one around them could hear. He waited for her to process what he'd said before continuing. At first, she smiled, looking ready to make a joke about all the hundreds of other Colonists around them. Then she grasped the implication of his words, and her expression shifted.

"Wells, are you saying . . ." Glass trailed off.

"Yes. There are other people here on Earth. People who were born here."

Glass's eyes grew large and round. "What?" She swiveled her head from side to side, as if expecting to see people watching her from the trees. "Are you serious? You can't be serious."

"I'm one hundred percent serious. But it's okay. They're very peaceful and kind. Well, most of them. There's a small group that broke off about a year ago, and they're dangerous. But the rest of them are just like us." Wells thought of Sasha and couldn't suppress a smile. "They're actually pretty inspiring. The Earthborns are good people, maybe better people than we are. I think we have a lot to learn from them. I just have to figure out a way to let the others know without scaring anyone."

Glass was staring at him, but it was no longer with confusion. "Wells," she said slowly, a small smile forming at the corners of her mouth, "is there something you're not telling me?"

He gave her a sidelong look. "Yes, there's obviously a ton I haven't told you yet. There was this terrible attack, and a fire, and then people started getting sick, and you'll *never* guess what happened when—"

"No," she said, cutting him off. "Something you're not telling me about these Earthborns. Or maybe one in particular?"

"What? No." He was usually pretty adept at hiding his thoughts, but something about Glass's tone made his cheeks redden.

"Oh my god," she whispered. "There's a girl. An *Earth* girl." Her voice was equal parts shock and delight.

"You're crazy. There's no Earth—" He cut himself off with a smile and shook his head. "How could you possibly have known that?"

Glass reached out and squeezed his arm. "You can't keep secrets from me, Wells Jaha. It was the way you were talking about these *inspiring* Earthborns. You had the same look on your face that you got when you used to talk about Clarke." Her expression grew less playful as her brow furrowed. "Does that mean you two broke up? What happened?"

Wells sighed. "It's a long story, but I'm fine." He smiled, thinking about the previous evening, lying with his head in Sasha's lap as they stared up at the stars. "More than fine, actually. I can't wait for you to meet Sasha."

"Sasha," Glass repeated, seeming slightly disappointed that it wasn't a more exotic name. "Where is she?"

Before Wells could reply, a tall boy in a guard's uniform approached, carrying a small water container with one hand, his other arm bound in a sling. Glass's face lit up at the sight of him, and she didn't look away as he passed the container to her and waited for her to take a sip. "Thanks," she said, smiling at him before finally turning back to Wells. "Wells, this is Luke."

Wells extended his arm and shook the guard's good hand firmly. "I'm Wells. Nice to meet you."

"I know. I recognize you, of course, and Glass has told me all about you. It's really good to meet you, man," Luke said, grinning as he released Wells's hand and clapped him on the shoulder.

Glass hooked her arm through Luke's and glanced back and forth between the two boys, beaming.

Wells grinned. He had no idea how Glass had ended up with a guard, let alone one who wasn't from Phoenix, but none of that mattered down here. Besides, there was something about Luke that Wells liked right away. He seemed solid, sincere. Nothing like the slimy Phoenicians Glass used to date. She was clearly in love, and that was all Wells needed to know.

"Welcome to Earth," Wells said with a smile, gesturing to the sky and trees and water all around them. As he did so, he noticed the blood covering Glass's shirt. He inhaled sharply. Had she been hurt without realizing it? He pointed at her. "Glass, are you okay?"

Glass looked down at her shirt, and her face paled. "Yes, I'm fine," she said quietly. "That's . . . that's not mine." Luke wrapped an arm around her shoulders and pulled her in tight.

Wells's stomach plummeted as he braced for the terrible news he could already feel hovering in the air, as if Glass's pain were radiating out from the dark place she'd hidden it away.

Glass took a deep breath and tried to compose herself, but before she was able to form any more words, she crumpled and buried her face in Luke's shirt. He whispered something into her ear that Wells couldn't hear and stroked Glass's hair.

Wells stared in horror. Part of him wanted to wrap his arms around his best friend, but that clearly wasn't his place anymore. So he stood, waiting, until Luke turned to face him. "It's her mother," he whispered. "She's dead."

CHAPTER 5

Glass

Glass had never felt more out of place in her life. Not as a Phoenician visiting Luke on Walden. Not as the daughter of a man who abandoned his family. Not even as a recently freed convict back on Phoenix for the first time. She stood by the fire pit, shivering though the sun was high overhead, and watched the frenzy of activity around camp. Everywhere she looked, kids her age or younger were busy with crucial tasks.

People darted in and out of the hospital cabin, bringing water for Clarke's patients and carrying out bloodstained bandages to burn or bury in the woods. Some of the kids spilled into the clearing, carrying axes and firewood they'd chopped themselves, while others were laying the foundation for a new cabin. A few hours earlier, a group of grim-faced volunteers had headed down to the lake to start digging graves for the passengers who hadn't survived. There were too many to fit in the cemetery on the far side of the clearing, and there was no point to carrying the bodies all the way to the camp.

Although the new Colonists had left without much warning, the dropships had all been prestocked with enough basic supplies to make the first-wave kids act like they'd been given the key to everlasting life. One of the girls Wells had assigned to take inventory looked like she was going to cry while running her hand along a new hammer, treating it with the same reverence other girls showed toward a beautiful piece of jewelry at the Exchange.

Glass was desperate to make herself useful, but she was completely out of her element. She was too afraid even to ask where—or worse, how—she was supposed to go to the bathroom. Luke had been called away with the rest of the guards, and although he'd been reluctant to leave Glass on her own, they both knew now wasn't the moment for him to shirk his duty.

A group of girls Glass's age were walking toward the fire, whispering urgently, but as they passed Glass, they fell silent and stared at her warily. "Hi," Glass said, eager to start out on the right foot. "Is there anything I can do to help?"

One of the girls, a tall brunette whose carefully torn shorts showed off her long, unbelievably toned legs, narrowed her eyes as she looked Glass up and down. "You were supposed to be on the dropship with us, weren't you?"

Glass nodded. "Yes, I was taken from the detention center, just like the rest of you." It was the first time she'd voluntarily confessed to having been Confined. "But I snuck off at the last minute." *Snuck off* was a somewhat inaccurate way to describe her life-or-death sprint onto Walden to find Luke, but she sensed that now wasn't the time for a play-by-play of her dramatic escape.

"Yeah, snuck off, okay," a girl with an Arcadian accent said, exchanging glances with her friends. "Must be nice to know people who can call in favors."

Glass bit her lips, wishing there were some way to make it clear how much she'd gone through, that she hadn't exactly spent the past few weeks living it up on Phoenix. She had almost asphyxiated on Walden and barely made it onto the last ship. She had just watched her own mother *die*, the reality of which was still pummeling her chest with alternating waves of searing pain and suffocating numbness.

"You should just hang out with the others," one of the girls said, a little more kindly. She gestured toward a group of other recent arrivals who were clustered on the other side of the fire, staring at their shocking new surroundings in wide-eyed wonder.

Glass nodded and watched the girls walk off, knowing full well she wasn't welcome among the recent arrivals either. Most of them had seen her board the dropship with Vice Chancellor Rhodes, taking the seat the others had so desperately hoped would be filled by one of the friends and family members they'd been forced to leave behind. If only her mom were here. She'd had a special gift for making herself at home in any social situation and helping everyone around her feel at ease as well. Sonja might not have known how to light a fire or chop wood any more than Glass did, but her warm smile and musical laugh would've been just as valuable.

Glass wrapped her arms around herself and glanced up at the dizzyingly tall trees. Swaying in the wind, they almost seemed to be looking down at her, making her feel like a little kid lost in a sea of oblivious grown-ups.

She watched as Wells stepped out of the hospital cabin, and even from a distance, she could tell his expression was grim. He ran his fingers through his hair and rubbed his temples. Despite the gravity of the situation, Glass couldn't help but smile at the familiar gesture—the same one she'd seen the Chancellor perform nearly every evening she'd spent studying at Wells's flat. A pang of regret washed over her as she thought about the Chancellor, left behind on the dying ship. He'd never get the chance to see everything his son had accomplished on Earth.

Glass had always known Wells was a natural-born leader, and it made her heart swell with pride to see how much everyone seemed to rely on him, though she felt a wistful twinge of sadness. It was a selfish thought, but she missed the days when Wells belonged to her most of all.

"Watch this," Glass called over her shoulder to Wells, who lagged behind her on the gravity track. She looked around to make sure the fitness monitor wasn't watching, then ran over to the control panel, grabbed the lever, and pushed it up a few notches. She felt immediately lighter and giggled as she pushed off the floor and hovered in the air for a moment before floating down slowly.

She bent her knees, pushed off with more force, extended her arms out, and rotated them through the air one at a time. "Look! I'm swimming!" She pinched her nose and puffed out her cheeks, before letting out a sputtering laugh. "That's how Earth kids got to school when it rained."

Wells bounced toward her with a grin. "How about this one?" he asked breathlessly, raising his left arm out in front of himself, pushing his right foot behind him, then switching his arms and legs in midair. "I'm skiing!"

Glass did her best imitation of an ancient Earthborn. "I'm just *skiing* over to the *grocery store*," she singsonged in a fancy old-lady voice, "where I will pick fresh *vegetables* from a *tree* and then drive my *vehicle* to the *beach* for a *picnic.*"

"With my pet bear, Fido, and my six children!" Wells added.

Glass and Wells collapsed onto the track in a fit of laughter so loud it brought the fitness monitor hurrying out of his office. "What do you think you're doing?" he scolded. "You know you're not allowed to touch the gravity settings." He strode to them, his face stern, but it was impossible to take him seriously when every angry step sent him bouncing into the air. As he got closer and realized that Wells was the Chancellor's son, his anger subsided slightly, replaced by the stiff smile most adults gave Wells when he caught them unaware.

"Young lady. Mr. Jaha." He turned from side to side, scanning the fitness center for a guard. "I won't write you up this time, but don't test me again. The gravity track isn't a play area, okay?"

They nodded and watched him turn around with as much dignity as he could muster while floating above the ground.

Glass and Wells pressed their lips tightly together, snorting sharp breaths through their noses until he was far enough away. When he was safely out of earshot, they burst out laughing until their sides ached and tears streamed down their young faces.

Glass wandered over to the edge of the clearing and sat down on a log. If she couldn't be helpful, at least she could stay out of the way. The only thing that made Glass feel like she wasn't a complete waste of space was the fact that Luke had quickly been recruited to the Vice Chancellor's personal guard, which was why she had barely seen him since they landed. He was off somewhere at a briefing about setting up a security perimeter around their camp.

Glass caught another glimpse of Wells at the far end of the clearing, this time walking with a girl who had to be Sasha. Wells threw his arm around the girl's shoulders and kissed the top of her head. It was startling to see Wells so outwardly affectionate and even more startling to think that his girlfriend was an *Earthborn*. All the questions Glass hadn't even thought to ask bubbled up to the surface. Did she speak English? Where did she live? What did she eat? And, more important, where did she get her clothes? Glass looked enviously at Sasha's tight black leggings, which seemed to be made of animal skin, and ran her hands along her own torn, dirty pants.

It was also incredibly disorienting to see Wells kiss anyone but Clarke. Last time she had seen her best friend, he was still so head over heels in love with Clarke that he could barely talk about anything else. But then again, if Glass had learned anything over the last couple of weeks, it was that people can surprise you. She had even surprised herself.

Glass laughed to herself before blushing and looking around to see if anyone noticed. She had to remember to tell

Wells that she'd actually spacewalked, alone, along the out-side of the ship. Not to mention her several suffocating trips through an air vent from Walden to Phoenix and back again. *He'd never believe me,* she thought. Then she corrected her-self. *He never would have believed me before. But now we'll both believe anything.*

With a sigh, Glass skimmed her eyes across the clearing again. She needed to find something to do. Her eyes fell on the hospital cabin. She gathered her courage and started across the clearing toward it, taking care to steer clear of two boys who were carrying something large between them. At first, she thought it was another injured passenger, but then she realized that what she'd taken to be two skinny arms and two long legs were actually *four* legs. And they were covered with hair, not skin. Glass gasped. It was an animal, a deer, maybe. She shuddered as her gaze landed on its enormous, lifeless brown eyes, and felt a pang of regret that the first animal she saw was a dead one. Earth was nothing like she'd imagined. It was cold and strange, and instead of dazzling Glass with its beauty, it only seemed to be full of death.

Glass turned away and walked up to the infirmary cabin, pausing at the door for a moment before taking a deep breath and stepping inside. From the first instance, she was over-whelmed by the efficiency of the operation, even in such a small space. It was a swirl of activity: Felix and Eric zipped across the room, handing off bandages and rummaging through a bin with small vials and bottles of medications. Octavia tilted a water container to the lips of a boy about her age, who lay on a cot with his leg propped up on a hunk of repurposed plastic from the wreckage. Crash survivors crammed the cots, sprawled across the floor, and even leaned on the wall. And at the center of it all was Clarke, who seemed to be in three places at once. She gave Octavia instructions without looking in her direction, passed Eric a shard of metal they were using to cut bandages, helped an older woman sit up, and pressed her hand against the forehead of a little girl nearby, all without seeming the least bit flustered. Glass had never seen Clarke looking so in control—so in her element.

"Hi, Clarke," Glass said. The greeting felt humorously inadequate given that it was the first time they'd come face-to-face on Earth, but now wasn't really the time to say, *Hi, Clarke, I hope you're doing well, and that you aren't too upset about breaking up with Wells after a traumatic journey to Earth. And, oh yeah, sorry for being such a bitch to you when we were kids.*

Clarke's head shot up, a flash of suspicion crossing her face, then disappearing behind her businesslike demeanor. "Glass. Do you need something? Are you hurt?"

Glass tried not to bristle at Clarke's curt tone. They had never been particularly friendly—Glass had always found

Clarke a little too serious for her taste. Glass was always more concerned with tracking down pretty accessories at the Exchange, while Clarke was preoccupied with learning how to save lives. But they had always shared a deep affection for Wells and a concern for his well-being. And at this point, any familiar face seemed like a friendly one. Glass had nothing left to lose.

"Oh, no—sorry. I'm fine. I just wondered if you needed any help," Glass stammered.

Clarke stared at Glass for a moment, as if trying to determine whether she was being serious. Glass waited awkwardly, until Clarke finally said, "Sure. Definitely. The more hands the better."

"Great," Glass exhaled. She cast her eyes around the room, searching for a task that needed doing. She spotted a teetering pile of dirty metal bins and cups. She pointed at them. "I could clean those."

Clarke nodded before turning back to the woman in front of her. "That would be great," she said to Glass over her shoulder. "Just be sure to take them to the south stream, not the one we get our drinking water from. But they need to be sterilized over the fire first. You just have to use a stick and hold them over the flame for five minutes or so."

"Got it." Glass scooped up the first few items from the top of the stack and moved toward the door.

"Glass," Clarke called after her. "Do you know how to get to the south stream?"

Glass shook her head, her cheeks burning with embarrassment. "No, sorry. I was just going to ask someone . . ."

Clarke gave her patient a few instructions, then grabbed an armful of metal bins and followed Glass. "I'll show you," Clarke said. "I could use some air."

The girls stepped into the sunlight together, squinting and taking in big gulps of cool air that seemed almost refreshing after the stuffy cabin.

As she and Clarke walked toward the fire pit at the center of camp, Glass caught a quick flash of movement from the corner of her eye. She whipped her head toward the tree line and squinted. Back in the shadows, about ten feet into the woods, a tall, dark-haired boy stood halfway behind a tree. He was staring at them. Glass sucked in her breath, startled, and stopped walking.

"What is it?" Clarke asked. She followed Glass's gaze and spotted the boy.

"Should we tell someone?" Glass asked nervously. "Is that—is that one of the Earthborns who want to hurt us?"

Clarke shook her head. "No, that's Bellamy. He's one of us, but he's not supposed to be here right now."

Glass heard something in Clarke's voice—was it worry? Fear? Much to Glass's surprise, Clarke furrowed her brow and shot Bellamy a strange look—almost like a warning. But the boy just met Clarke's eyes and grinned, unruffled by her serious expression.

Bellamy took a few bouncing steps forward, as if he were heading into camp. Clarke shook her head firmly this time. He stopped, though he didn't look happy about it. Clarke mouthed a few words and gestured toward him, as if waving him away. He shrugged, and just before he stepped farther back, he gave a little mocking salute before disappearing into the trees.

Glass turned to look at Clarke, who was blushing slightly. She knew Wells was with Sasha, but it hadn't occurred to her that Clarke could also have met someone new so quickly. Things certainly moved fast down on Earth.

"So, why are you keeping Bellamy in the woods?" Glass teased. "Do you want to make sure you get him all to yourself?" She meant it as an icebreaker, an attempt to tell Clarke that she knew she and Wells had moved on. As soon as Glass uttered the words, though, she realized it hadn't come out that way.

"I'm not *keeping* him anywhere," Clarke said, shooting Glass the same look she used to give her when she said something ditzy during tutorial.

Glass flinched. "I'm sorry. I didn't mean—"

Clarke must have realized how harsh she'd sounded. Her

face softened. "No, I'm sorry," she said, exhaling. "That wasn't fair. There's just . . . there's just a lot going on that we haven't told you about yet."

Glass let out a small laugh. "Yeah, I'm starting to figure that out."

"Does that mean you know about Wells?"

"About him and . . ." Glass trailed off, not sure whether Wells's secret was hers to share.

". . . and Sasha," Clarke finished for her.

Glass nodded, relieved that Clarke knew as well. "So, you're okay with all that?" she asked hesitantly.

Before Clarke could respond, a boy with red hair and freckles dashed over. "Clarke, one of the new people says he can't breathe and he needs a shot of something."

She let out a small sigh. "He said all that?" The boy nodded. "If he can talk, he's fine. It's probably just a mild panic attack. Tell him I'll be there in a second." The boy nodded again and ran off.

"Yes, I'm definitely happy for Wells and Sasha. Things with Bellamy are . . . I mean, I know it hasn't been that long, but it almost feels like—"

"It's okay," Glass said, cutting her off with a smile. Clarke might be all composed and in control when in doctor mode, but talking about boys made her endearingly flustered.

Clarke looked like she was weighing whether to speak or not. "Did Wells tell you anything about Bellamy yet?"

Glass shook her head.

"I'd better let him talk to you first, then."

Glass scanned the bustling camp and turned back to Clarke. "I think it's going to be a while before Wells has time to gossip with me. What's going on?"

Clarke hesitated, biting her lip.

"Come on, Clarke," Glass cajoled, slightly amused by the fact that although she'd known Clarke for most of her life, they were having their first proper chat on *Earth*. "I'm sure Wells won't care if you're talking about your own boyfriend."

"It's a little more complicated than that." She looked from side to side to make sure no one else was in earshot, then turned back to Glass with a small smile. "So, this is crazy, but what do you think the odds are that the second guy I fell for would turn out to be the secret half brother of the first guy I fell for?"

Glass stared at Clarke, certain she'd misunderstood. "Wells has a *brother*?" she said slowly, bracing for Clarke to burst out laughing and correct her.

But to her amazement, Clarke nodded. "The Chancellor and Bellamy's mother had a secret affair before he married Wells's mother."

Glass had heard a lot of confusing things come out of

Clarke Griffin's mouth over the years, especially during math tutorial, but nothing as mind-blowing as this. "I can't believe it."

"I couldn't either at first, but it seems to be true. And that's only the beginning." In a surprisingly calm voice, she told Glass about what Bellamy had done to get on the drop-ship with his sister, Octavia, how he'd taken the Chancellor hostage before knowing that he was his father. Clarke's face grew even more serious when she told Glass her biggest fear, her worries about what the guards would do to Bellamy when they discovered that he was responsible for the Chancellor's shooting. "I've been trying to get him to leave camp, but he refuses," she said in a tone Glass couldn't quite read, a strange mixture of frustration and pride.

Glass struggled to take it all in and made a mental note to talk to Luke. Maybe there was something he could do to throw the other guards off Bellamy's scent. "Wow," she said, shaking her head. "That's even crazier than my spacewalk."

"You spacewalked?" Clarke's eyes widened in astonishment.

"I spacewalked," Glass said, a tiny hint of pleasure sneaking into her voice. "It was the only way to get to Phoenix. Otherwise my boyfriend Luke and I plus a whole lot of other people would have died on Walden."

The girls stood in silence for a moment, each struggling

to process the momentous news the other had just shared. Then the door to the hospital cabin opened behind them, and Octavia stepped out.

"Clarke," she called. "We need you in here for a sec."

"Coming," Clarke replied. She turned to Glass. "I'm glad you're here, Glass."

"Me too," Glass said with a smile. It was true that she was pleased to see Clarke. Whether she was happy to be on Earth was another matter entirely, but at least it wasn't quite as cold and lonely as she'd always imagined, staring down at the thick shroud of gray clouds from the ship. Especially now that it seemed like she might have a friend.

CHAPTER 6

Bellamy

"Screw this," Bellamy grumbled to himself, kicking a clump of dirt into the air. He watched it sail in a smooth arc between two trees before landing with a plop a few meters away. Footsteps pierced the silence of the woods, where he lurked behind a cluster of tall trees, keeping himself out of sight. He peered through the foliage into the clearing, watching three of the new arrivals—a man and two women—wrinkle their noses at the deer roasting over the fire. The deer Bellamy had killed that morning and had passed to Antonio to take back to the camp. They could either learn to eat meat or starve to death. Or, better yet, let them find their own food.

When the hundred landed, there was no one there to greet

them or show them the ropes. No one *taught* Bellamy how to track animals, use a bow and arrow, or skin a two-headed deer. He'd figured it out himself, the way Clarke had figured out how to treat injuries and illnesses she'd never seen before. The way Wells figured out how to build a cabin. Even Graham, that otherwise useless slimeball, had figured out how to make a spear. If Graham could do it, these helpless fools could do it too.

Bellamy would have given his best bow to strut right into the middle of camp, his head held high, and defy the bastards out there to just *try* to arrest him. He knew that once the smoke cleared and the Colonists' ears stopped ringing, one of them would recognize him as the boy who had held the Chancellor hostage on the launch deck. It didn't matter that Bellamy hadn't pulled the trigger—he was the reason the Chancellor got shot. He hadn't had a chance to ask Wells if there had been any news on his father . . . correction: *their* father. Would he ever get used to that idea? He certainly wasn't going to find out if the man had lived or died by standing out in the woods by himself.

This camp was Bellamy's home. He had helped build it with his bare hands, side by side with the rest of the hundred. He'd carried logs from the woods and laid them down to build a foundation. He had single-handedly kept the group alive with the animals he hunted. He wasn't going to leave it all behind just because he'd had the audacity to try to protect his sister. It wasn't his fault the Colony had some stupid population rule that made Octavia a freak of nature and gave other people permission to treat her like a criminal.

A branch snapped, and Bellamy spun around with his fist raised, then lowered it bashfully when he saw a little boy staring up at him. "What are you doing out here?" Bellamy asked, looking around to make sure he wasn't being trailed by anyone else. It was bizarre seeing adults in the camp, but it was even stranger seeing little kids.

"I wanted to see the fishes," he said, though his lisp made the word sound like *fithith*.

Bellamy crouched down so he was eye level with the boy, who looked to be about three or four. "Sorry, buddy. The fish live in the lake. That's a long way from here. But look." He pointed toward the trees. "There are birds up there. Want to see some birds?"

The boy nodded. Bellamy stood up and craned his head back. "There," he said, pointing to a spot where the leaves were rustling. "You see?"

The boy shook his head. "No."

"Let me help you get a closer look." Bellamy reached down, scooped the boy into his arms, and lifted him onto his shoulders, making the toddler squeal with delight. "Keep it down, okay? No one's supposed to know I'm out here. Now, look, there's the bird. See the birdie?" Bellamy couldn't see the boy's face, so he took the silence as a yes. "So where are your parents? Do they know where you went?"

Bellamy crouched down so the boy could slide off his back, then turned to face him. "What's your name?"

"Leo?" a girl's voice called. "Where'd you go?"

"Shit," Bellamy said under his breath, but before he had time to move, a girl with long dark hair hurried into sight. He exhaled. It was just Octavia.

She cocked her head to the side and smiled. "Already luring children into the woods like a real creepy hermit, are we? That didn't take long."

Bellamy rolled his eyes, but he was secretly glad to see Octavia in such good spirits. She'd had a tough few weeks, and just when she'd returned to camp, the rest of the Colony had suddenly arrived. If nothing else, Octavia was adaptable. She had spent her first five years living in a freaking closet, and the rest of her life proving she deserved to be alive.

"You know this kid?" Bellamy asked.

"That's Leo."

"Where are his parents?"

Octavia shot a glance at Leo, then shook her head sadly.

Bellamy let out a long breath and looked at Leo, who was busy tugging at a large vine encircling a nearby tree. "So he's all on his own?"

Octavia nodded. "I think so. There are a bunch of them. I guess their parents didn't make it onto the dropships, or else . . ." She didn't have to finish the sentence. He knew they were both thinking of the freshly dug, still unmarked graves down by the lake. "I've been looking after them all, until we can figure out what to do."

"That's really sweet of you, O," Bellamy said.

She shrugged. "No big deal. The little kids aren't the ones we should be pissed at. It's their parents who locked us up." She was trying to sound blasé, but Bellamy knew that growing up in the Colony's care center had given her a soft spot for orphaned kids. "Come on, Leo," she said, reaching out for his hand. "I'll show you where the bunny lives." She looked at Bellamy. "You going to be okay out here?" she asked.

Bellamy nodded. "It's just for today. Once things settle down, we'll come up with a plan."

"Okay . . . be careful." She smiled and turned to Leo. "Let's go, kiddo."

Bellamy stared after them and felt something in his chest twinge as he watched Octavia hop down the slope, pretending to be a rabbit in order to make Leo laugh.

She had always been on the outside looking in. No one but Bellamy had ever treated her fairly, or even kindly. Until now. She had finally been given the chance to be a normal teenager, with friends and crushes and, if he was being totally honest, a seriously smart mouth. He wasn't going to leave her behind, obviously. And he wasn't going to take her away. So what choice did that leave him? She deserved the chance to stay here, where she had made her first real home. Their first real home.

Bellamy had a sudden flash of the expression on Clarke's face as she urged him to hide, and his stomach balled up into a knot. It took a lot to frighten that girl—a brilliant doctor with a warrior's spirit who just happened to be breathtakingly beautiful, especially when the light hit her blond hair—but the thought of the guards aiming their guns at him had been enough to fill her luminous green eyes with fear.

Bellamy exhaled slowly, trying to calm himself. Clarke was just looking out for his best interests. Keeping him alive was a pretty basic one. But her frantic pleas for him to stay safe and out of sight kindled more anger in him than anything else. Not at Clarke, but at this whole messed-up situation. It was getting dark. Was he going to spend the entire night in the forest?

He was just about to walk back into the clearing and resume his rightful place when he saw Wells enter from the other side of the tree line, leading another group of stunned survivors. Bellamy studied Wells's upright bearing, his brisk pace, and the confident way he addressed the shambling group as if he were their leader, not a convicted criminal half their age. It was hard for Bellamy to get his head around the fact that mini-Chancellor was his actual, real-life brother. . . . It wasn't every day that you not only realized that you'd gotten your father shot but also that you had not one, but two illegal siblings.

Everyone in the clearing suddenly fell silent, and all heads snapped toward the spot from which Wells had just emerged. Bellamy followed their gaze and saw Vice Chancellor Rhodes striding through the trees and into the camp. He moved silently among the hundred and the other survivors with his shoulders thrown back, wearing the slightly bored expression that always made him look like a douche back on the ship. Here it just made him look like a moron. He'd narrowly escaped death less than twenty-four hours ago and now he was on the ground for the first time in his entire life. Would it kill him to show the slightest bit of relief or, hell, excitement?

No one dared speak to the Vice Chancellor as he walked around the clearing in a slow circle, flanked by four guards, surveying the camp they had worked so hard to build. Dozens of people held their breath at once, waiting for him to do or say something. After a long moment, the Vice Chancellor stepped inside the nearest cabin. He was out of sight for a moment, then came back into the sunlight, one corner of his mouth twitching with amusement.

Bellamy wanted to fly across the clearing and punch the sadistic little power grubber right in the face. But one look at the guards who followed him at a short distance, forming a half circle around Rhodes at all times, was enough to keep Bellamy's feet in place. Not only were there a lot more guards than he'd expected—at least twenty, not counting the ones who were injured and still making their way back from the crash site—they all seemed to have guns. Bellamy swallowed hard. The abstract threat of guards with orders to shoot him was one thing. Staring down the barrel of a real gun here on Earth was another. Bellamy wasn't exactly more afraid than he had been before the newcomers got here. He was just more certain than ever that he and Octavia had to look out for themselves, because no one else would do it for them.

Eventually, Rhodes made his way into the center of the clearing and turned to address the group that had gathered around him. He paused, keeping his audience waiting. Octavia stood in the front of the group, eyeing the Vice Chancellor skeptically. Wells moved off to one side, his arms crossed over his chest, his expression unreadable. Clarke remained at the very back of the crowd, leaning against the wall of the hospital cabin. She looked exhausted, which made Bellamy all the more furious. He'd give anything to be able to put his arm around her and tell her that she'd done an amazing job.

The people gathered around looked at Rhodes, their

dirt-smeared faces filled with expectation—and, Bellamy realized with some surprise, relief. Most of the hundred seemed *glad* Rhodes and his minions were here. They actually thought he was here to help them.

Finally, Rhodes began. "My fellow citizens, this is a sad day, a day we will mourn for generations, but it is also a great day. I am so honored to stand here with you, at long last, on the soil of Earth. The contributions of those of you who came down on the first dropship will not soon be forgotten. You have bravely forged ahead where none of our people have set foot in hundreds of years."

Bellamy studied Clarke's face. She betrayed no reaction, but he knew they were thinking exactly the same thing. There were plenty of humans who had set foot here, not all of them Earthborns. Clarke's parents, for example, and the others who had come to Earth with them. So far, though, none of the hundred knew Clarke's parents were alive besides Bellamy and Wells.

"You have proven that human life can, indeed, exist again on Earth. That is magnificent. But our lives do not depend solely on safe water or clean air." He paused for dramatic effect and looked around the crowd, locking eyes with one person after another. "Our lives depend on each other," he continued. Several people in the crowd nodded emphatically, and Bellamy wanted to gag.

"And in order to protect each other and ourselves, we must follow certain rules," Rhodes said. *Here it comes,* thought Bellamy, clenching his hands into fists, as if he could somehow hold back the words he knew would change everything. "Life on the Colony was peaceful. Everyone was safe and provided for"—clearly this man had never lived on Arcadia or Walden—"and we were able to keep our species alive because we respected authority, did what was expected of us, and maintained order. Just because we now live on Earth does not mean we can abandon that adherence to a code that is more important than any one of us." Rhodes paused again, letting his words sink in.

Bellamy took in Wells's and Clarke's faces, and he could tell from their expressions that they were all on the same page. Rhodes was full of shit. He had said nothing about the hundred being forgiven for their crimes—which they had all been promised in exchange for their "service" to humanity when they came down here on the first dropship. And based on the number of happy reunions Bellamy had witnessed that day—one or two among the non-Phoenicians—obviously none of their families had been given priority on the next wave of ships. The number of lies this man was spewing in one short speech was repulsive. But even worse, it seemed like a lot of people were eating it up. *Open your eyes,* Bellamy wanted to shout at them. *We survived fine here without these idiots, and we'll be fine without them. Don't listen to a word this jerk says.*

"I trust that each and every one of you"—Rhodes was wrapping up, his words flowery but his tone ice cold—"will recognize the greater good and do exactly what is expected of you, for your own personal well-being but also for the continuation of our very race. Thank you."

A chill shot down Bellamy's spine. This wasn't a warm and fuzzy motivational speech. This was a warning. *Do what I say or you will be removed from the herd,* the Vice Chancellor was threatening them. Bellamy didn't trust himself to toe the line, that was for sure. He had never been much of a rule follower on the Colony. And now, here on Earth, where he had spent entire days and nights alone, deep in the woods, there wasn't a chance in hell he'd obey anyone ever again. For the first time in his life—in all their lives—Bellamy was free. They all were.

But Rhodes was never going to forgive Bellamy's act of treason on the launch deck. Bellamy saw that clearly now. Instead, the Vice Chancellor and his followers would make an example of him, which meant execution. Probably publicly.

A decision appeared whole in Bellamy's mind, already considered and made. He had to get out of here. He would come back for Octavia when it was safe. Clarke and Wells would look after her for now. Bellamy took a large step backward, farther into the woods, his eyes locked on the back of Rhodes's head. On his second step, he backed right into a tree, smacking it hard. He fell forward with a grunt and struggled to keep his balance. He managed to stay upright but stepped, heavily, on a pile of dry sticks near his feet. They cracked loudly, the snap-snap-snapping echoing right out into the clearing.

Hundreds of heads popped up to follow the sound. The guards raised their guns to their shoulders and zigzagged the barrels at the tree line. With surprisingly quick reflexes, Rhodes turned and scanned the landscape for the source of the sound. Bellamy was stuck. He couldn't move, or he'd definitely be spotted. His only option was to stay perfectly still and hope that Rhodes and his guards all had terrible eyesight.

No such luck. Rhodes spotted him almost instantly, his face pinching into a delighted grimace. They stared at each other for a long moment, during which Bellamy wasn't sure if the Vice Chancellor recognized him as the one who had held the Chancellor hostage. Then a flash of sheer joy passed across his usually inscrutable face.

"There!" Rhodes yelled to his guards, pointing straight at Bellamy. The uniformed crew crossed the clearing in record time. Bellamy spun around, counting on his knowledge of the woods to put him at an advantage. He could sprint over tree stumps and duck under low branches at top speed. But he'd gone no more than a few meters when he felt one, then two bodies throwing themselves against his, knocking him to the ground. The guard who landed on him grunted and scrambled to get his hands around Bellamy's arms. Bellamy fought back, hard, shoving and kicking as he wrestled his way to his knees, then to a standing position. His heart pounded so hard he actually felt his ribs vibrating with each beat. Adrenaline coursed through his limbs. He felt like one of the animals he'd tracked and killed to keep the hundred alive.

More guards arrived and began to surround Bellamy. He took a couple of short steps toward one of them, but at the last second, he ducked, whirled around, and ran in the opposite direction. The guards scrambled to keep up. Bellamy bolted a few steps farther into the shady woods, still hopeful that he could shake them.

But they didn't use their bodies to stop him this time. A sharp *crack* pinged off the tree trunks, and dozens of startled birds fluttered out of the highest branches. Bellamy cried out as a piercing pain tore through his shoulder.

They had shot him.

Bellamy fell to the ground and was instantly swarmed with guards, who roughly lifted him up and bound his arms behind his back with no regard to the blood pouring from his wound. They dragged him into the clearing.

"Bellamy!" He heard Clarke's voice as if from a long distance. Through hazy vision, he saw her pushing her way through the crowd, yelling at the guards as she approached. "Leave him alone. You shot him—isn't that enough? Please, let me look at him. He needs medical attention."

The guards parted, allowing Clarke through. She wrapped her arms around Bellamy's chest and helped him sink to the ground. "It's okay," she said, her breath ragged. She ripped his shirt at the neck and pulled it off his shoulder. "I don't think it's too serious—I think the bullet passed right through." Bellamy nodded but couldn't speak through his gritted teeth.

"Your orders, sir?" one of the guards called out across the clearing to Rhodes.

Bellamy didn't hear the answer. He had only one thought as he sank into unconsciousness: He'd rather die than live on Earth as a prisoner.

CHAPTER 7

Wells

Wells normally slept outside, preferring the silent, star-filled clearing to the overcrowded cabins, but he'd spent the past two nights on the floor in the infirmary cabin, barely sleeping at all.

Clarke spent every possible moment at Bellamy's side, cleaning his wound, checking for fever, and saying whatever silly things she could to distract him from the pain. But she also had dozens of other patients to tend to, and so Wells pitched in as much as he could. He made sure Bellamy was drinking water and, in Bellamy's more lucid moments, kept him informed about what'd been going on in camp.

Wells suppressed a groan as he rose to his feet, yawning

while he rubbed his shoulder. There weren't nearly enough cots to go around, and Wells had made sure they went to the injured. He glanced down at Bellamy, who'd finally fallen asleep after a painful, restless night. There didn't seem to be any blood leaking through his bandage, which was a good thing, but Clarke was growing increasingly worried about infection.

He looked at Bellamy's pale face and felt a new surge of fury toward the Vice Chancellor. His father would've *never* let the guards shoot Bellamy, regardless of whether he realized their target was his son. Rhodes had a lot to say about order and justice, but he didn't seem particularly concerned about practicing what he preached.

Wells slipped outside, careful not to let the door slam. Early mornings used to be his favorite time on Earth. He'd have an hour to himself to watch the sunrise, before the rest of the camp would wake up and begin the day's routine: The kids on water duty were up first, heading down to the stream with empty containers and messy hair. The firewood team was next, always racing through the chopping to see who could get it done fastest. They had quickly settled into a community, with their own customs and traditions. In many ways, it was a happier, freer life than anything they had known on the Colony.

But although it'd been less than seventy-two hours since

the other Colonists arrived, those mornings felt like a distant memory. He hadn't seen Sasha in days. They'd both agreed that it was safer for her to stay at Mount Weather until Wells figured out the right way to tell Rhodes about the Earthborns. He felt her absence as a physical ache.

The normally empty clearing was scattered with groups of miserable-looking people—new arrivals who hadn't secured spots in the cabins and had spent a sleepless night staring terrified at the unfamiliar sky, or disgruntled members of the hundred who had chosen to brave the wet grass and frigid air rather than deal with the intruders who'd invaded their space.

A few adults were already standing around the cold fire pit, clearly waiting for someone to come light it for them. A group of guards stood off to the side, deep in conversation as they gestured toward the ridge where the splinter Earthborns had first appeared. After weighing the pros and cons of revealing that there were other people on Earth, Wells had told Rhodes about the two groups yesterday—about the peaceful ones led by Sasha's father, and the violent ones who'd killed Asher and Priya. Ever since, Rhodes had stationed around-the-clock guards at the edges of the clearing.

Wells walked over to the fire pit and forced a smile. "Good morning," he said.

The group nodded at him, but no one spoke. He knew how

they felt, because he'd felt the same way during his first days here—disoriented, traumatized by the journey to Earth, but also haunted by the loss of the people left behind. He also knew that the only way to move forward was to keep busy.

"Who wants to learn how to start a fire?" he asked. They all accepted his offer, with varying degrees of enthusiasm, but only one—a woman in her twenties—hung around long enough to try it on her own. Wells stacked logs in her arms and steered her back toward the fire pit. He showed her how to stack the logs in a pyramid to get the best airflow and walked her through the steps of lighting them. When they were done, she smiled, and he saw a tiny spark of life return to her eyes.

"Great job," Wells said. "Keep an eye on that, and when there's some food to cook, we'll build it up a little more." He headed toward the small groups who had gathered for hunting duty, passing the cluster of guards on the way. He felt their eyes on him and stopped. They stood with their guns over their shoulders, waiting for someone to tell them what to do.

Although he'd been stripped of his officer's rank when he was Confined, he cleared his throat and addressed them with the same voice he'd learned during training. "One of you should head out with each hunting party. We've got a lot of people to feed, and those guns could come in handy."

The guards looked at each other as if checking for permission, then shrugged and followed him. Wells divided them up and gave them a few tips on walking quietly so they didn't scare off their prey. The only two who stayed behind were the ones Rhodes had assigned to guard the infirmary cabin, to ensure that Bellamy didn't escape.

The clearing grew increasingly noisy as hungry people spilled out of the overcrowded cabins, searching for something to eat for breakfast.

They were in desperate need of several more cabins, which would require a massive harvesting of logs and at least a week of building. He'd have to train twenty or thirty of the new arrivals to get it done quickly, before the weather got cooler. They also needed more water buckets, which they'd have to shape from metal wreckage. He made a mental note to send a group over to the crash site to get at least ten good pieces that could work. None of this would matter, though, if they didn't get more food here, and fast. With Bellamy out of commission, that was going to be harder than ever. Wells exhaled slowly and organized his thoughts, letting the morning sunlight warm his face for a moment.

Opening his eyes, he crossed to the supply cabin and stopped to talk to the Arcadian boy who stood out front, reviewing a list. They had started keeping an inventory and assigning shifts to track what came in and out. Wells was about to ask the boy how they were doing on spare clothing when someone cleared his throat behind him. Wells turned and found himself face-to-face with Vice Chancellor Rhodes. Rhodes was studying Wells with a curious look, his lips pressed together in a tight smile that didn't seem to reflect any actual happiness. Two older guards flanked the Vice Chancellor. Wells recognized them from his officer training—one had been his firearms instructor, and the other had once made him do five hundred push-ups. He grimaced at the memory.

"Good morning, Officer Jaha."

"Good morning, Vice Chancellor Rhodes. Officers." Wells saluted them, a gesture that felt out of place beneath the vast blue sky and soft clouds that floated overhead, instead of the harsh lights of Phoenix.

Rhodes held out his hand to Wells, and Wells took it. Rhodes gripped his fingers a bit too hard and shook his hand for a moment too long. Wells had always been a model guard and officer, respectful of his superiors and the rules. He had excelled at every stage of training, usually landing in the top spot in his class. He had taken pride in knowing and following protocol, even if it meant the other trainees ribbed him—or worse, whispered behind his back that the Chancellor's son was sucking up to their teachers. But Wells didn't care. He wanted to prove himself on his own merits, and he had. No one could deny that Wells was a first-class officer. But today, standing in the clearing, his hand held hostage by the Vice Chancellor, Wells suddenly felt nothing but disgust. It was as if he knew what was about to come out of Rhodes's mouth before he even spoke.

"You have shown remarkable leadership, Officer Jaha."

"Thank you, sir." Wells braced himself.

"Particularly for one so *young*." Rhodes emphasized the last word, twisting it into an insult. "On behalf of the Council, I would like to thank you for your service, young man." Wells said nothing. "You have set up a satisfactory—if temporary—camp here on Earth." The Vice Chancellor's top lip curled in disdain. "But you have taken on far too much responsibility for someone your age, when you should be enjoying your youth."

Wells pictured the arrow piercing Asher's neck just inches from his own, saw Priya's bloated body hanging from a tree, felt the gurgling and terrifying hunger pangs they'd all shared in those first few days. *Some youth*, he wanted to spit at Rhodes. But he kept his lips pressed together.

"We more experienced leaders will take over now," Rhodes continued, "while you enjoy a well-deserved break."

Wells's nostrils flared, and he felt his cheeks get hot. He struggled to keep his expression soldier-neutral. Rhodes was taking control—but he clearly had no idea what he was getting into. Neither had Wells at first, but now he had several weeks of crucial knowledge that he could share. His voice steady, his tone diplomatic, Wells said, "With all due respect, sir, those of us who came down on the first ship have learned quite a bit in a very short period of time. Things are more complicated down here than they may seem, something we learned the hard way. We can save you a lot of time and trouble. Allowing us to share what we've learned will serve the greater good of everyone here."

Rhodes's smile grew tighter, and he let out a choked laugh. "*With all due respect*, Officer, I think we are well qualified to handle anything that may arise. The sooner we bring order back to this community, the sooner we can all feel safe."

Wells knew the look in Rhodes's eye. It was the special combination of disdain, mockery, and envy that he'd been seeing in people's faces his entire life. Being the Chancellor's son had never been simple. Rhodes looked at Wells and saw a spoiled, know-it-all child. Wells could single-handedly build a cabin for each of the new Colonists, and Rhodes would still see him as an entitled show-off. As the son of the one person who had stood between the Vice Chancellor and the top job, Wells was the symbol of Rhodes's frustration.

Any goodwill Wells may have earned as the person who kept the hundred alive for the first few weeks was quickly dissipating, along with his influence. If this was his last chance to speak directly with Rhodes, then he was going to use it well.

"Yes, sir," Wells said in his most respectful tone. Rhodes saluted him stiffly, clearly pleased with himself. He spun on his heel and began to walk away, the guards trailing him like obedient pets. "There is just one thing," Wells called to Rhodes's back. The Vice Chancellor stopped and turned back, looking annoyed. "The prisoner, Bellamy Blake."

Rhodes's eyes narrowed. "What about him?"

"He is vital to the survival of this camp."

"Excuse me, Officer?" Rhodes shook his head in disbelief. "Are you referring to the young man who almost got your father killed?"

"Yes, I am, sir. Bellamy is by far the best hunter we have. He has kept us all alive. We need him."

The smile fell from Rhodes's face, and his expression grew cold. "That boy," Rhodes said slowly, "is a murderer."

"He's not," Wells said, trying hard to sound calmer than he felt. "He didn't mean to hurt anyone. He was just trying to protect his sister." He'd hoped Bellamy's protectiveness would strike a chord with the Vice Chancellor, but the word *sister* only prompted a sneer. Wells could only imagine what would happen if, out of desperation, he admitted that Bellamy was his brother.

"He's the reason your father isn't here," Rhodes spat. "The reason *I'm in charge*." With that, he spun around and stormed away.

Wells watched him go, his heart sinking. There would be no leniency for Bellamy. No mercy.

CHAPTER 8

Clarke

The stitches weren't holding. Clarke clenched her jaw as she cleaned the wound on Bellamy's shoulder for the third time that day. She knew objectively that her frustration wasn't helping, but she was half out of her mind trying to figure out what to do next. She could take her chances and hope Bellamy's body fought off an infection and began to heal despite the stitches. Or she could remove the stitches and put new ones in—but that would put him at risk for reopening the wound inside, which could set him back.

She took a deep breath, exhaled slowly, and tried to focus. Though Bellamy had been lucky that the bullet had made a clean exit, it had entered in the worst possible place, within millimeters of a major artery. It would have been a tricky spot to stitch up if they had been back on the ship with a sterile surgical suite and bright lights. But in this dark cabin, with two guards hovering over Bellamy and bumping into Clarke every time she tried to check his wound, it was nearly impossible.

This was why doctors weren't supposed to operate on people they cared about. She could barely keep her hands from shaking, let alone make an objective decision under pressure. She felt Bellamy's forehead with the back of her hand. His fever had come down, which was a good sign, but he was still disoriented and in a lot of pain. It made Clarke sick to think of how much he was suffering—and how little she could do to help him.

"Clarke?" a weak voice called from across the room. "Clarke? I need you, please." It was Marin, an older woman with a deep gash in her leg. Clarke had cleaned and stitched the wound, but they were running desperately low on painkillers, which meant they could only be used in the most dire cases.

"I'll be right there," Clarke said. It killed her to leave Bellamy, but there were still so many people who needed serious medical care that Clarke couldn't spend more than a few minutes with him at a time. She squeezed his hand, and he half opened his eyes, smiled, and gave her hand a weak squeeze in return. She gently placed his arm back down on the cot and turned, bumping into one of the guards.

"Excuse me." Clarke could barely keep the irritation out of her voice. The constant security wasn't just excessive—it was hampering her ability to care for her patients. Where was Bellamy supposed to go while semiconscious and half-delirious with fever?

"Clarke, please? It hurts." The voice was plaintive, desperate now.

Clarke didn't have time to wallow. She had dressings to change and medicine to administer. Yet while she was grateful for the chance to be helpful, the exhausting, around-the-clock care she had to provide wasn't enough to clear her mind of worry. Every time she caught a glimpse of Rhodes, her body seized with fury and disgust. Not only had he nearly killed Bellamy, but he was essentially keeping her prisoner. There was no way she could leave the camp with Bellamy in danger, and every hour that passed was one that could've been spent tracking down her parents. As far as they knew, she was still on the Colony, not standing on the same ground, under the same sky. It was a thought almost too frustrating to contemplate.

Clarke crossed the room and leaned over Marin. As she lifted the bandage from her leg, she pushed away thoughts of how she was letting her parents down by standing here, in this cramped cabin, instead of setting off on her own to find them.

"I'm sorry you're in so much pain," Clarke said softly. "I know it hurts, but the good news is that this is healing beautifully." Marin looked miserable, her face pale and clammy, but she managed a nod and a quiet *thank you*.

Clarke had spent so many nights on Phoenix leaning over her textbooks, marveling at the sophistication of medicine on the ship. Most major diseases had been eradicated—there was no more cancer or heart disease, not even the flu—and they had developed ways to regrow skin and rapidly fuse bones. She was awestruck to live in a time of such medical brilliance. She wanted to live up to the doctors who had come before her, so she worked hard, memorizing procedures and medications and physiological processes.

What Clarke wouldn't give to have even a tenth of that medical equipment right then. She was essentially practicing in the dark, with fumbling hands instead of razor-edged scalpels, and flimsy assurances instead of bacteria-killing medicines. She might as well have offered her patients a wooden spoon to bite, like they did in the Middle Ages. She looked around at the faces of the bewildered adults and shell-shocked kids who groaned and wept and just stared off into the distance. There were hundreds more like them right outside. Could she care for all these people, day after day, all by herself?

And these were the lucky few who had somehow managed to secure a spot on one of the dropships. By the looks on some of their faces, the cost of saving themselves had been horrifyingly high. She could see the pain of leaving loved ones, friends, and neighbors behind—of letting others die so they could survive—written in their eyes. Clarke crouched down next to a boy, Keith, who lay quietly on a low cot at the back of the room. She smiled at him, and he gave her a little wave. Last night, she had asked Keith if his mom or dad were here with him, and he had shaken his head silently. Clarke could tell from his haunted expression that he was on Earth alone, and she stopped asking questions.

She wondered what would happen to him after he left her care. His broken ribs would heal soon, and he would leave the relative quiet of the hospital cabin. So far, Octavia had been taking care of the parentless children, but there was only so much one teenage girl could do. Who would teach him how to hunt or tell if the water was clean enough to drink? Would he be scared the first night he slept under the stars? Clarke brushed his sweaty hair back from his forehead and tapped the tip of his nose. "Get some rest, buddy," she whispered. Keith closed his eyes, though Clarke doubted he would be able to rest.

Just seeing him so tiny and alone made Clarke grateful for the people she knew on Earth. There had been quite a few familiar faces among the latest arrivals—Dr. Lahiri, for one, and a few people from her residence corridor. Even Glass. Though they'd never really been friends, the girls had known each other their entire lives. There was something comforting about seeing a face you've seen all your life, about knowing that Glass had brought many of the same memories with her from the dying ship. Almost like Clarke didn't have to remember everything herself—she had someone to share the load.

Although her limbs were heavy with exhaustion and anxiety, she forced herself to continue on to her next patient. It was Dr. Lahiri, whose shoulder was still causing him an unnerving amount of pain.

He lifted his head from the cot. His normally immaculately kept gray hair was greasy and tangled, which was almost more upsetting than the wound in his shoulder. "Hello, Clarke," he said wearily.

"Hi, Dr. Lahiri. How's your head?"

"Better. The dizziness has subsided, and I'm only seeing one of you at the moment."

Clarke smiled. "Well that's an improvement. Though I wish there were two of me, frankly."

Dr. Lahiri studied her carefully for a moment. "You're doing a great job here, Clarke. I hope you realize that. Your parents would be very proud of you."

Clarke's heart swelled—with sadness or gratitude, she

wasn't sure. For a few glorious days, she'd been absolutely sure she'd see her parents again and had spent long hours imagining all the things she would tell them, unloading all the thoughts and stories she'd tucked away, having no one to share them with. But now, the odds seemed slimmer and slimmer that she'd ever find the information she needed to track them down.

"I have to ask you something," Clarke said quietly, looking around to make sure the guards were out of earshot. "I found something the other day, something that made me think my parents might be alive." She watched Dr. Lahiri's eyes widen, but it wasn't with shock or even disbelief. Could he have known about this already? "And I think they're on Earth," she continued, taking a deep breath. "I know they are. I just need to figure out how to find them. Do you . . . do you know anything? Anything that could point me in the right direction?"

Dr. Lahiri sighed. "Clarke, I know you want—"

They were interrupted by a commotion by the door. Clarke spun around to see Vice Chancellor Rhodes standing at the front of the room. A murmur rippled across the cots as patients lifted their heads and saw who had entered. Clarke looked back at Dr. Lahiri desperately, wishing they could finish their conversation. He nodded at her, as if to say they would talk more later.

Clarke crossed toward the Vice Chancellor. She stopped

in front of him, her hands on her hips, feeling protective of her patients and her infirmary. Guards fanned out in a semicircle around him, blocking out all light from the doorway. The room had darkened, in more ways than one. Just the sight of Rhodes's smug face filled Clarke with rage. She didn't think she'd ever felt this strongly about anything before. Rhodes was the one who had ordered her parents to test the effects of radiation on human subjects. On *children*. Rhodes was the one who had threatened to kill Clarke if they didn't comply, then denied any involvement in the horrific experiments. He had sentenced her parents to die. And now he was here for Bellamy.

"Vice Chancellor," Clarke said, not bothering to try to hide her disdain. "How can I help you?"

"Clarke, this doesn't concern you. We're here about Bellamy Blake." He brushed against her shoulder as he stepped past her and farther into the room. Clarke clenched her hands into fists, her fingernails digging hard into her palms. The blood ran hot in her veins, and she had to take a couple of quick breaths to make sure she didn't do something she'd regret. As corrupt and immoral as Rhodes was, he was also dangerous. Her parents had learned that the hard way.

Clarke watched as Rhodes approached Bellamy, who was, mercifully, asleep. The Vice Chancellor studied him for a moment, then turned and stepped briskly toward the door again. As he passed his guards, he spoke without looking at them. "Put the prisoner in solitary confinement until his trial."

"Sir," ventured one of the guards, "where will we keep him?"

Rhodes stopped and spun slowly to look at him with narrowed eyes. "Figure it out," he snapped before disappearing through the door.

"Yes, sir," the guard said to Rhodes's retreating back.

Clarke's stomach did a slow turn as she recognized the voice. It was Scott. She looked up to see him staring at Bellamy, his face unreadable. Normally the sight of his blotchy skin and watery eyes made her want to take a long, hot shower. But this time, she didn't feel her usual revulsion. This time she felt more hope than disdain, because Scott had given her an idea. No one—especially not Vice Chancellor Rhodes—was going to hurt Bellamy. Clarke would see to that.

CHAPTER 9

Glass

Glass knew she was lucky to be on Earth, but a part of her wondered if she'd have fought quite so hard to get here if she'd known she was going to spend the rest of her life peeing in the woods. Glass stepped out of the tiny shed, which really wasn't much more than a lean-to with a tree as the fourth wall, and headed back toward camp. At least, she thought she was heading toward camp. All the trees looked the same, and she was still getting her bearings.

The distant sound of voices reassured her she was getting closer. She stepped into the clearing, reluctantly leaving behind the comforting quiet of the woods. Glass stopped in her tracks, suddenly disoriented. She wasn't in the right place. She was used to arriving between the infirmary and the supply cabins, but somehow she had ended up on the opposite side of the camp, near one of the new dormitory-like structures that was going up. She sighed at her own miscalculation, making a mental note to be more careful next time. Luke had already lectured her several times about staying alert and not going off into the woods alone. But he was working all the time, and Glass wasn't comfortable enough with anyone else in camp to ask them to come with her to the bathroom.

Glass rounded the construction site and came up behind two men talking in low voices near the tree line. They were engrossed in conversation and didn't seem to notice she was there. She stopped, unsure whether to alert them to her presence, stay still until they were done, or just keep walking past them. Before she had a chance to decide, she realized that one of the men was familiar—it was Vice Chancellor Rhodes.

Glass froze as her brain unleashed a storm of conflicting emotions. Something about him had always made Glass's skin prickle, and watching him order his guards to shoot Bellamy certainly hadn't helped matters. Yet at the same time, he was the reason Glass was alive. When he'd spotted Glass and her mother in the crush of people trying in vain to make their way to the dropships, he'd swept them along with his entourage and secured them the final two seats.

Glass hadn't been near enough to Rhodes to speak to him since that moment, but now a thousand unspoken questions bubbled up in her throat. Why had he helped them? What was his relationship with her mother? Had she spoken of how much Glass had disappointed her, back on the Colony?

The Vice Chancellor's voice snapped Glass out of her thoughts. "We'll hold the trial in the center of camp. Make sure everyone knows attendance is mandatory. I want them to see up close that treason or self-serving treachery of any kind will not be tolerated."

Glass stifled a gasp. He was talking about Bellamy.

"Yes, sir," said the other man, who wore a ripped and dirt-dusted officer's uniform. Glass recognized him as the Vice Chancellor's second-in-command, Burnett—the man who had grabbed her arm and pulled Glass and her mother to safety on the launch deck. "And have you thought about where we will house him long-term if his sentence is Confinement?"

Rhodes let out a harsh, dry laugh. "*Confinement*? There's only one outcome to this trial, and I assure you, it is not Confinement."

Burnett nodded. "I see."

"You and I will sit on the Council, as will a couple of the elder Phoenicians who came down with us," Rhodes continued. "I've already spoken to them. They understand what they need to do. We will execute the prisoner, which should serve as a clear reminder to all that maintaining order here on Earth is just as important—indeed, more so—than it was on the Colony."

"I understand, sir. But as to the logistics. We can't exactly float the prisoner down here. How would you like to handle the execution? We have firearms, but . . ." Burnett hesitated for only the briefest of moments. "Will you pull the trigger yourself?"

Glass shut her eyes as a wave of nausea crashed over her. She couldn't believe her ears. They were talking about executing Bellamy in the same off-hand manner they might have used to discuss electricity rations or an upcoming Remembrance Day celebration.

"I've been giving that some thought, and I believe I have just the person for the job. He's a rule abider, and he's an excellent guard. A member of the engineering corps in fact. But he's displayed some rebellious tendencies lately, harboring a fugitive, among other things, and I think this task will do nicely to remind him where his loyalties lie."

Glass's head started to spin, as if someone had cut off the oxygen supply to her brain, and she reached out a hand to steady herself on the nearest tree trunk. *Luke.* The Vice Chancellor was going to force Luke to execute Bellamy to prove his loyalty. But Luke would never kill someone—she knew he couldn't possibly pull the trigger. What would

Rhodes do to him then? Would he question more than just Luke's allegiance? Would he wonder if Luke could be trusted at all? Because it had become crystal clear what Rhodes did to people he couldn't trust.

Rhodes and Burnett began walking toward a small cluster of guards she didn't recognize. As soon as they were out of earshot, Glass let out a long breath that ended in a choked sob. She had to find Luke. She scanned the campsite but didn't see him anywhere. Panic began to rise in her chest. *Stay calm,* she told herself. *Freaking out will solve nothing. You kept it together during a spacewalk—you can certainly keep it together long enough to find Luke.*

Glass forced herself to walk calmly across the center of camp, headed for the infirmary cabin. Maybe Clarke had seen Luke. She stepped inside. It took a moment for her eyes to adjust to the dim, windowless cabin, and she felt momentarily blinded. When her vision returned, she saw Luke standing across from her, his back to her. He was on duty, guarding Bellamy. The relief she felt upon seeing him nearly brought tears to her eyes. But then an image of Luke raising a gun and pointing it at Bellamy, pulling the trigger, the loud *pop* as he fired it, flooded her mind. She couldn't let it happen. She couldn't let them force Luke to make that decision—and she wasn't going to stand by while they threatened to hurt him too.

Glass crossed the room in three big steps and grabbed Luke's arm. He spun around, his fists up in a defensive gesture, then laughed when he saw her.

"Hi," he said, dropping his arms to his sides. "You trying to get me in trouble?" His smile fell when he saw the expression on Glass's face. "Are you okay?" Luke said in a low voice, leaning toward her so no one else could hear their conversation.

"Can we talk?" She nodded toward the door. "Outside?"

"Sure." Luke turned to the other guard. "Hey, man, I need to step out for a second. You okay?" The guard shrugged, looked at Bellamy, who lay sound asleep and strapped down to the cot, and turned back to Luke and nodded. Luke followed Glass out into the sunlight.

They stepped behind the cabin, and after checking to make sure no one was listening, Glass told Luke everything she had heard Rhodes say. She hated seeing the pained look on his face as he absorbed the full weight of her words. He looked away from her, casting his gaze far out over the treetops. He was silent for a long moment, and Glass held her breath. Birds chirped, the sound of an ax splicing wood echoed across the camp.

Finally Luke turned back to her, his jaw tight and his eyes burning with resolve. "I won't do it," he said firmly.

Glass's heart fluttered with love and pride at Luke's clear sense of right and wrong. She admired his integrity and honor—it was one of the first things she had been drawn to. But she would never—*could* never—let him jeopardize himself to save someone else.

"But, Luke, you understand what that means, right? They'll punish you." Glass's voice trembled with fear. "I know he saved my life, but Rhodes is dangerous. You should have seen the way he talked about executing Bellamy. It was . . . awful. Who knows what he's capable of?"

"I know." Luke's jaw clenched and unclenched.

They were both quiet for a moment. Glass took his hand and squeezed it. He felt far away, distant, like he did when he was preparing for a spacewalk.

"Luke." She squeezed his hand again. Slowly he turned to look at her. "It can't end this way." After all they had been through, after all they had fought for and survived, it'd be madness to let Rhodes turn either of them into scapegoats just like he was doing to Bellamy.

"It won't," Luke said, pulling her into a tight embrace.

She breathed in his familiar scent, which was now layered with earthy smells that she was growing to love as she began to associate them more and more with Luke. His heart beat a steady rhythm against her cheek. Her blood pressure began to fall, her pulse slowed, and the adrenaline in her veins subsided. This was all she needed. *He* was all she needed.

Glass pulled away suddenly. Luke's head shot around, his instincts programed to check for danger.

"I know what to do," Glass said.

Luke looked down at her, his brows knit together. "What?"

"We'll leave."

"What do you mean 'leave'? Where would we go?"

"I don't know, but we'll figure it out. Wells can help us. He and Sasha can tell us which way to go. We can hide out for a while—as long as it takes for us to be sure that when we get back, all this will have been forgotten."

"What about the Earthborns? The dangerous ones?" Luke asked, looking at her as if she'd gone completely insane.

"We'll have to take our chances."

Luke stared at her for a long moment, and Glass braced for the weary shake of his head, and some vagaries about not abandoning his duties. But to her surprise, a small smile crept across his face. "We'd have to go tonight, then. We don't want to give Rhodes the chance to find me."

Glass looked at him, startled. "Seriously? You really want to go off on our own?"

He placed his uninjured hand on her waist. "Do you know what's kept me going this last year? All the time you were in Confinement, those nights on Walden when I was certain we were dying? It was the thought of being on Earth with you. Even when I was sure it was just a fantasy, I couldn't stop imagining exploring the planet with you. Just us." He let go of her waist and ran his fingers through her hair. "It's incredibly risky, though. You know that."

She nodded. "I know. But I'd rather be in danger out there with you than risk being here without you." She smiled up at him and ran her hand softly across his stubbly cheek. He took her hand in his and kissed her fingertips.

"And I'd rather be out there with you than cause anyone else more pain," he said.

"Then let's go get ready. We'll take whatever supplies we can grab without attracting attention and then head out."

"I have to finish this shift. You get some water and whatever food you can hide in your clothes, and we'll meet back here after sundown. While everyone's eating dinner."

"Okay," Glass agreed. "I'll find Wells. And I think we should tell Clarke too. She needs to know what they're planning for Bellamy. Because if it isn't you, it's going to be someone else."

"Can we trust her?"

"Yes." Glass was emphatic. "We can trust her."

"Good." Luke bent his head to give Glass a quick, soft kiss. "We'll be just like Adam and Eve," he said with a smile.

"There's no way I'm dressing in leaves, no matter how long we're alone in the woods."

Luke made a show of looking her up and down, then

grinned mischievously, making it clear exactly where his mind was. "Go get ready," he said, tapping her elbow. With one last lingering look, he turned around and headed back to the infirmary cabin.

CHAPTER *10*

Clarke

For one fleeting, blissful moment, Clarke was happy. As Keith stood up for the first time since the dropships landed and took a few steps, everyone in the infirmary cabin cheered. Clarke stood in front of him, holding out her arms as he hobbled forward. He had one skinny arm wrapped protectively around his ribs, the other waving out to the side for balance. He stepped into Clarke's arms, and she hugged him gently. The boy was going to be fine.

"Okay, buddy, let's get you back to bed. That's enough for one day," Clarke said.

"Thanks, Dr. Clarke." Keith's smile was big enough to light up the room.

"Just 'Clarke.'" She smiled, easing him back down onto the cot. Out of the corner of her eye, she glimpsed the one unoccupied cot in the cabin, and all the temporary happiness flooded out of her, leaving only panic and despair in its wake. Guards had come that afternoon to move Bellamy to a new prison cabin they'd built on the edge of the clearing, a dismal, windowless shack made of sheet metal salvaged from the crash site. He was locked up by himself, with two armed men outside the door at all times. Clarke wasn't sure exactly what Rhodes had planned, but she knew it was just going to get worse. Either Bellamy would succumb to infection from a lack of proper medical care, or else Rhodes would expedite his demise by . . .

She shook the thought out of her head. It was too terrible to contemplate. She would figure something out. She *had* to.

As Keith gingerly settled himself, Clarke turned to Marin, whose leg had shown huge improvement. The wound had begun to heal with no hint of infection. "You're next, Marin," Clarke said. "We'll get you up and walking in no time."

"I can't wait." Marin grinned. "How long have I been on this planet, and I still haven't seen so much as a tree or a leaf?"

"Well, that's what you get for being unconscious when we brought you in here," Clarke teased, her light tone belying the dread building in her stomach. "But I'll bring you a few samples later, to tide you over."

"Clarke?" someone called from the doorway, a desperate tinge to the voice.

Clarke spun around to see a pale, anxious-looking Glass shifting her weight from side to side. "Glass, what's wrong?"

"I . . . I need to talk to you for a sec."

"Sure." Clarke hurried over to her as quickly as her overtaxed legs would allow. Glass's face was drawn and pale. "Is everything okay?" Clarke's heart seized a little. Had something happened to Wells?

"I think we should go outside," Glass said, shooting a nervous look around the cabin.

Clarke nodded and, without another word, followed Glass through the door and into the clearing. The late-afternoon sun seemed to mellow the frenetic scene somewhat, although everywhere she looked, Clarke could see signs of strain— people arguing over rations, guards casting uneasy glances toward the trees, and, in the distance, people bending their heads to avoid meeting the eyes of the two guards standing to attention in front of Bellamy's prison. The idea of him in there, alone and ill, made Clarke want to break into a sprint and crash through the door, guards be damned.

She tore her eyes away and turned her attention to Glass. "What's going on?"

"It's about Luke . . . and Bellamy."

Clarke scrunched up her face in confusion. What could

Bellamy and Luke possibly have to do with each other? Bellamy had basically been unconscious or asleep since Luke landed on Earth—had they even met?

Glass inhaled and exhaled slowly, as if summoning the courage to speak. "Clarke, I just—I thought you should know. They're planning to execute Bellamy." Her voice had grown faint, as if saying the terrible word took a physical toll.

Clarke's stomach dropped out, and she bit her lip to stifle a cry. "Execute him?" she whispered. Glass nodded.

It wasn't as if Clarke hadn't expected something like this. Her medical training had taught her to consider every eventuality and face even the grimmest head-on. But there was an enormous difference between forcing herself to imagine the worst-case scenario and actually hearing it articulated on another person's lips.

"They're planning to hold a trial, but it's going to be a total sham," Glass continued, her face growing more pained with each word. She explained that Rhodes was going to make Luke kill Bellamy. "But we're not going to let them force Luke to do it," she said quickly. "We're leaving camp. Tonight. That should buy you some time."

"How . . . how will that help us?"

"If Luke isn't there to carry out Rhodes's orders, they'll have to rethink the execution. It's not a permanent solution, but it might buy you an extra day to figure something out."

"Is that . . . is that why you're leaving? So Luke won't have to kill Bellamy?"

Glass nodded, unhinging something in Clarke's chest, allowing a surge of unprecedented affection and gratitude to rush forth. Clarke wanted to grab Glass's hand and beg her forgiveness for every snide comment, every time she'd giggled inwardly at one of Glass's mistakes in school. She'd never judged a person so unfairly. But she couldn't move, could barely speak. They were going to kill Bellamy. They were going to drag the boy she loved into the clearing, point a gun at the kindest, bravest person she'd ever met, and end his life with the twitch of a finger.

But then Clarke's brain kicked into another gear, and she felt other instincts taking over. *No.* She refused to let this happen. She saved lives; she didn't stand by and watch them fade into oblivion. She would save Bellamy. If Glass could find the courage to flee the camp with Luke, Clarke could find the courage to do whatever was necessary.

At that thought, the gravity of Glass's plan began to sink in. "Glass, there has to be another way. It's too dangerous. You guys don't know the terrain, and there are—there are . . . people . . . out there who want to hurt us."

"Wells told us about the other faction of Earthborns. We'll be careful, I promise." She forced a smile that didn't reach her wide, sad blue eyes. "But listen, Clarke," Glass said, putting her hand on Clarke's arm. "Just because Luke isn't here doesn't mean Bellamy will be safe. They'll find someone else to do it."

Clarke nodded, her mind whirring. "I know. I think I have a plan." She thought of Scott's sour breath and penetrating stare. A shudder passed through her, but her resolve was firm: She would use whatever powers of persuasion she had to get Scott to free Bellamy.

"Can I help?" Glass asked, her face full of hope and concern. "I mean, before we leave?"

Clarke ran through the plan forming in her head one more time, then nodded slowly before stammering what she needed Glass to do. For a second, Clarke worried that she'd said too much. Glass was staring at her with enormous eyes, her mind turning behind them. But something in Glass's face shifted, and a look of understanding and resolve took over. It was clear she understood the lengths Clarke was willing to go to in order to save Bellamy.

She could only hope it was enough.

CHAPTER 11

Wells

Wells had never set out to be in charge. It had just evolved. He saw things that needed to be done, and he did them. If he thought something could be done better, he suggested it. It wasn't a power thing, like it clearly was with Rhodes. It was just the best way Wells had found to keep people alive.

He stepped into the supply shed and surveyed the stacks of odds and ends they'd collected from the crash sites. He knew Rhodes wouldn't want him assessing their inventory, but the Vice Chancellor had been conspicuously absent for most of the day, and Wells figured he could always come up with some excuse if he were caught. He needed to do something to keep busy. He could hardly stand to be in the clearing.

The sight of the armed guards in front of the new prison made him physically ill. He racked his brain trying to come up with a way to help Bellamy, but he couldn't think of a way to talk to Rhodes without making the situation even worse.

So until he came up with a plan that didn't involve getting both him and Bellamy killed, he'd take inventory.

There hadn't been much in the way of actual supplies prepared and loaded onto the hundred's dropship by whoever was in charge up there on the Colony. It seemed as if they hadn't believed the hundred would survive the trip, let alone spend more than a month on Earth. There had been a smattering of useful things—one case of medicine and first-aid tools; two cartons of protein paste, which were long gone; and a handful of blankets, water containers, cooking utensils, and weapons. The second round of dropships hadn't carried much more. Wells figured that was the result of having no advance notice when they left the Colony.

But somehow, the hundred and the newcomers had managed to stockpile an impressive number of supplies. They had repurposed broken seats and shards of metal into water buckets, cots, chairs, and tables. They had used straps and wires to bind canvas and upholstery into tarps and tents and blankets. They had foraged for wide, flat leaves they could dry out and use for multiple purposes—from woven baskets to plates and bowls. They used everything they could find to cook, clean, and protect themselves. It was awe-inspiring, really, that all these people had put their heads together and figured out how to survive. Wells had never been so aware of how easy they'd had it on the ship.

The quiet of the supply shed was a welcome change from the hubbub outside. Wells took his time assessing their inventory, making a mental note that they needed to start gathering more leaves and small pieces of wood for kindling. They were doing okay on berries and plants, and a whole new crew was training to track animals—which was good, considering that it'd be a long time before Bellamy would be able to go hunting.

Wells stood up and stretched his arms over his head. He heard a soft *thunk* against the side of the building. Maybe it was Felix dragging the rain barrels over, as Wells had asked him to. He stepped outside to see if he could help. Moving around the side of the shed, his eyes landed on Kendall and his body went rigid. The younger girl had seemed sweet at first and had paid so much attention to Wells he'd thought she'd had a harmless crush on him. But over the past week, he'd grown more concerned with her behavior. Nothing about her quite added up, from her strange accent, to the way her story about ending up in Confinement kept changing.

But that wasn't the most troubling part. Wells's skin prickled as he thought about Priya, his friend who'd been violently killed and left hanging from a tree. They'd all thought the Earthborns had done it, of course, just like they'd murdered Asher. But even the horrific details of that terrible day didn't add up. Priya had been strung up with a rope from the hundred's own camp, and the gruesome letters carved into her feet bore a startling resemblance to the handwriting on her grave maker—a marker Kendall had fashioned herself.

Part of Wells thought he was just being paranoid, that he'd been rattled by the traumatic events. But there was also part of him that knew not to let Kendall out of his sight.

She stood alone, her back to him, leaning over one of the rain barrels. She was reaching down into it.

"Hey, Kendall," Wells said, trying to keep his tone neutral.

Kendall jumped at the sound of his voice and faced him with a large smile plastered on her face.

"Oh, hi, Wells," she said smoothly.

"What's going on? What's up with the rain barrel?"

"Nothing. Just checking to see how much was in there. Felix just rolled these over. I don't know how he did it with so much water in them."

"It's not hard if you get it at the right angle," Wells replied. "Why do you need to check the water level?"

Kendall looked up at the sky and held up her hands near her shoulders, palms up, as if checking the air for moisture.

"It doesn't look like we're going to have any rain today, and I wanted to be sure we had enough."

Wells studied her face. Something about her was out of synch—it was almost as if her semiclueless voice and her piercing stare belonged to two different people but had accidentally ended up together.

"Did you find something in there?"

Kendall tittered. "In the rain barrel? No. Why?"

"What were you doing with your hand in it, then?"

"Wells, I don't know what you're talking about. I didn't have my hand in the barrel."

"Kendall, I saw you standing there reaching into it."

She narrowed her eyes and pursed her lips. For a moment so brief Wells thought he might be imagining it, her expression transformed from innocent and awkward to cool and calculating. Then she opened her eyes wide again, smiled shyly, and shrugged. "Wells, I don't know what to tell you. I wasn't reaching into the barrel. I have to get to my hunting shift." Before Wells could say another word, she turned on her heel and scurried back to the center of camp.

Wells felt uneasy. Something wasn't right. He looked down into the barrel, but all he saw was crystal clear water, about halfway up the side. With a frustrated slap of his palms against the side of the barrel, Wells decided he needed to tell Rhodes what he'd just seen. Making sure the water was safe to drink was more important than some stupid power struggle.

It wasn't hard to track down the Vice Chancellor. He just had to spot the clump of guards gathered around, waiting for orders. With an *excuse me* or two, he made his way to the front of the group and stood behind Rhodes, who was talking to Officer Burnett, his second-in-command.

"Sir?" Wells said in his well-trained officer's respectful tone.

Rhodes spun around and looked Wells over from head to toe. He seemed surprised to see Wells again. "Yes, Officer Jaha? How can I help you?"

Wells felt the eyes of the guards on him. "I witnessed something I think you should know about, sir."

"Did you?"

"Yes. I saw a girl named Kendall dropping something into one of the rain barrels. I believe she was putting something into our water supply."

"And what do you think this Kendall was putting into our water supply?" Rhodes asked coolly.

"I don't know, sir. But there's something about her that doesn't feel quite right. She's just a little . . . off."

Rhodes let out a dry chuckle. "She's 'off'?"

Wells nodded.

Rhodes looked from Wells to Burnett, then back again. "Well, Jaha. Thank you for bringing this very critical piece of intelligence to my attention. I will be sure to have my men investigate anyone who may seem a little *off*. We can't have that."

The men gathered around snickered. Wells felt his cheeks burn.

"It's not a joke," Wells said firmly. "She was up to something. I just don't think she's as innocent as she seems."

Rhodes pinned Wells with a cold stare. "I realize that your brief time as leader here on Earth was very satisfying for you. And one day, if you manage to keep your desperation in check, perhaps you'll be in charge again. But right now I find it shameful that you would make up accusations against an innocent girl simply because you would like to feel important."

Any sense of embarrassment Wells felt was gone in a flash, replaced by pure disgust. He wasn't the one playing games here—and he wasn't the one letting power go to his head. Rhodes was putting all their lives at risk because he was . . . what? Threatened by a teenager? He wasn't going to give Rhodes the satisfaction of letting his frustration show. As hard as it was, he ignored Rhodes's accusations and focused on giving him concrete evidence so he'd have to act, regardless of whatever personal beef he had with Wells.

"Sir. Before you arrived here, two members of our group were killed."

"Yes, I heard about those unfortunate incidents." Rhodes waved his hand dismissively at Wells. "But I understand that you were not properly protected. We've established a security perimeter that will prevent that from happening again."

"I'm not sure how a *perimeter* would prevent an arrow from hitting someone in the neck. Sir. And I'm not sure how a perimeter would help if one of their people has already infiltrated our camp. My friend Priya was strung up from a tree like an animal. We couldn't understand how someone could have snuck into camp for long enough to do that to her without anyone noticing a stranger among us. But I think I've figured it out. I think that the culprit was already here, not an outsider at all. I think it was Kendall."

Rhodes looked at Wells like he was a scrap of trash stuck to his boot. "That's enough. Come back to me when you're ready to help. I don't have time to listen to your conspiracy theories and delusions. I have a settlement to run. If you can tell us where to find an ample food supply, then I'm happy to listen to you. Now go."

Without a word, Wells stormed away. As he rounded the corner of the nearest hut, he slammed directly into someone.

"Sorry," he said, looking up into a familiar face. Kendall. She had been standing right there and had heard everything he said to Rhodes. Wells braced himself for a harsh exchange of some kind. But instead, all Kendall did was shoot him a strange, unreadable smile before turning around and heading off into the woods. Wells watched her get swallowed up by the trees, his heart pounding in his chest, somehow knowing in his gut that she wasn't coming back.

CHAPTER *12*

Clarke

Clarke didn't have the stomach to tell Wells all the details about her plan to rescue Bellamy. She needed his help, but there was a limit to what your ex-boyfriend needed to know. Especially when the plan essentially consisted of one step: flirt dangerously with a sociopathic guard. And particularly when your ex-boyfriend was the protective and occasionally self-righteous type, who also happened to be the de facto leader of the camp.

"So what exactly is it you want me to do?" Wells asked, surveying her with an expression that made it very clear he knew she wasn't telling him everything.

"Someone has to create a distraction so Bellamy and I can get out of camp without anyone noticing."

"I can certainly create a distraction, but how exactly do you plan on getting past the guards?"

"I have a plan. Don't you trust me?"

Wells sighed and ran his hand through his hair. "Of course I trust you, Clarke, but what I don't understand is why you won't trust me. Why won't you tell me what's going on? I know he's your boyfriend, but he's also my brother." The word sounded strange coming from Wells's lips, but it nonetheless landed in a soft spot deep inside her heart.

"I know, Wells. That's why I need you to believe me. The less you know, the better chance this has of working."

Wells shook his head, then gave her a wry smile. "You could convince me to do pretty much anything. You know that, right?"

Clarke grinned. "Good. Because I have one more favor to ask."

"Anything you want, Griffin."

"Once we get out of here, we'll need somewhere to go. Do you think Sasha would ask the Earthborns to take us in—at least for the time being?"

"I'll talk to her," Wells said. He and Sasha had agreed to meet in the woods at noon each day, a temporary measure until it was safe for her to visit the camp again. "I'm sure she'll do it."

"Thank you." She ran through her mental checklist again. Nearly all the pieces of her plan were in place.

Her only regret was that leaving camp would mean leaving behind Dr. Lahiri. They hadn't had a chance to finish their conversation, and she knew there was something he hadn't told her about her parents.

"What is it, Clarke?" Wells asked, apparently reading the concern in her face. He'd always been able to tell what she'd been thinking, a skill that had made the beginning of their relationship so magical, and the end of it so heartbreaking.

"What's wrong?"

"Besides the fact that I have to drag Bellamy and his open wound through the woods to get away from that maniac Rhodes?"

"Yeah, besides that."

She filled him in on what Dr. Lahiri had looked like when she'd asked him about her parents, but how she hadn't had a chance to finish the conversation.

Wells put his hand on her shoulder. "Clarke, I'm sorry."

"For what?"

"For everything. For being naïve. For not getting how sick Rhodes is. I really thought they would do what was right. It sounds so stupid now."

Clarke wanted to take Wells in her arms and hug him—out

of gratitude, out of appreciation, out of empathy. But that wasn't her place anymore.

"Don't ever apologize for seeing the best in people, Wells. That's an amazing quality."

He looked away from her and cleared his throat. "Bellamy's my brother. I'll do anything to help." He settled his gaze back on Clarke, his eyes glinting with a spark she'd never seen there before. "And if it happens to undermine Rhodes's authority in the process, well, that's just a two-for-one deal."

———

An hour later, after Clarke had rinsed off in the stream, then changed into slightly less filthy clothes, she set off on her mission. *It's just for show,* she repeated to herself, trying to slow her pounding heart. *Nothing's actually going to happen.* The repetition soothed her, and soon the words blended into a melody in her head.

She stopped in her tracks. There he was, leaning against the supply shed, his thumbs hooked in his belt, a smug smile squirming across his face. He was talking to an Arcadian girl about Clarke's age, with the same color hair and general build as Clarke too. *Well, at least he has a type,* she thought. *Gross.*

Clarke took a slow breath, braced herself, and reviewed her plan, hoping for the millionth time it would work, that she wasn't just about to re-create one of her own nightmares.

"Hi, Scott," Clarke said as she headed for the supply cabin door. Instead of avoiding eye contact and walking past him as quickly as possible, like she'd normally do, she forced herself to let her gaze linger on his face, and she flashed him what she hoped was a beaming smile, though it could've well been a grimace.

"Hello, Doc," he drawled, giving her a quick look up and down. The girl Scott was talking to turned to glare at Clarke and, when it was clear Scott's attention was now fixed elsewhere, stormed away.

He's all yours, honey, Clarke thought. *Just as soon as I get what I need.*

Adrenaline pumped through her body as she stopped in the cabin entryway, just a few inches from Scott. His intense expression made her nervous—he looked suspicious. Was she coming on too strong? Flirting was not her specialty. She'd always been much more comfortable using scalpels and microscopes than smiles and sauntering strides.

Scott's mouth slithered higher at the corners, and his eyebrows shot up, as if asking her a silent question. "To what do I owe the honor?" he asked, reaching out to hold the door for her.

"I was just looking for something in here," Clarke said. "Do you mind helping me?"

"Sure, no problem." He followed her inside and pulled the door shut behind him with a thud that made Clarke's stomach churn, but she had to keep going.

She flipped her hair over her shoulder and turned to face him. "Listen, I wanted to apologize."

He looked momentarily startled, but then smirked and said, "What could you have to apologize for, sweetheart?"

His voice made Clarke's skin crawl, but she continued. "For not always giving you proper medical attention. I . . ." This was it, she couldn't screw it up now. She lowered her voice and tried to make it as breathy as possible. "I still get a little nervous, around certain patients."

He raised an eyebrow. "Yeah, what kind of patients?"

She forced herself to place her hand on his arm. "The ones who make me feel more like a schoolgirl with a crush than a real doctor."

Scott's eyes popped in a way that gave Clarke a whole new sense of the expression *his eyes lit up.* If they hadn't been Scott's eyes, she would have been flattered to have a guy look at her like that. A flash of guilt cut through her as she realized Bellamy *did* look at her that way.

"Really?" His voice was tinged with a note of disbelief, but that didn't stop him from putting his hand on her waist.

Clarke nodded, ignoring the pressure of his touch, though it was like letting a spider crawl across her arm.

"Do you forgive me? I promise to be more . . . professional going forward."

Scott placed his other hand on her hip, then let both hands slide around until they were on her butt. It took a considerable amount of willpower for Clarke not to pull away. "Professional might be overrated."

Steeling herself, she leaned over to whisper in his ear. "Well, in that case, want to go on a little walk with me? There's a part of the woods I've been dying to explore."

He tightened his grip for a moment before letting her go and shooting her an oily smile. "Absolutely."

They stepped back outside, and Clarke hoped Scott didn't notice how she shuddered as he placed his hand on the small of her back. "Lead the way, Doctor."

Clarke turned toward the woods just in time to see Octavia cross over the tree line, leading two small children by the hand. To Clarke's horror, Bellamy's sister was staring straight at her, a look of pure loathing burning on her face. Octavia didn't know about Clarke's plan to use Scott. She probably thought this scene was exactly what it looked like: Clarke cheating on Bellamy with a guard.

Clarke locked eyes with Octavia, wishing they still had cornea slips and she could send the girl a message. But the only way to communicate with her on Earth was to speak to her, and that would never work. She had Scott on the hook, and she couldn't break the momentum now. She didn't want to do anything to arouse his suspicions. It was too risky to talk to Octavia. All Clarke could do was hope Octavia wouldn't get to Bellamy before she did. If Octavia told him what she had seen, Bellamy would never leave camp with Clarke that night. Octavia turned and stomped back toward the fire pit.

Clarke watched Octavia walk off, then took a deep breath and turned back to Scott. She held his gaze for an extra beat, brushed her hand against his, and said in a throaty voice, "Follow me." She tipped her head toward the woods. Scott's eyes grew big and round.

"I'm right behind you," he breathed into her ear. His breath was hot and damp on her face. Clarke suppressed her gag reflex and reminded herself that Bellamy would die if she didn't go through with this. She grabbed Scott's hand and tugged him toward the trees.

They ducked into the dim forest, the branches brushing against their shoulders. She led Scott into a particularly dense area of woods, where the leaves grew in a thick tangle. They would hear someone approaching before they could be seen. She turned to face Scott, who bumped right into her in his excitement. He pressed his chest against her and wrapped his arms around her shoulders.

He wasn't wasting any time. Clarke tried to focus on Bellamy. All this was for him. For them.

"Are you in a rush?" Clarke managed to say just before he planted a firm, wet kiss on her. She reflexively turned her face, and his lips slid off hers and onto her cheek.

"I've wanted to do this for a long time," Scott said, grabbing her face with both hands and repositioning it.

"And I've wanted to do *this* for a long time," Clarke said as she raised her hand in the air and slammed it down into his neck, the syringe puncturing his skin with a small pop. She pressed the plunger hard with her thumb, administering a massive dose of sedative right into his bloodstream. For a millisecond, Scott's eyes filled with confusion and betrayal. Then he released his hold on her and slid to the ground with a dull thud.

Clarke wiped her slobbery face with her sleeve and got to work. She knelt down and fumbled around in Scott's uniform and utility belt. Her hands were shaking, but she finally managed to wrap her fingers around his heavy key ring and the cold, smooth metal of his gun. Without so much as a backward glance, she hopped up and headed back through the trees, leaving him unconscious on the ground. Clarke wanted to be far away from him when he woke up.

She pushed Scott from her mind and slipped back into the clearing. She ran her eyes around the camp, checking for guards and looking for Wells. He was in the arranged spot.

Clarke closed her eyes and listened hard—yes—she could hear the lower whistle from the trees that was their signal from Sasha. She'd gotten the message. Clarke steeled herself. It was go time.

CHAPTER *13*

Bellamy

The pain was searing and constant, unlike anything he'd ever felt before. It was much worse than the time he'd fallen down a flight of stairs during a fight and broken his collarbone. This was a deep, throbbing pain, like the inside of his bones were on fire. Bellamy slumped against the cold metal wall—a wall that must've been built around him while he was unconscious, because it sure as hell hadn't been there when he was shot.

His stomach rumbled loudly, although the thought of swallowing anything added a layer of nausea to the waves of pain. He couldn't remember the last time he'd eaten; he had a vague recollection of Clarke encouraging him to take a few mouthfuls of protein paste but had no idea how long ago that'd been.

Bellamy squeezed his eyes shut and tried to distract himself by replaying his favorite moments with Clarke over again in his mind. The first time she'd kissed him, when she'd shed her reserved, serious-doctor persona like a set of binding clothes and thrown her arms around him in the woods. The night they went swimming in the lake and it'd felt like the entire planet belonged to him and the glistening girl with a mischievous spark in her eyes. He even reminisced over the past few days in the infirmary cabin, feeling his pain abate every time she stroked his cheek, or followed a tender kiss on the forehead with a decidedly undoctorlike kiss on his neck. Hell, taking a bullet to the shoulder almost seemed like a fair price to pay for one of her surprisingly diverting sponge baths.

It worked for a moment, but the pain inevitably returned with renewed fury. He started to raise a hand to adjust his bandage and realized his wrists were bound together and attached to the wall behind him. With a groan, he twisted around to investigate, his shoulder throbbing in protest at the movement, but the pain wasn't quite enough to overwhelm his curiosity. He'd never seen anything like these cuffs before. They were lightweight, made of a thin metal cord that looked as delicate as thread, with a slim lock binding them together. He tried to pull his hands apart, but the fiber held strong and dug into his skin. As he tugged, he felt the tension in the cord getting stronger and watched in amazement as his wrists slammed together. *The metal was reacting to his movements*. He held very still and slowly the cord released its grip, until he was able to wiggle his hands again.

Bellamy's shoulder burned, and he scooted himself further up the wall, trying to find a comfortable position. Grunting with the effort, he settled in and leaned his head back. He was exhausted, but the pain made it impossible to sleep for more than a few minutes at a time.

Narrow shafts of sunlight filtered through the cracks between the sheets of metal that formed the walls and roof of the cabin. He studied the angle of the light and listened carefully to the sounds outside, trying to figure out where the prison was located. The far-off *thwack* of an ax hitting firewood told him he was a good distance from the woodpile. A group of boys walked by, right on the other side of the wall, chatting about a Walden girl. Under their voices, he could hear water sloshing, which meant he was near the path people used to get to the stream.

Bellamy strained to identify every sound he could make out. Logs clattering together, blankets and tarps snapping as someone shook them out, a guard's officious tone as he corrected someone's stacking technique. But there was only one sound Bellamy wanted to hear, and he held his breath, frustration building in his chest. Octavia's voice. He wanted—needed—to hear his sister. He would be able to tell from just a few words whether she was happy or scared, in danger or safe. But he didn't recognize any of the voices floating across the clearing. The place was overrun with newcomers.

Bellamy didn't even have the strength to be angry anymore. He only cared about Octavia, Clarke, and Wells. If it weren't for them, he wouldn't care if he lived or died, if he was executed or set free to live alone in the woods. But what would happen to his sister if he were killed? Who would look after her once he was gone? The hundred had formed a community, but now that Rhodes and all the others were here, all bets were off. He couldn't be sure anyone would look out for his kid sister when they were all busy looking out for themselves. Just like everyone else had been back on the ship.

A loud *thud* against the side of the cabin made Bellamy jerk to the side—which sent shooting pain through his upper body. "Jesus," he grunted. Then he heard scuffling, followed by loud voices. One familiar voice rose above the rest: It was Wells.

"Put the shackles on," Wells said in a voice Bellamy had never heard before, low and menacing. "Do it *now*," he snapped, "and don't make a sound. If you do so much as open your mouth, I'll shoot you." And although it contradicted everything Bellamy knew about his half brother, it sounded like Wells meant it.

Shit, Bellamy thought. *Mini-Chancellor is starting to sound like a mini–Vice Chancellor.*

There was silence as, presumably, the guard complied with Wells's order. A few seconds later, two figures burst through the cabin door—a stony-faced, iron-jawed Wells and a flushed, rapidly-breathing Clarke. They fell into the room and rushed over to him, as Bellamy's head swam with confusion and relief. Were they actually here to *rescue* him? How the hell had they managed that?

Bellamy's chest swelled with a feeling he'd never really known before—gratitude. No one had ever done anything this dangerous for him, no one had ever thought he was worth that kind of risk. He'd spent his whole life taking reckless action to protect Octavia, but no one had ever done so much as transfer him a ration point or sneak out past curfew to check on him the few times he'd gotten sick.

Yet here they were, the girl he never would've dared *dream* about back on the ship, and the brother he never knew existed, putting their lives on the line for him.

Clarke sank to her knees next to him. "Bellamy," she said, her voice cracking as she ran her hand along his cheek. "Are you okay?" She'd never sounded so afraid, so fragile. Yet there was nothing vulnerable about a girl who'd face down a clearing full of armed guards.

Bellamy nodded, then winced as Wells tugged on the cuffs attached to the peg on the wall. "How are you going to get those off?" Bellamy asked, his voice hoarse. The guard outside would alert the others any second. If they didn't get out of there fast, not a single one of them would live to see another sunset.

"Don't worry," Wells said. "She has the key."

Clarke reached into her pocket and pulled out a slim key, made of the same flexible metal as the cuffs.

"How the hell did you—you know what? Forget it. I don't want to know," Bellamy said. "Just get them off."

Wells took the key from Clarke and began fumbling with the restraints while Clarke switched back into doctor mode and quickly examined his shoulder, muttering to herself as she peeled back the blood-stained bandage. Bellamy couldn't take his eyes off her. Her brow was furrowed in concentration and a thin sheen of sweat misted her face, but she'd never looked more beautiful.

"Got it," Wells said as the cuffs sprang open. "Let's go." He reached down, wrapped an arm behind Bellamy, and hauled him to his feet. Clarke slipped under Bellamy's other arm, and helped him hurry across the cabin. When they reached the door, Clarke held up her hand and signaled for them to wait while she listened for sounds outside. At first, Bellamy wasn't sure what they were waiting for, but then he heard it. A loud crash and series of cries echoed from the far side of the clearing, followed by shouts of "We're under attack!" and "Guards—fall in!"

A stampede of heavy footsteps thudded past the cabin, toward the commotion.

Clarke turned to Wells and grinned. "She did it! Go, Sasha."

"What'd she do?" Bellamy asked as he leaned a little harder on Wells. He hadn't walked in days, and his muscles felt like jelly.

"She rigged up something in the trees to make it sound like the Earthborns were attacking the camp. If everything goes according to plan, Rhodes will have sent all the guards into the woods, and we'll be able to sneak out the other side."

"Your girl's pretty badass, Wells," Bellamy said with a weak smile. "Will she be okay?"

"She'll be fine. She's far enough out in the woods that they'll never get to her in time."

Clarke listened at the door for another moment, then waved at them urgently. "Let's move."

They slipped out the door. The coast was clear—everyone

in camp was facing the other direction or racing toward the commotion on the far side. Bellamy, Clarke, and Wells hurried around the back of the cabin and, before anyone could notice they were gone, disappeared into the cover of the woods.

CHAPTER 14

Wells

There was no sound except the sharp intake of breath and the crunch of twigs and dried leaves under their feet. Wells, Bellamy, and Clarke had run until their sides cramped, eventually slowing to a walk. Wells glanced over his shoulder to check on Bellamy, whose shoulder was clearly hurting him, although he refused to complain, and who seemed much more anxious about Octavia than he was about his injury.

"You're sure she doesn't think I abandoned her?" Bellamy said as he allowed Clarke to help him step over a moss-covered log blocking their path.

"Positive," Wells said, glad he could provide at least that modicum of comfort. "We told her the plan, and she agreed that it was better for someone to remain at the camp and keep tabs on Rhodes for a while."

"She would've come if it weren't for the kids," Clarke chimed in. "She's the only one who's looking after them. It's really amazing, what she's done."

Wells watched as pride momentarily chased away the fear in Bellamy's face. "I always knew she had it in her."

"Where did Sasha say she'd meet us?" Clarke asked, scanning the trees nervously. Although she and Bellamy had stumbled across Mount Weather once before, Wells knew neither of them were confident about finding it again.

"She'll find us," Wells said.

There was a rustling in the tree ahead of them, and a moment later, a figure dropped down from the branches, landing silently on her feet.

"Okay, that was kinda creepy," Wells said with a grin as Sasha walked toward them. He still hadn't gotten used to how Sasha managed to blend in with her surroundings. It was almost as if she changed color, like the lizards he'd read about when he was a kid. But she didn't, of course—it was something about the way she breathed, her stillness. She just became part of the woods.

He pulled her into his arms, burying his face in her long dark hair that always smelled like rain and cedar. "Thank you for your help," he said, cupping his hand under her chin and raising it for a kiss. "That was amazing."

"Does that mean it worked?" Sasha asked, breaking away to look from Wells to Clarke and Bellamy.

"It worked perfectly," Wells said.

"So what's the plan now?" Bellamy asked, clearly in pain. His face was pale, and his breathing had grown ragged.

"I'm taking you all back to Mount Weather with me," Sasha said. "You can stay there as long as you need."

"They won't mind?" Bellamy asked, looking nervously from Clarke to Sasha.

Sasha shook her head. "As long as you're with me, it'll be fine," she assured him.

"We shouldn't stop for long," Wells said, his voice strained. "Once they realize you're missing, they're going to come after us."

"Bel, are you okay to keep moving?" Clarke asked gently.

"I'm good," he said, though he wouldn't meet Clarke's eye.

They followed Sasha as she darted, quickly and quietly, through the darkening forest. "So are you all right?" Sasha asked when they were a few meters ahead of Clarke and Bellamy. With the rush to free Bellamy, he and Sasha had barely had time to talk about anything besides the actual logistics.

"I don't know." That was the truth. It'd all happened so quickly, he hadn't had time to process the implications of disobeying Rhodes, of leaving the camp. Wells certainly wasn't going to stand by and watch Rhodes execute his brother in cold blood. But it was still hard to fathom that they'd been forced to leave their new home behind—the home, the community, that *they* had built with their bare hands, from nothing.

"It won't be forever. As soon as your father gets better, he'll come down on one of the other dropships and everything will be okay."

"No, it won't. Sasha, my dad's in a coma, and there aren't extra dropships just lying around." His tone was sharp and bitter, but he didn't care. This wasn't a situation he could count on anyone to fix. He'd been an idiot to trust Rhodes. He should've acted sooner, before everything spiraled out of control.

Another girl might've been hurt—or worse, apologized as if she'd done something wrong. But Sasha just took Wells's hand and gave it a squeeze. It was deeply unfair. Bellamy had only been trying to save his sister. He hadn't even been the one to pull the trigger—one of Rhodes's own precious guards had done that. Besides, it was Wells's father who had gotten shot, and if Wells didn't think Bellamy should pay for that, then who was Rhodes to say otherwise?

Actually, Wells smiled grimly, it was *Bellamy's* father too. If only Rhodes knew that, he'd probably have an aneurysm. Wells couldn't deny that the image brought him some pleasure.

Sasha raised an eyebrow, clearly curious about what he was thinking. "I was just imagining what would happen if Rhodes found out that Bellamy and I were brothers," Wells said.

Sasha laughed. "He'd probably have a heart attack. Actually, that might be the best plan. I'll head back to your camp, shout the news, and wait for Rhodes to drop dead. Problem solved."

Wells squeezed her hand back. "Your tactical mind never ceases to amaze me."

They walked on, with Wells only half listening as Sasha pointed out various geographic features. At one point, Clarke began peppering Sasha with questions about different animal species, but Wells could tell she doing it more to distract Bellamy.

They walked for what seemed like hours. Finally Sasha pointed to a small rise in the ground, so subtle they would never have noticed it on their own.

"That way," she said. They followed her, picking their way carefully among the branches. Wells felt the ground beneath him slowly sloping downward, and he adjusted his gait to keep from toppling forward. They rounded a curve and Wells's breath caught in his chest as he took in the sight spread out before him. At the bottom of the hill, in a wide valley, was an entire town, just like he'd spent his entire life reading about. Just like he'd imagined building with the hundred on Earth.

Wells had never seen anything so remarkable since he'd

arrived on the planet—not the endless trees reaching to the horizon, not the lake or the sky. Nature was beautiful in a way he'd never imagined, but this . . . this was *life*. Signs of vibrancy and energy were everywhere: light-filled windows with the shadows of families inside; animals stomping their hooves, harnesses jangling; smoke curling out of a dozen chimneys in a coordinated dance toward the sky; wheelbarrows tipped on their sides, as if they'd just been dropped moments ago; balls and toys at rest, the echoes of children's laughter floating in the air around them.

Wells let out an astonished laugh. Clarke turned to him and smiled. "Pretty cool, right?" He was glad that she was here to share this moment. She was one of the only people in the solar system who knew how much this meant to him.

"It's spectacular."

Sasha slipped her hand into his and squeezed. "Let's go." She led them down the hill and onto the dirt road that ran through the center of her town. Wells breathed in the smell of roasting meat and something lighter and sweeter—was someone baking bread?

Sasha walked up to the front door of the last house on a row and entered without knocking. They stepped through the doorway and into a room lit by a small lamp and a flickering fire. The first thing Wells noticed was the enormous oil painting of a star-filled sky on the wall. Back on the ship, something like that would've been behind a foot of bullet-proof glass, maybe inside an oxygen-free chamber, but here it hung unadorned, just a few meters from the ash-spewing fire. Yet Wells could tell that the firelight somehow brought it to life more than the harsh, fluorescent lights of Phoenix ever could, making the stars appear to glow.

Wells pulled his gaze from the painting and turned his attention to the gray-bearded man who'd just stood to greet them. He was standing next to a plain wooden table that was covered with electronics, most of which Wells didn't recognize. The only piece that looked at all familiar was an ancient laptop that'd been welded onto an enormous solar panel, and not particularly neatly.

"Hi, Dad," Sasha said, stepping forward to kiss her father's cheek. "You remember Clarke and Bellamy, right?"

The man raised a bushy eyebrow. "How could I forget?" He turned to his guests and nodded. "Welcome back."

"Thank you," Bellamy said, slightly bashful. "Sorry I keep showing up like this."

Sasha's father glanced at his heavily bandaged arm. "Somehow, I don't think it's entirely your fault, although you do seem to have a special talent for finding trouble."

"Talent is one word for it," Clarke said, reaching her arm forward. "It's nice to see you again, Mr. Walgrove."

"Dad, this is Wells." Sasha caught Wells's eye for a brief

moment and shot him an encouraging look.

"Nice to meet you, sir." Wells stepped forward and held out his hand.

"Nice to meet you too, Wells." Sasha's dad gripped Wells's hand in a firm shake. "Call me Max."

Max turned back to Bellamy. "Where's your sister?" He said the word casually, without twisting his lips with disdain like Rhodes would've done. In this world, having a sibling didn't mark your family as deviants.

"She didn't come with us," Bellamy told Max, trying to keep his voice steady as he shot Clarke an anguished look.

Sasha led them back outside and explained that there was only one spare cabin at the moment, and it only had one bed. Wells quickly said that Bellamy should take it, and he helped Clarke walk Bellamy over while Sasha ran to get Clarke some medical supplies.

Once Bellamy and Clarke were safely inside, Sasha took Wells's hand and interlaced her fingers through his. "So . . . where to? You can crash on the floor at my dad's house, or if you don't mind the cold, I can take you to my favorite spot."

"Hmmm," Wells said, pretending to weigh the choices. "While sleeping a few meters from your father sounds amazing, I'll have to go with option B."

Sasha smiled and led Wells back through the tiny town and into a small patch of trees that grew between the cabins and the hill leading up to Mount Weather. "I hope I can find it in the dark," Sasha said, running her hand along the trunk of one of the larger trees.

"Find what?" Wells asked.

"This." Sasha's voice was triumphant. In the dim light, Wells could just make out some kind of ladder, made from ragged rope. "Follow me." Silently, Sasha scaled the tree, disappearing into the branches before calling down to Wells. "Come on, slowpoke."

Wells grabbed on to the rope hesitantly. It hardly looked capable of supporting his weight, but there was no way he was going to wimp out in front of Sasha. With a deep breath, he slipped his foot into the first rung, and, holding on to the tree to steady himself, took a big step. He swayed from side to side but managed to keep climbing, wincing slightly as the rope cut into his hands.

Without looking down, he moved up the ladder and eventually saw Sasha resting on a small wooden platform tucked among the branches. "Like it?" she asked, grinning as if she'd just invited Wells into the most magnificent palace.

Carefully, he slipped off the ladder and crawled over next to her. "Love it," he said with a smile. "Did you make it yourself?"

"I was pretty little, so my dad helped."

"And he won't mind if we spend the night here?"

"Wells, my father is in charge of our entire society. He's a little too busy to care about where I sleep."

Wells snorted. "No father is *that* busy."

"It's *fine*. Though we can certainly go back if it'll make you more comfortable."

In response, Wells reached his arm around Sasha and pulled her close. "I'm pretty comfortable here, actually."

She smiled and gave him a quick, light kiss. "Good."

"I've missed you these past few days," Wells said, lowering himself onto the wooden platform and pulling her down with him.

"I've missed you too." Her voice was muffled as she snuggled into his chest.

"Thank you . . . for everything. I never meant for you to get caught up in all this, let alone impose on your people."

Sasha sat up slowly and looked at him. She traced her hand along the side of his face and then began running it through his hair. "You don't have to thank me, Wells. I want to keep you all safe too, you know."

"I know." He took her hand and kissed it. "So . . ." he said, looking around. "This seems like a nice place to sleep."

"Are you tired?"

"Exhausted," he said, wrapping his hand behind her, and pulling her in for another kiss. "You?"

"Maybe not quite *that* tired."

She kissed him again, and the rest of the world slipped

away. There were no new Colonists. No Earthborns. No Rhodes. Just Sasha. Just their breath. Just their lips.

The camp suddenly felt light-years away, as distant as Earth used to look from the Colony. "You make me feel legitimately crazy. You know that, right?" Wells whispered, running his hand down her back.

"Why? Because I'm seducing you in a tree?"

"Because no matter what else is going on, being with you makes me perfectly happy. It's crazy, switching gears that fast." Wells ran his hand along her cheek. "You're like a drug."

Sasha smiled. "I think you need to work on your compliments, space boy."

"I've never been the best with words. I'm much better at showing what I mean."

"Is that so?" Sasha breathed as Wells brought his other hand to her stomach. "I guess I'll have to take your word for it." Wells let his fingers drop a little lower, and she shuddered. "Okay, now you're the one making me feel crazy."

"Good," Wells whispered into her ear, thinking that things on Earth weren't quite as dire as he'd feared. As long as he had Sasha, it would always feel like home.

CHAPTER 15

Glass

Glass looked around her, feeling genuine awe for the first time since setting foot on the ground. Sunlight filtered through the trees, showering the ground with golden dots of light, like thousands of little gemstones. This was how Earth was supposed to look—peaceful, beautiful, and full of wonder.

Luke took Glass's hand to steady her as they made their way down a steep slope. There was a narrow stream at the bottom, the water perfectly clear except for the red and yellow leaves dancing in the current. When they reached the bottom, Glass hesitated, turning from side to side as she scanned the bank for the best place to cross. But as she took a hesitant step toward the edge, Luke picked her up with his good arm and crossed the stream with an easy bound, despite the fact that they were both carrying heavy packs.

When they reached the other side, Luke lowered her carefully to the ground, then took her hand again as they continued. At first, they'd kept up nearly constant conversation as they exclaimed and pointed out different trees, and signs of various animal life. But after a while, they'd fallen silent, too overwhelmed by the beauty around them to fumble with the inadequate words they had to express it. Glass almost liked it better that way. She loved watching Luke's face light up each time his eyes settled on a new wonder.

It had taken a couple of hours for Glass's heart rate to come down after they'd slipped away from the camp. The quiet had scared her initially. Every snap of a twig or rustling of leaves boomed in her ears and made her jump. She knew it was just a matter of time before Rhodes realized they were gone and sent a search party to hunt them down.

But after a few hours, her stress faded away, and she began to savor the silence, the freedom of being completely alone with Luke. Glass couldn't believe they'd ever considered staying at camp. The air was fragrant with damp leaves and musky tree bark. It was a riot of sensory input that Glass had never experienced before. She couldn't have imagined how much brighter and more saturated the colors were on Earth, how much sweeter the air, or how the rich smells would compete for her attention.

They'd walked long into the night and slept for a few hours before setting off again, eager to put as much distance between them and Rhodes as possible before the Vice Chancellor sent a search party after them. Every half hour or so, Luke would stop, fish a compass out of his pocket, and set it on the ground, checking to make sure they were still heading due north. Sasha had told him that the splinter Earthborns, the violent ones, had claimed a vast area to the south of the Colonists' camp as their territory. It was no guarantee, of course, but heading north at least wouldn't lead them directly into harm's way.

The trees grew close together, creating a canopy of leaves so thick it almost blocked the sky. But the amber light spilling through the branches and the rapidly cooling air made it clear that the day was nearly over.

"I think we made it," Glass said wearily. The fear and adrenaline that had kept her going yesterday had drained away, and exhaustion had set in. "They're not sending anyone after us, are they?"

"It doesn't seem like it," Luke said with a sigh. He reached over and slid Glass's pack off her shoulder. "Let's rest for a little bit."

They dropped the packs and walked toward an enormous, moss-covered tree whose huge, twisty roots stuck out of the ground. Luke raised his arms over his head and stretched before lowering himself onto the root. "Come here," he said, grabbing Glass's hand and pulling her onto his lap.

Glass laughed and pressed her hand against his chest. "We have the whole planet to ourselves, and you want to share the same seat."

"We don't have the *whole* planet, you little imperialist," Luke said, twisting a strand of her hair around his finger. "We have to leave some room for the Earthborns."

"Oh, right." Glass nodded with mock gravity. "In that case, we better conserve space." She smiled and swung her leg over Luke's so they were facing each other.

"Good plan," he said, wrapping his arms around her waist, closing the narrow distance between them. He kissed her gently on the lips and then brought his mouth down to her chin, her neck. Glass let out a small sigh, and Luke grinned. He kissed the spot where her jaw met her neck and raised his head to whisper in her ear. "It feels good to be selfless, doesn't it?"

"It has its benefits," Glass breathed, running her hand down Luke's back. Their joking aside, it felt incredible to be so alone. On the ship, there were thousands of people packed into a space originally designed for hundreds. There were always ears listening, eyes watching, and bodies brushing up against each other. People knew your name, your family, and your actions. But out here, there was no one watching them. No one judging them.

"Oh, look," Glass said, pointing over Luke's shoulder at a cluster of small pink flowers she hadn't noticed before. He twisted around and extended his arm, reaching for one. But just as his fingers were about to close around the stem, he pulled back and let his hand fall back to his side.

"It doesn't seem right to pick it," he said, turning back to Glass with a sheepish expression on his face.

"I agree." She smiled and placed her hand on the back of his head, bringing his lips back to hers.

"It's a shame, though," Luke murmured. "It would've looked beautiful in your hair."

"Better just to imagine it."

Luke kissed her again, then slid his arm under her and stood up, lifting her into the air. "Luke!" she laughed. "What are you doing?"

He took a few steps and, without a word, lowered her to the ground, laying her gently in the patch of flowers. Glass's breath quickened as she watched Luke kneel beside her. The playfulness in his face had disappeared, replaced by something closer to reverence. He reached down and ran his fingers through her hair, allowing it to fan out across the pink blossoms.

Glass's heart was pounding, but she forced herself to stay still as Luke bent down to kiss her, using his good hand to support his weight. She parted her lips slightly, then reached her arms around to pull him closer. She took a deep breath, savoring the heady combination of the flowers, the forest air, and *Luke*.

"We should get going," Luke said finally, looking up at the darkening sky. "We're going to need to find a place to stay tonight."

Glass let out a long, contented sigh. "Can't we just stay right here forever?"

"I wish. But we're not actually safe out here in the dark. We should find a spot that's more protected."

They walked on with renewed energy for a few more hours as the sky went from a deep grayish purple to a rich, velvety black. The moon was so bright, it blocked out most of the stars and painted strangely beautiful shadows on the forest floor. It was so beautiful, it made Glass's heart ache, as each new wonder served to remind her how much her mother was missing, how much she'd never get to see.

Luke came to a sudden halt and held out his hand to stop her. He cocked his head, listening, though Glass didn't hear anything. After a moment, Luke whispered, "Do you see that?"

At first, all she could see was a shadowy landscape of trees, but then she spotted it: It was a small building. Right there in the middle of nowhere.

"What is it?" she asked, suddenly nervous that they'd wandered somewhere they weren't meant to be.

"It looks like a cabin," Luke said, tightening his hold on her hand as he led her forward, stepping slowly and silently. They made their way toward it, moving in a wide arc before approaching it from the side. It wasn't a cabin; it was a tiny stone house, remarkably intact. The sides were covered with vines and moss, but it was clear that the walls were sturdy and strong.

They stopped a few feet away. A sudden breeze rustled the trees, and then it fell silent. Both Luke and Glass held their breath, waiting for any sign of life, but none came.

Luke stepped up to the door, pressed his ear against it for a moment, then pushed it open and stepped inside before beckoning for Glass to join him. She took a deep breath, adjusted her pack, and crossed over the threshold. There was just enough light coming through the cracked, dust-caked windows for them to see the frozen tableau inside.

"Oh," Glass murmured, half in surprise, half in sorrow. It was as if whoever lived there had stepped out for a moment but never come back. A small bed rested in the far corner. Next to it, stacked wooden boxes formed a dresser. Glass's eyes darted across the tiny space. Opposite the bed was a kitchen that looked sized for a doll family. Pots and pans hung from nails in the wall. A lopsided wooden table sat, waiting for someone to join it, by the cold fireplace. A basin rested against a far wall, with clean dishes piled up on one side. The house seemed lonely, like it had been waiting for a long time for its family to come back.

Glass walked over to the table and ran her hand over its rough surface. Her hand came away dusty. She turned back to Luke.

"Can we stay here?" she asked, scared it might be too good to be true.

Luke nodded. "I think we should. It seems abandoned, and it's clearly safer than staying out there."

"Good," Glass said, looking around, grateful for their good luck and for the chance to dispel the sense of loneliness that clung heavier than the dust. She dropped her pack to the floor and then reached for Luke's hand. "Welcome home," she said, rising onto her toes to kiss his cheek.

He smiled. "Welcome home."

They went back outside to look for firewood and any supplies that might've survived. There was a tiny, half-collapsed wooden shed behind the house, but the only tool they found was a mangled shovel, rusted beyond use. Luckily, there were enough dried branches on the ground that they didn't need an ax, at least not for now.

The faint sound of running water called out to them through the darkness. Glass took Luke's hand and pulled him toward it. While the house was surrounded by trees on three sides, there was a slope at the back that led down to a river. "Look," Luke said, pointing at a chunk of jagged wood that stuck out over the water. "It looks like they built something on the river. I wonder why."

He tightened his grip on Glass's hand and led her a little closer, taking care not to lose their footing in the dark. "Is that . . ." He trailed off as he pointed at an oddly-shaped shadow, a strange combination of sharp edges and curved lines.

"It's a boat, isn't it?" Glass said, taking a few steps closer to run a finger along it. It was cold, almost like metal but lighter. It had once been white, but most of the paint had peeled off, leaving nothing but large patches of rust. She peered inside and saw what appeared to be a paddle resting on the bottom. "Do you think it still works?"

Luke walked around the side, staring at it. "There doesn't seem to be an engine, just the paddle. I guess that means if it still floats, it'll work." He turned to Glass and smiled. "Maybe when my wrist is better, we'll give it a try."

"Well, *I* have two functioning wrists. Unless you think I'm not up to the task."

"You know there's *nothing* I think you can't do, my little spacewalker. I just thought it'd be romantic to take you for a boat ride."

Glass leaned against him, nestling into his side. "That sounds wonderful."

They stood there for a moment, watching the moonlight rippling on the water, then went back inside the house.

Using the matches he'd taken from the camp, Luke built a small fire in the fireplace while Glass took out their tiny supply of food. Neither had felt comfortable taking more than a few days of rations. "This is crazy," Glass said, passing Luke a piece of dried fruit from her pack. "It's like something out of a fairy tale. A house in the woods."

Luke took a sip of water from his canteen, then passed it to Glass. "I wish we knew what happened to the people who lived here, whether they tried to make it through the Cataclysm, or whether they evacuated." He looked around. "It seems like they might've left in a hurry." There was a note of wistfulness in his voice that made it clear he'd been thinking the same thing as Glass.

"I know, it's like the house held on to their memories long after they were gone."

Growing up on the ship, believing in ghosts had seemed like the most foolish thing in the world. But here, on Earth, in this house, Glass was beginning to understand how someone could believe in a lingering presence.

"Well, then it's our responsibility to replace them with some happy memories," Luke said with a smile. He scooted closer to

Glass and wrapped his arm around her. "Aren't you warm in front of the fire? Don't you want to take off your jacket?"

Glass grinned as he unzipped her jacket. She closed her eyes as he began kissing her, softly at first, then with more urgency. But as much as she wanted to lose herself in his touch, she couldn't shake the nagging thought building in the back of her mind. Luke was wrong. You couldn't replace sad memories with happy ones.

That was the thing about heartache. You never could erase it. You carried it with you, always.

Luke's rhythmic breath was like a lullaby. Glass's head rose and fell on his chest as he inhaled, exhaled. She had always envied his ability to pass out cold—the sleep of the innocent, her mother had always called it. Glass's head was spinning too fast for her to fall asleep. She wished she could just enjoy the moment, savor the magic of lying next to Luke, but she could barely look at him without feeling a heavy pang of sorrow bang against her heart. They didn't have much longer. Soon, Glass would have to end it, before Luke discovered the secret that would get them both killed.

Tears sprang to Glass's eyes, and she was grateful that he couldn't see her face. He didn't know that their future together didn't involve anything but pain and sorrow. She took a couple of deep breaths, steadying herself.

"You okay, baby?" Luke mumbled, his voice thick with sleep.

"Fine," she whispered.

He extended his arm, and without opening his eyes, pulled her closer to him and kissed the top of her head. "I love you."

"I love you too," she managed to say before her voice cracked.

After a few moments, she could tell from the rhythm of his breath that he had drifted back off to sleep. She took his hand and gently placed it on her belly, letting his warmth seep through her skin. She watched his face as he slept. He always looked like a little boy when he was asleep, his long lashes practically brushing his cheeks. If only she could tell him about their child, the one growing inside her as they lay there.

But he could never know. Whereas at seventeen, Glass had a wisp of a chance of being forgiven for violating the Gaia Doctrine, at nineteen, Luke would be floated—executed after a cursory trial. She would have to leave him, cut off all contact so the Council couldn't trace him back to her.

"I'm sorry," Glass whispered as the tears slid down her cheeks, wondering which one of them her heart ached for the most.

Luke sighed in his sleep. Glass shifted her weight and brushed her hand against his cheek, wishing she could tell what he was thinking. In the chaos of their escape from the Colony, and the trauma of their crash landing on Earth, there hadn't been any time to talk about their devastating fight on the ship. Or maybe Luke wanted it that way.

Glass had tried to conceal her pregnancy, but she was eventually found out. Violating the ship's strict population control rules was one of the most serious crimes of all, and even after suffering a miscarriage, Glass still had to face the Chancellor. When he'd insisted that Glass reveal the father, she'd panicked and lied. Instead of Luke, she'd given the name of his roommate, Carter, a manipulative, dangerous older boy who had tried to assault Glass when Luke was away.

But although Carter was a vile slimeball, he hadn't deserved to die. But that was exactly what had happened. The Chancellor had taken Glass's word, sending Glass, a minor, into Confinement, and ordering Carter's execution.

Glass would never forget the look of fury and disgust in Luke's face when he'd discovered the truth. And even though he'd forgiven her, she worried she'd broken something that couldn't be fully repaired—Luke's trust.

He sighed again and, without opening his eyes, pulled her closer to him. She smiled, allowing the reassuring thud of his heartbeat to drown out her other thoughts. Coming to Earth was a chance to start over, to put the horror of the past behind them.

Glass closed her eyes and was just beginning to drift off to sleep when a loud noise startled her awake. All her senses fired up, she sat up in bed and looked around. The cabin was empty. Had she dreamed the sound? What was it? She replayed it in her head—it wasn't quite a howl, and it wasn't quite a voice. It was something else—like a call, a signal, but not words. Just a . . . communication of some kind. Between what kinds of creatures, she had no idea. Camp was miles away, and they'd seen no other signs of civilization out here. They were totally alone. It was probably just the sound of the wind against the cabin roof or something. She had nothing to worry about.

Glass lay back down, pressed herself into Luke's warm, relaxed body, and finally fell asleep.

CHAPTER 16

Bellamy

Bellamy wasn't used to sitting on his ass, doing nothing. He didn't like feeling helpless. Useless. He was used to fighting for the things he needed—food, safety, his sister, life itself—and having to depend on other people drove him crazy. Yet that tendency was what got him into this mess in the first place. If he hadn't been in such a rush to get on the dropship with Octavia, the Chancellor—his father—never would've been shot. And then a few weeks later, Bellamy could've come down with the second wave of Colonists, as a citizen instead of a condemned prisoner.

He sat on a wooden bench on the village green, a small grassy area in the center of Sasha and Max's town. He watched a group of kids a few years his junior walk by on their way to the schoolhouse. Three boys punched each other on the shoulders. He could hear their teasing tone. One took off running, and the other two chased him, laughing. An older boy and girl held hands, drawing out their good-bye, sharing a private joke and a blush-inducing kiss.

But then again, he'd had no idea that the Colony was running out of oxygen and that they'd been weeks away from an emergency evacuation. And it's not like some nineteen-year-old nobody from Walden would've been first in line for a spot on the dropship. Forcing his way to Earth had been the right decision. He'd been able to keep an eye on Octavia. And he'd met a beautiful, intense, intimidatingly smart girl who made him start and end every day with the same goofy grin on his face. That is, when she wasn't driving him totally crazy.

He lifted his head and looked around for Clarke, who'd been asked to examine a kid's broken arm. Under other circumstances, staying in this town wouldn't suck. It was both orderly and relaxed. Everyone had a place to live and enough to eat, and there were no power-tripping guards running around, scrutinizing everyone's movements. Sasha's father was clearly in charge, but he wasn't like Rhodes, or even like the Chancellor. He listened closely to his advisors, and from what Bellamy could tell, most important decisions were put to a vote. The other bonus was that here no one even thought it was weird that he had a sister—they all had siblings, lots of them.

Yet the peacefulness had an ominous quality in light of recent events. What if Rhodes came after them? What if Bellamy accidentally turned the Earthborns' quiet village into some kind of war zone? He'd never forgive himself if innocent people got hurt because of him.

Bellamy bounced his leg nervously. His stomach had been in knots since they'd arrived here three days ago. He didn't know what to do. Max, Sasha, and their people wanted him to stay. They wanted to protect him. And it wasn't all that bad, staying in a place with a real roof over his head and delicious food that he hadn't had to track, kill, and skin himself. Bellamy couldn't deny it: A little kernel in his chest longed for a life this simple. He wanted Rhodes to forget about him, for his past to go away, for his life to be as easy as it was for those kids.

He scanned the tree line and the path leading into town, searching for signs of intruders. Nothing. He'd hardly been able to sleep since he got here. He was too busy straining his ears in the overnight quiet, listening for the sound of approaching footsteps, the rustle of leaves that would tell him they were about to be attacked—that he was about to be taken.

This was no way to live. The anticipation and dread were getting to him, and even the little town was starting to feel like a prison. Since he'd been on Earth, Bellamy had gotten used to spending hours of every day out in the woods by himself. Being confined to the village was certainly better than being stuck on a ship in space, but still.

He leaned back against the bench with a sigh and looked up at the blue expanse above. What the hell was he going to do all day? He couldn't hunt; he couldn't even wander off by himself. The kids were in school, so he couldn't play ball with them. Everyone else had something to do. He looked around at the people busily going about their tasks—building, fixing, washing, tending to the animals, and so on. And they were all so pleasant; it made him kind of uncomfortable. Every single person he passed wished him a good day. He didn't know what to say or do with his face—was he supposed to smile back? Say hi? Or just nod?

At least he knew Octavia was okay. Sasha had been back to the camp twice to check on her from afar and had gotten a message to Octavia letting her know that Bellamy was safe. For whatever reason, Rhodes had chosen not to take out his vengeance on Octavia, at least not yet. There was only so long Bellamy was willing to stay away from her, though. He couldn't rely on Rhodes's goodwill, if that's what it was, for long.

"Morning." Max had approached without Bellamy realizing it.

"Morning," Bellamy replied, happy to be shaken from his miserable thoughts.

"May I join you?"

"Sure." Bellamy scooted over, and Max dropped onto the bench next to him. Steam rose from a metal cup in his hand. They sat in silence for a long moment, watching the last of the children running late into school.

"How's the shoulder?" Max asked.

"Better. Thanks for giving Clarke all that stuff to use. I know it's pretty valuable, and you've done so much for us already." He paused, wondering if it were noble or foolish to share his concerns about sticking around. "I don't think it's a good idea for me to stay here, though."

"Where do you plan to go?" Max didn't sound surprised, and Bellamy appreciated the lack of judgment in his tone.

"I haven't figured that part out yet. All I know is that I can't just sit here and wait for them to come get me, and I can't let anyone here risk getting hurt for me."

"I understand how you must feel, knowing that there are people out there who want to harm you. But they don't have the right to take your life, Bellamy. No one does." Max paused. "And no one here is doing anything they don't want to do. The truth is, I don't think you're any safer out there," Max went on, tipping his head toward the woods. "There are greater dangers than Rhodes. I'm not sure how much you know about the others?" Max raised his eyebrows. "The people from our group who left us."

"A little." The last time he'd been here, when he'd come to rescue Octavia, Bellamy had heard the story about the Colonists who'd come down from the ship, way before the hundred had arrived. The Earthborns had taken them in, shared their food, but not everyone had been happy about welcoming the strangers, especially since the strangers were the descendants of the people who'd fled the dying Earth in a spaceship, leaving everyone else to perish.

The two groups had established an uneasy peace, but then something happened. An Earthborn child died, and chaos broke out. There was a faction of Max's people who blamed the Colonists, and who blamed Max for letting strangers into their home. They demanded retribution, and when Max refused to let them kill the Colonists, they split off to live on their own, outside of Max's authority.

The craziest part of the whole story was that Clarke's parents—who she had thought were dead, sentenced to floating from the Colony—had been among that first wave of Colonists. They had been banished along with the others after the child's death.

Max took another sip of his drink. "I grew up with them. We raised our children together, I thought I knew them." He paused for a moment, as if letting the memories play out in his mind before continuing. "But now they've become unrecognizable. They've become obsessed with violence and claiming as much land as possible as their own. They're angry, and they have nothing to lose. Which makes them very, very dangerous."

"What do they want?" Bellamy asked, not even sure he wanted to know the answer.

"I wish I knew." Max sighed and ran a hand along his gray beard. "Revenge? Power? What could they want that we didn't have right here?"

They were silent for a moment.

"Clarke wants to go find her parents," Bellamy said.

"I know she does. But it's not safe. If the splinter group is willing to hurt their own neighbors and friends, they certainly won't hesitate to hurt Clarke. And if they find out that she is their daughter—well, I'd hate to think of what they might do. The Griffins had nothing to do with the boy's death, but these aren't rational people we're talking about here." Max turned and locked eyes with Bellamy. "Do you think she understands the risks?"

Bellamy shook his head. "I don't know. But she's not going to stay here and wait around forever. She wants to find her mom and dad. Soon. I tried to convince her to wait until it's safe for me to go with her. We need to find out more about where they might have gone. But she's determined."

"I don't blame her." Max sighed. "I'd want to find them too."

"Yeah." Bellamy knew what it was like to feel a desperate, primal urge to find someone you love. He got why Clarke wanted to start tracking her parents. But was he willing to let her die for it?

Bellamy's thoughts were interrupted as a man raced toward them.

"Max," the man said breathlessly, coming to a sudden halt in front of their bench. "There's a group approaching the town. They're about a hundred meters out. They'll be here in a few minutes. And—Max—they're armed."

Bellamy's heart leapt into his throat as a wave of guilt crashed over him. *They're here for me.*

Max jumped to his feet. "Send out the signal. And dispatch a group to meet them and bring them in. *Peacefully.*" The man nodded and ran off. Max turned back to Bellamy. "Follow me."

Bellamy tried to remain calm, but a surge of anger and fear welled up inside of him, the same combination of feelings that generally prompted him to do something stupid. He trailed Max closely as they jogged down the path and toward the town's main hall, where people were already gathering, many bearing guns and spears. Clarke, Wells, and Sasha ran inside a few minutes later, looking anxious but determined. Sasha joined her father at the front of the room, while Wells and Clarke wended their way through the crowd to stand with Bellamy at the back.

"Don't worry," Wells said to Bellamy as the crowd chattered anxiously all around them. "We're not going to let them take you."

But that wasn't what Bellamy was worried about, not really. He was more worried about what would happen when the Earthborns refused to hand him over—what Rhodes would do if he didn't get his way.

Max raised a hand, and the room fell silent.

"As most of you know, we have some visitors coming," he called out, his voice commanding but calm. "They're being brought in now. We will meet with them, hear what they want, and then we will decide what to do."

A tide of murmurs and muffled questions rose up from the crowd. Max held up his hand again, and everyone quieted down. "I know you have a lot of questions. I do too. But let's start by listening. Remember, there is no peace without peaceful exchange."

A tense silence settled over the room. A few minutes later, a handful of Earthborns led in a group of Rhodes's guards. They had been relieved of their weapons but not restrained in any way.

"Welcome," Max said. The guards were stony-faced and silent, their eyes darting around the room, strategizing and assessing. "Please make yourselves comfortable and tell us why you've come."

The guards exchanged glances. The eldest, a middle-aged man named Burnett who Bellamy recognized from the prison cabin, stepped forward.

"We are not here to harm your people," Burnett said in the same cold, flat voice Bellamy had heard countless guards use before dragging someone off to Confinement, making them disappear forever. He scanned the room until his eyes landed on Bellamy. Every muscle in Bellamy's body tensed up, and he had to fight the urge to bolt to the front of the hall and wrap his hands around Burnett's thick neck. "We are under orders to collect our prisoner, that's all. You are harboring a fugitive, who must answer for his crimes. Hand him over, and we'll leave you in peace."

Clarke grabbed Bellamy's hand and held it tight. He knew she'd do anything to keep him safe, but at this point, all he wanted to do was spare her any more pain.

Max surveyed Burnett carefully, pausing before he spoke. "My friend, I appreciate that you have come here under orders. And it is not our intention to cause trouble in any way." Max shot Bellamy a look over the sea of heads that separated them, his expression unreadable. "But it's my understanding that the *prisoner*, as you call him, will not be receiving any sort of just sentence. If he returns to your camp, he will be executed."

A sea of shocked gasps and whispers rippled over the crowd. An Earthborn woman near Clarke and Bellamy turned to stare at them, taking in their frightened expressions and clasped hands, and her expression changed from confusion to resolve. Three men who'd been standing near Bellamy's side exchanged glances, then took a few steps so they were standing between Bellamy and the guards. "And we are not in the business of sending young men to their deaths," Max finished.

Burnett shot an amused look at one of the other guards, and a small smile crept across his face. "It wasn't a request," he said. "You understand that there will be consequences to your refusal, don't you?"

"Yes," Max replied calmly, though his eyes had grown cold. "You've made yourself very clear." He turned toward the other Earthborns. "I believe I can speak for everyone here when I say that we will not be accomplices to this unjust punishment. But I will allow them to decide."

There was a long pause. Bellamy felt suddenly queasy as he looked around at the faces of these people—these strangers—who held his fate in their hands. Was it fair to make them decide—to ask them to put their own safety on the line to protect him?

He was steeling himself to rise and surrender himself to Rhodes when Max cleared his throat. "All those in favor of letting our visitors take the boy with him, please raise your hands."

One of the guards smirked, while the man next to him cracked his knuckles. They were clearly relishing this, eager to watch the Earthborns relinquish Bellamy to his grim fate.

But to Bellamy's shock, no one raised their arm. "What the . . ." he whispered as Clarke squeezed his hand.

"All in favor of letting Bellamy, Clarke, and Wells stay here, under our protection?"

Countless hands shot into the air, blocking Max, Burnett, and the other guards from view. Bellamy's knees began to buckle as an overwhelming tide of gratitude rose within him. The adults back at the Colony had never offered Bellamy so much as a crumb of kindness. Never, not even when he and Octavia were practically starving. But these people were willing to risk everything for him—a total stranger.

That's what made it worse. These were good people. They didn't deserve to die for some kid who'd spent nineteen years making nothing but terrible decisions.

Clarke slid her arm around his waist and leaned into him, helping to support his weight.

"It's okay," she whispered into his ear.

"No," Bellamy said under his breath, as much to himself as to her. Then, "*No*," he called out, louder. No one heard him over the clamor in the room. Except Clarke and Wells.

Clarke's hand fell away from him, and she and Wells stared at him in confusion.

"Bellamy!" Clarke said, her eyes wide. "What are you doing?"

"I can't just stand here and let all these innocent people put their asses on the line for me. They have kids; they have families. They don't need this shit."

Wells stepped forward and put a firm hand on Bellamy's shoulder. "Hey," he said. "Hey, just relax." Bellamy tried to shake free of Wells's grasp, but Wells wouldn't let him. "Bellamy, I get it. You're not used to accepting help. But this isn't Confinement for selling stolen goods at the Exchange. This is the death penalty. Rhodes is going to *kill* you."

Bellamy leaned over and put his hands on his knees. He took a few deep, steadying breaths. He knew that Max and Sasha's people believed in something bigger than themselves. He had seen it in their kindness toward each other, in the way they welcomed three strangers into their lives. He had seen it in Max's leadership. But he didn't know how he could ever bear the burden of their generosity.

Clarke took Bellamy's hand again and looked into his eyes. "Even if you won't do it for you, will you do it for me? Please?" Her voice was trembling, and something in Bellamy's chest shifted. He'd never heard her sound so vulnerable, so scared. He'd never heard her beg anyone for anything. Anything she wanted, she went after herself. But that wouldn't be enough this time. She needed help.

"And for me." Wells clapped his hand on Bellamy's good shoulder.

Bellamy turned from Clarke to Wells. How had this happened? When he and Octavia had left the Colony, it'd been them against the universe. And now he had people who cared about him. He had a family.

"Okay," he said with a nod, fighting back the tears threatening to make an appearance. He forced a smile. "But just this one time. Next time I'm sentenced to death for being a hotheaded idiot, you have to let them take me."

"Deal," Wells said, stepping back with a grin.

"No way. You're my hotheaded idiot." Clarke rose onto her toes and kissed him. Bellamy wrapped his arm around her and kissed her back, too moved to be embarrassed by the prickle of tears in his eyes.

CHAPTER 17

Glass

Glass shoved the cabin door open with her shoulder. Both her hands were full, one with a bucket of water from the river, the other with a sack of berries she'd found growing nearby. She dropped the food on the uneven wooden table and carried the water over to the basin. Without having to think about it, Glass reached up and took down a small bowl from the shelf. After just two days, she was already so comfortable in their little house that it felt as if she and Luke had been settled there forever.

Their first morning in the cabin, they had stepped outside cautiously, scanning for signs of Earthborns. But there was no hint of any other human life. Slowly their comfort and confidence grew, and they trekked a few meters away in an attempt to find food.

They were both so focused on their search, they almost didn't notice a deer grazing nearby. Glass raised her head to call Luke over, and just before his name left her lips, she saw it, standing just feet from her. It was young—*was there a special name for a baby deer?* Glass strained to remember—and so beautiful. Its soft brown muzzle twitched as it sniffed the air, and its wide brown eyes were sweet and sad. Glass was afraid to move, for fear of scaring it away. She wanted Luke to see it too, but she couldn't make a sound. She and the deer stared at each other for a long moment, until finally Luke turned and saw it. He froze. She could tell from the look on his face that he was as awestruck by the animal as she was.

The three of them stood there, locked in a silent exchange. Finally, a distant rustle in the trees sent the deer bolting off into the woods with barely a sound. Glass let out a sigh as it disappeared. "That was incredible," she said.

"Yeah," Luke agreed, but his expression was serious.

"What's wrong?" she asked, surprised at his reaction.

"It's just—if we don't find something to eat, we're going to have to, you know . . ." He trailed off.

Glass's heart sank. She had been so transfixed by the deer's expressive eyes; she hadn't stopped to think that she might be forced to eat it. The thought made her stomach turn. "Let's not worry about that now," she said. "Just keep looking."

Luckily they'd found the berries, and so far they'd been okay. But she knew deep down it was only a matter of time before something changed. They were running low on water-purifying tablets, and there was no pot in the house that would enable them to boil any water. There were weird bugs that scuttled across the floor in the predawn hours, waking Glass from a dead sleep and giving her goose bumps. Luke just laughed at her as she scooted closer to him and pulled the blankets tighter over them both. And there had been the constant, nagging worry about what would happen next. Would they be able to stay here? Could it really be that simple? She remembered learning about Earth seasons—the pretty fall leaves meant that, soon enough, winter would come, and they'd have to figure out how to survive the cold. She did her best to push those thoughts away, though. Winter was a worry for another day. Today she just wanted to live out the fairy tale, in their fantasy cabin under the tall canopy of trees.

Luke stepped through the doorway, stomping mud off his boots. Leaves clung to his thick, wavy hair. A waft of piney crispness floated off of him and filled her nose. Glass inhaled deeply. Just being this close to him and breathing in his scent made every nerve in her body tingle.

"Dinner?" She held up the dish of berries with mock solemnity. "I made you something special tonight."

"Ah, berry stew." Luke grinned. "My favorite. Is it a special occasion?"

She cocked her head to the side and smiled mischievously. "It can be."

Luke stepped across the room in a couple of quick strides, hugged her, and pulled her into a deep kiss that felt like it would never end.

———

Later that night, they fell asleep entwined together by the fire. Glass had nodded off quickly. With each night they'd spent in the woods, Glass had grown more and more relaxed, the anxiety and stress of the past few weeks slowly fading from her memory. She had started to sleep deeply, almost hungrily, as if sleep offered her a nourishment she had long craved.

When the first noise came through the window, Glass incorporated it into her dream. She only woke when Luke sat upright next to her, her body rolling off his as he jumped up in a panic. She opened her eyes, snapping instantly into consciousness. That's when she saw it: a face at the window of the cabin. Someone was staring at them—an Earthborn, she saw in the reflected light of the dying fire. She could tell from the long hair and bulky clothes. None of the Colonists dressed like that. They didn't carry themselves like that. Terror and adrenaline shot through her body, flooding her veins and firing up her brain. She heard screaming in the distance, but it took her a moment to realize the sound was coming from her own mouth.

Luke jumped up and reached for the gun he had taken from camp. Shirtless and barefoot, he whipped open the front door to the cabin and bolted into the darkness.

"Luke, no!" Glass called after him, a note of desperation in her voice. "Don't go out there!" But he had already disappeared from view. Panic gripped her chest, threatening to bring her to the ground, but she pressed forward, stumbling after Luke, gasping for air as she tried to call his name.

Glass ran outside, searching blindly in the dark until her eyes adjusted. She was flooded with relief when she saw Luke standing a few meters away, his back to her. He held the gun high in the air, pointed at the sky. Facing him, forming a half circle, were three men and one woman. They were dressed similarly to Sasha, in a combination of animal skins and wool, but that was where the similarities ended. Their faces were like cruel masks, and their eyes glinted with malice as they exchanged delighted glances with one another.

Luke and the Earthborns were engaged in a silent standoff.

The Earthborns stood with their arms raised, spears poised at shoulder-height, ready to attack. They seemed to be waiting for some kind of signal. Before he could stop her, Glass ran toward Luke. He wrapped a strong arm around her and pushed her behind him. She could feel every muscle in his body tensed, ready for a fight.

She stuck her head out from behind him and called out to the Earthborns. "Please," she said, her voice cracking. "We're not here to hurt anyone. We're friends of Sasha's. Please don't hurt us."

"Oh, you're friends with Sasha, are you?" one of the men said, his voice harsh and mocking. "Well, in that case, we'll kill you right away instead of leaving you half dead for the animals. It's only polite."

Luke tried to push her further behind him. There was a long, terrifying pause, as each side waited for the other one to act. Finally, one of the Earthborns—the man whose face she'd seen at the window—stepped forward menacingly. "We tried warning your friends. We showed mercy by only killing one of them. Yet instead of realizing that you aren't welcome here, you brought down *more* of your kind. Enough is enough," he spat.

"That's not what happened," Glass cried. "We didn't know . . . there was no way to communicate with them.

But there are no more of us coming, I promise." Her voice broke, both from fear and from the sad realization that it was true. Whoever hadn't made it onto one of the drop-ships was gone forever.

The Earthborn woman sneered at Glass. "You *promise*?" She snorted. "We learned the hard way what happens when you trust outsiders." She nodded at the man, who raised his arm and aimed his spear directly at Luke's heart, cocking his arm back.

"Don't move!" Luke shouted. "Please. I don't want to hurt you, but I have a gun. Don't force me to use it."

The man paused, as if considering Luke's words, but only for a moment. Then he took another careful step forward.

Glass's ears rang with the sharp crack of the bullet. It echoed off the tree trunks and bounced back at them. Luke had fired into the sky, pointing the gun away from the Earthborns, but it had been enough to scare them. They jumped and scattered, disappearing into the darkness.

Glass was so relieved to see them retreating that at first she didn't realize what had happened. There had been a little flurry of motion right as Luke fired the shot. Had one of them thrown something? She turned back to Luke, and her blood froze in her veins. He stood facing her, his eyes wide and startled. His mouth was open, but no sound came out. She ran her eyes down his body, following his arms down to his hands, which grasped his left leg tightly. Blood poured out from between his fingers. A wooden spear lay on the ground near his foot.

"*Luke!*" she cried. "Luke—no!"

Luke sank to his knees.

Glass ran to him, throwing herself on the ground next him. "Luke!" She grabbed his arm, as if trying to keep him with her, to stop him from slipping away somewhere she couldn't follow.

"You'll be okay," she said, willing herself to push the panic from her voice. Luke needed her to stay calm. He needed her to figure something out. "Let's just get you inside." She looked down and blanched. Even in the faint moonlight, she could see the grass around Luke's leg turning dark red.

She reached under Luke's arms and gave an experimental tug but stopped abruptly when he let out a cry of pain. "Just help me up," Luke grunted through clenched teeth. "We'll deal with the rest when we get inside."

Uneasily, he rose onto one leg. She tried to keep her breathing steady, tried to forget the fact that they were two days' walk from medical help. How could they have been so foolish to go off on their own?

"Don't worry," Luke said, wincing with each awkward

hop. He twisted around, scanning the dark trees for signs of the Earthborns. "It's not that bad." But even Luke couldn't keep the fear out of his voice.

They both knew he was lying. And they both knew what would happen if he didn't get better.

Glass would be entirely on her own.

CHAPTER *18*

Clarke

The mood in the Earthborns' camp had shifted dramatically. As the sun sank, so did the fevered excitement that had made everyone's blood run fast and hot during the confrontation with Rhodes's men. They were still committed to protecting Bellamy—if anything, the encounter had made it clear how dangerous it would be to acquiesce to the Colonists—but their faces had grown grave, their voices hushed and urgent as they herded their children into their homes and bolted the doors.

Clarke was sitting outside the cabin, racing against the fading light as she prepared to repair the stiches Bellamy had torn during the escape. "Take off your shirt," she said as

they settled onto a patch of grass that lay beyond the length-
ening shadows.

Bellamy looked taken aback as he turned his head from
side to side, scanning the dirt road for people. "What? Here?"

"Yes, here. It's too dark inside the cabin." He hesitated,
and Clarke raised an eyebrow. "Since when does Bellamy
Blake have to be asked twice to take his shirt off?"

"Come on, Clarke. They already think I'm some insane
fugitive who's going to get them all killed. Do I have to be an
insane, *shirtless* fugitive as well?"

"Yes, unless you want them to see you as an insane, *dead*
fugitive. I need to fix those stitches."

He sighed dramatically and, with his good arm, grabbed
on to the edge of his shirt and pulled it over his head.

"Thank you," Clarke said, suppressing a smile. As a
patient, Bellamy bore a striking similarity to some of the
little kids she used to treat back in the medical center. But
that was one of the things she loved about him. He could
be a deer-hunting, arrow-shooting warrior one moment, and
a goofy kid splashing around in the stream the next. She
admired the way he threw himself into every role, living
every moment to the fullest. The last few weeks on Earth
had been exhausting and terrifying, but also completely
magical as she learned to see the untamed planet through
Bellamy's unexpectedly romantic viewpoint. Unlike most

of the hundred, who'd always choose gossiping around the fire over exploring the woods, Bellamy seemed to prefer the company of trees to people. Clarke loved walking with him in the forest, watching his brash attitude slip away as he looked around in wonder.

She had Bellamy lie down while she threaded the needle she'd just sterilized over the fire. "Do you want me to see if they have painkillers?" Clarke asked, placing her hand on Bellamy's arm.

He squeezed his eyes shut and shook his head. "No. I've caused enough trouble already. I'm not taking their medicine."

Clarke pressed her lips together but didn't argue. She knew better than to go head-to-head with Bellamy when he was in one of his stubborn moods. She pressed a little harder on his arm, both to keep him still and to steady herself. "Okay. Take a deep breath."

She slid the needle into his skin, forcing herself not to move as Bellamy flinched and groaned. The best she could do was to work quickly and accurately, and make the procedure as short as possible. "You're doing great," she told him as she brought the needle back around and prepared for a second stitch.

"If I didn't know better, I'd think you're enjoying this," Bellamy said through gritted teeth.

"Everything okay here?" a voice called. Clarke didn't turn around, but she could hear Max, Wells, and possibly Sasha walking toward them.

"Super," Bellamy said before she could answer. "Just indulging Clarke's sadistic side. Pretty standard." He let out another groan. "I let her do this to me every night."

"Don't move," Clarke said. She tugged gently on the thread and watched in satisfaction as the skin pulled tight. "You don't want me to slip and accidentally sew your lips shut."

She could hear the smile in Sasha's voice as she said, "You two make a strange couple."

"Says the Earth girl dating a boy who fell out of the sky," Bellamy managed through clenched teeth.

Clarke tied a small knot and snapped off the extra string. "All done." She squeezed Bellamy's knee to let him know to sit back up.

He looked down at the stitches and nodded. "Nice job, Doctor," he said loudly so the others could hear. Then he smiled and pulled her close. "Thank you," he whispered before kissing the top of her head, then reaching for his shirt.

"You should head inside," Max said, shooting a glance at the trees surrounding the village. "I don't think your people are going to cause any trouble tonight, but there's no reason to make it easy for them if they do."

Wells cleared his throat. "I wanted to talk to you about that. We know it's only a matter of time before the guards come back, most likely with more people and a lot more guns. And from what we know about Rhodes, he won't be overly concerned about hurting innocent people. He'll consider harboring Bellamy to be an act of war." He paused and glanced at Sasha, who gave him a small nod. "I think it'd be safer to move everyone back inside. Underground—into Mount Weather."

Max stared at him. "Underground," he repeated bitterly, twisting his mouth just as Rhodes did when he said the word *sister*.

"It's a fortress, isn't it?" Clarke said. "If it could keep out a hundred kilotons of radiation, surely it could keep out a few guards."

Max shot Sasha a look Clarke couldn't quite read, but it was enough to make her bite her lip nervously. When he spoke, his voice was strained. "We're well aware of Mount Weather's capabilities. Our people lived there for centuries, entire generations entombed. They lived and died without ever glimpsing the sky. When we finally came back above ground, we vowed to stay there. We'd never let anything—or anyone—force us underground again."

As someone who'd grown up on a space station, who still got a thrill from her first breath of fresh morning air, Clarke could understand where Max was coming from. But if it came down to living underground or dying above, then the choice was clear. "Rhodes isn't going to stop until he gets what he wants," she said. "And he won't care how many of your people he has to kill along the way."

Max's face hardened. "We've fought off attackers before," he said. "We know how to defend ourselves."

"Not against people like this," Wells said. "These are trained soldiers—a small army. I know the other Earthborns are dangerous, but they've got nothing on Rhodes's men."

Max fell silent, and although his expression remained stern, Clarke could tell he was considering Wells's words.

Sasha spoke first. "Dad, we should listen to Wells. He knows what he's talking about. I don't want to go underground any more than you do, but in this case, I think it's the right thing to do."

Max stared at her with a look of mild surprise, then something in his face shifted, as if he were looking at his daughter in a new light, accepting that she'd gone from child to confidante. Clarke's heart throbbed painfully as she thought about her own father and the long hours they'd spent discussing Clarke's medical training or his own research. In the year leading up to his arrest, he'd begun treating her like a trusted colleague, a friend. Would she ever get the chance to tell him all about her adventures on Earth? Would she ever get to share the questions she'd been saving especially for him?

Finally, Max nodded. "Okay. We'll do this calmly. And we need to emphasize to our people that this is only a precaution. We'll send out the signal and get everyone moving right away. Wells, you come with me. You can brief us on Rhodes and his strategy while we evacuate."

After conferring with some of his advisors, Max decided to move everyone inside Mount Weather that night. He sent a few engineers ahead to make sure that the fortress was ready for an influx of people, and spent the rest of the evening going from house to house, explaining the situation.

By midnight, everyone in the community had gathered at the base of the mountain, prepared to spend the night in its depths for the first time in decades. Most people carried food and clothes, leading children who clutched their favorite toys.

Max stood by the enormous metal door built into the hillside, which had been propped open to let the stream of people file in. Bellamy and Clarke hung back until nearly everyone was inside, as did Wells, who was standing watch with Sasha. "Is there anything I can do?" Clarke asked Max as they approached.

"Just make sure everyone's settled. There are more than enough rooms, but some of them are hard to find. If anyone seems lost, you can tell them to wait for me. I'll be down in a few minutes."

Clarke nodded, took Bellamy's hand, and led him through the door and down the first flight of steep, narrow stairs that seemed to descend down into the belly of the Earth. They'd both been inside Mount Weather before, but that was when they'd believed the Earthborns were their enemy, so they hadn't spent a great deal of time admiring the incredible setup. This was no dark cave—this was a sophisticated bunker that had been built by the best engineers in America to withstand the Cataclysm.

Clarke and Bellamy made their way down the first residential corridor, a brightly lit hall lined with bedrooms on either side. At the end, a woman stood holding the hands of two small, scared-looking girls. "Do you need any help?" Clarke asked.

"All these rooms are full," the woman said, a note of anxiety in her voice.

"Don't worry. There's a whole other section the next level down," Clarke said. "If you just wait here, I'll run ahead and find it."

"My doll's tired," one of the little girls said, holding a wooden toy in the air. "She needs to go to bed."

"It won't take long. And you know what you can do in the meantime? You can tell my friend here all about your doll."

"What?" Bellamy shot her a look. "I'm coming with you."

"No extraneous activity for you. Doctor's orders."

Bellamy rolled his eyes, then sighed and turned to the little girl. "So . . ." she heard him say as she hurried off. "What's your doll's favorite way to hunt? Does she like spears or bows and arrows?"

Clarke grinned to herself as she imagined the look of confusion on the little girl's face, then took another flight of stairs down and turned in the direction she assumed led to the bedrooms, but the layout of this floor was different than the one above. She backtracked and tried going the other way but ended up even more turned around.

The corridors looked different in this wing. It had fewer doors and seemed more utilitarian, like it'd been built for equipment or supplies. Sure enough, the first door she reached had a sign reading PHYSICAL PLANT OPERATIONS: AUTHORIZED PERSONNEL ONLY. Since anyone authorized to open the door had been dead for at least a couple hundred years, she figured there was no harm in sneaking a peek. She jiggled the handle. It was locked.

Clarke moved along to the next door, on the opposite side of the hall. RADIO COMMUNICATIONS: AUTHORIZED PERSONNEL ONLY the sign read. Clarke froze. Radio? She hadn't thought about it before, but of course people would have wanted a way to communicate if they were locked down inside Mount Weather . . . but who would they have communicated *with*? If they were using this room, then presumably there wouldn't have been anyone left to take the call. Unless . . . had there been other bunkers maybe? Other versions of Mount Weather?

Clarke stared at the door for a long moment, a strange, distant thought tickling the back of her mind. She couldn't quite put her finger on it, but something about this door—that sign, those words—felt familiar. She tried the handle, but this room was locked too.

"Clarke? Did you find more rooms?" Bellamy's voice was faint, but there was a tinge of worry to it. "Clarke?"

"I'm here," she called back, spinning around and hurrying down the hallway toward his voice.

They finished helping everyone get settled, then went with Max, Wells, and Sasha to take inventory of the supplies. On their way to the old cafeteria, Max explained to them that his people had kept Mount Weather up and running all this time, just in case of an emergency like this.

"So you're pretty familiar with this place, then," Clarke said.

"I was born down here, actually," Max replied, to her surprise. "I was the last Mount Weather baby. A few months after I was born, it became clear that the radiation levels were finally safe, and we all moved back to the surface. I still spent a lot of time down here, though. It was my favorite place to explore because the adults hardly ever came inside."

"I can imagine. So, speaking of exploring," Clarke said

carefully, trying not to sound like she was snooping. "I found a radio room today. Do you know what it would've been used for?"

"Mostly for fiddling with, honestly," Max said with a shrug. "Every generation has had a system for sending out signals on a regular basis. But no one—not once—has gotten a reply. As far as we could tell, there was just no one out there to respond."

Clarke felt an unexpected wave of disappointment, but then another question surfaced through her sea of confused thoughts. "Did the scientists who came on the first dropship use it?"

Max looked at her quizzically, as if trying to figure out where she was going with her questions. "Actually, yes. Well, they tried anyway. They asked a lot of questions about the radio, and I even let them in to try it out but I told them what I just told you—"

Clarke cut him off. "You have the key?"

"Yes, I have the key. Do you want to go in?"

"Yes, please. That would be great, actually."

Bellamy shot Clarke a questioning look, but she looked away, letting her mind wander in pursuit of a memory she wasn't sure was ever hers to begin with.

Clarke forced herself to take a deep breath, just like she did before assisting Dr. Lahiri with a complicated surgical procedure. But this time, she wasn't about to use a scalpel to expose someone's tricuspid valve; she was bracing herself to enter the Exchange.

Clarke hated the vast hall that was always packed, no matter when you went. She hated haggling for a good price, and she really hated having to make small talk with the attendants, pretending like she cared whether a T-shirt was ten percent earth fibers or fifteen. But it was Wells's birthday tomorrow, and Clarke was desperate to find him the perfect present.

Yet just when she had gathered the courage to step inside, Glass and Cora came her way, prompting Clarke to duck around the corner. There was no way she could pick a present for Wells with them watching, making loud comments about her selections as if she couldn't hear them. She'd just have to come back later. They were scrutinizing scraps of fabrics with the same care Clarke reserved for tissue samples in the lab.

"I just don't see any harm in looking." A man's voice drifted down the hall, making Clarke stop in her tracks.

"David, you know there won't be anything even close to what we need at the Exchange. All that technology was snatched up *years* ago. We could check the black market on Walden, if you think it's worth the risk."

Clarke's breath caught in her chest as she peeked around the corner. It was her *parents*. Clarke's mother hadn't gone to the Exchange in years, and she couldn't remember her father ever going. What in the world were they doing here in the middle of the day, when they were supposed to be in their respective labs?

"The radio works," her father was saying. "We just need to find a way to amplify the signal. It'll be simple, really. We just need a few pieces of equipment."

"Which is all well and good, except for the fact that there's no one on the other end to hear us."

"If anyone made it to Mount Weather, or to one of the CDC bunkers, then they have access to a radio. We just need to make sure—"

"Do you know how crazy you sound?" her mother said, lowering her voice. "The chances of it working are infinitesimally small."

"But what if I'm not crazy? What if there are people down there, trying to make contact with us?" He fell quiet for a moment. "Don't you want to let them know that they're not alone?"

To their credit, Bellamy, Wells, and Sasha didn't balk when Clarke told them about her parents and how she thought they might've known about the radio in Mount Weather. It was crazy, but no crazier than Bellamy and Wells discovering that they were brothers, or Clarke learning that her parents had been on Earth the entire time she'd been mourning their deaths.

Max unlocked the door with a loud click. The door creaked open on old hinges. He stepped aside and held out his arm, signaling for Clarke to enter. She took a hesitant step inside. It was small, no more than three or four people could fit comfortably, and one entire wall was covered with speakers, switches, and dials. The other three walls were hung with various instructional signs. Clarke's eyes landed on a poster that showed various flags next to long strings of numbers. The labels read:

PARLIAMENT HILL, OTTAWA

CENTER FOR DISEASE CONTROL

10 DOWNING STREET, LONDON

PALACIO NACIONAL, MEXICO CITY

CIA

MI6

KANTEI, TOKYO

KREMLIN, MOSCOW

"When was the last time you tried to send out a signal?" Clarke asked.

"About a month ago," Max said. "We're due to try again in a couple of weeks. But honestly, we only do it as routine maintenance, mostly to make sure the equipment is still working. There's never been so much as a blip, Clarke."

"I know. But that doesn't mean my parents weren't onto something. Maybe being in here and using the same equipment they did will help me figure out where they went."

"Well," Max said, nodding, "I'll leave you to it, then. Good luck."

Clarke walked over to the controls, her hands trembling.

To the right, a tall stack of equipment towered over the room. Cables and cords of every color and width poured out of it like tentacles. Clarke ran her hands over the machinery, too afraid to push any one thing. She studied the markings, combinations of letters and numbers she'd never seen before: kHz, km, GHZ, μm.

One switch seemed straightforward enough: It read ON/OFF. Clarke took a deep breath and flicked it up with a *snap*. She sucked in her breath as the whole apparatus lit up like it had been shocked to life. Lights flashed. Its guts seemed to whir and grind. Clicks and crackles emanated from somewhere deep inside. Then, a low, soft hiss filled the room, growing louder and steadier. It was mesmerizing—the sound of possible life out there, somewhere. Clarke could tell why her parents would have come here. They would have wanted to see for themselves, to hear the vastness of this planet with their own ears. To hear the sound of hope.

She spotted a small drawer under the console. She tugged it open and to her surprise found a small booklet. It was a manual. The pages crackled as she opened it and ran her finger down the instructions.

She could have spent all night in the radio room. She had no idea how much time passed while she pushed buttons, gently nudged dials a millimeter or two in one direction or another. And each time she made the slightest adjustment, the hiss changed, just a tiny bit. It was almost indiscernible, but Clarke could hear it. It was like the subtle distinction between the accent of a Phoenician and a Waldenite. And in each moment, she felt something she never dreamed she'd feel again—the presence of her parents. They had listened to this same endless sound. They had tweaked it and plumbed its depths for hints of a life outside Mount Weather. She just had to spend enough time here to figure out what they had discovered—and where it led them.

By the time Bellamy came to check on her, Clarke was practically giddy with excitement.

"How's it go—" Before he could finish, she'd ran over and thrown her arms around him, prompting him to laugh and groan all at once as he gave her a one-armed hug.

"Sorry," she said, blushing. "Some doctor, right? Are you okay?"

He grinned. "I'm fine. So, what did you hear on that thing that's got you so excited?" he asked, gesturing toward the radio equipment.

"Nothing, just empty air," Clarke said with a huge smile. "It's amazing!"

Bellamy furrowed his brow in exaggerated confusion. "Uh, I know I'm no scientist or anything, but how is that amazing?"

She swatted his good arm. "The fact that it's working at all means I have a lead, finally. My parents thought there could have been more people out there"—she waved her hand up at the ceiling, at the world above them—"somewhere. And maybe this radio told them where to go next. I just have to figure out what they discovered. It's a start at least!"

"Wow," Bellamy said, beaming at her. "Clarke, that's incredible." But then his smile faded as a shadow of worry crossed his face.

"What's wrong?"

He shook his head. "I don't want to be a total buzzkill," he said apologetically. "And I'm really glad you found a lead. But that doesn't change how dangerous it is out there."

She grabbed his hand and interlaced his fingers with hers. "I know. But that's not going to stop me."

"Then I'll go with you."

Clarke smiled. "I was hoping you'd say that." She rose up onto the balls of her feet to kiss him.

"In fact, we should go soon. Tomorrow. Now."

Clarke stepped back to stare at him. "Bellamy, what are you talking about? We can't go *now*. Not after an entire village decamped into a mountain to keep you safe."

"That's the point. They shouldn't have done that. No one person is worth jeopardizing a whole society and *definitely* not me."

"We went over this," Clarke said, squeezing his hand. "It's more than—"

"Clarke, just listen, please." He sighed. "I don't know how to explain it. It's just—not a lot of people have loved me in my life. And it seems like every time someone cares about me, they get hurt. My mom, Lilly, Octavia . . ." He trailed off.

Clarke's heart ached for the little boy who had no one to look out for him, who grew up too fast. "Do you think if they knew that beforehand, it would have changed their love for you one tiny bit?" Clarke asked, holding his gaze.

"I just . . . I just hate being the reason people are always in danger. I'd never be able to live with myself if anything happened to you." He ran his finger along her cheek and gave her a sad smile. "I'm not like you. I can't stitch you back up again."

"Are you serious? I was a mess when I got here, after everything that had happened with my parents, Wells, Lilly . . . and then Thalia. I was broken, and you put me back together."

"You weren't broken," Bellamy said, his voice soft as a caress. "You were the strongest, most beautiful girl I'd ever seen. I still can't figure out what I did to get so lucky."

"What do I have to do to convince you that *I'm* the lucky one?" She kissed him, harder than before, letting her lips convey everything she hadn't found the words to say.

Bellamy broke away, then placed his hand on her waist and grinned. "I think you might be on the right track. Though

I could probably use a *little* more convincing." He pulled her to him, then stepped backward so he was against the wall, laughing as she grabbed on to his shirt and began to pull him down to the floor.

CHAPTER *19*

Wells

Wells hadn't slept all night. He'd tossed and turned for hours on the hard mattress. It wasn't so bad for an underground bunker, and it sure beat the ground back at camp, but his mind had been running nonstop, and he felt every bump and wrinkle beneath him. Two upsetting pictures jostled for control of his exhausted brain—a no-man's-land waiting to be claimed by the most terrifying thought. The first was an image of Bellamy's still, cold body alone in the woods, the moss stained red with his blood. The second was no better: dozens of Earthborns, sprawled out in the grass and on their front porches, many of them children, massacred by Rhodes and his men.

He must've drifted off at some point, though, because when he opened his eyes, his head was on Sasha's stomach, and she was running her fingers through his hair. "Are you okay?" she asked softly. "You were having a nightmare."

"Yeah . . . I'm fine," he said, though that couldn't have been further from the truth. Wells couldn't bear the thought of giving up his friend and brother, Bellamy. He would rather die himself than hand him over to a man like Rhodes. But he couldn't come to grips with the terrible risk the Earthborns had assumed by protecting Bellamy. As with so many decisions he had seen his father face, Wells knew there was no easy answer.

Sasha let out a long sigh but didn't say anything. She didn't have to. Wells loved how they could be on the same page without having to say anything at all. "It'll all be over soon," she said, still playing with his hair absentmindedly. "We'll scare Rhodes off, and he'll decide Bellamy's not worth all the trouble. And then everything will go back to normal."

Wells pushed himself up so he was leaning against the back of the bed, next to Sasha. "And what exactly does 'normal' mean for us?" he asked with a slightly embarrassed smile. "Until recently, you were locked up in our camp as a prisoner."

The hundred had caught Sasha lurking near the clearing when Octavia was still missing, and had mistaken her for one of their enemy's spies.

"I guess that means we get to choose a new normal. You'll stay here, teach us all those useless things you learned in space, and we'll teach you how to not die."

"Hey," Wells said, feigning hurt. "We had done a pretty good job not dying before you came along."

"Fine, Mr. Big Shot. In that case, maybe it's time to even the score and make you *my* prisoner." She swung one leg over so she was facing him, then pressed her hands against his chest.

"I'd happily spend the rest of my life as your prisoner if this is what it entails."

She smiled and hit his shoulder playfully. "I'm serious, though. You're going to stay here with us, right?"

Wells paused. He'd been so fixated on the immediate challenges—rescuing Bellamy and then staving off Rhodes—that he hadn't really stopped to think about what would happen after. He couldn't go back to the camp. That much was clear. He'd never wanted to set sights on Rhodes again, even if that meant abandoning everything he'd worked so hard to build. But could he stay with the Earthborns forever? What would he do? How would he make himself useful? But as his eyes met Sasha's, he knew he wasn't going anywhere. He wanted her face to be the first thing he saw every morning, and the last thing he saw before he drifted off to sleep every night. New images flooded his brain, ideas he'd never even thought of in passing, but that somehow made sense when he was looking at Sasha. Maybe someday they'd have a cabin of their own in the Earthborns' village. The thought made his chest tighten with a fierce longing he'd never felt before. *This* was the life he wanted. *This* was what he was fighting for.

"Yes," Wells said, reaching out to stroke her cheek. "I'm staying." Then, afraid that she'd somehow sensed the vision playing out in his head, he smiled and joked, "Your prisoner isn't going anywhere."

"Good." She grinned, rolled to the side, and slipped out of the bed. "So you won't object to staying here for a little bit."

Wells watched as she started to pull on her shoes. "Where are you going?"

"It turns out there's not as much food down here as we thought. I'm just going to run back up and grab some more from the storeroom."

"I'll come with you," he said, swinging his legs out of the bed.

"Absolutely not. If any of the Colonists see you out there, they'll be able to follow you right back to Bellamy. Besides"— she grabbed on to Wells's shins and hoisted his legs back onto the bed—"you should try to get a little sleep. We need our General at his sharpest."

"What are you talking about? *You're* the real brains of this operation. You're not going alone though, right?"

"I'll be faster and safer on my own. You know that." She smiled and kissed his cheek. "I'll be right back."

———

Wells spent the morning sorting through dusty old weapons that had been kept in a storeroom in Mount Weather. The Earthborns had only a few guns between them, and those had already been distributed to the best-trained fighters, but the more people they could arm, the better. Most of the blades were too dull to use, but there were some worth distributing to the Earthborns when the time came.

At lunchtime, he dropped his achy body onto a hard bench and chewed slowly on his small ration of fibrous dried meat. Where was Sasha? He scanned the cafeteria, expecting to see her bright eyes and jet-black hair everywhere he looked. She wasn't there.

Clarke and Bellamy sat close together at the far end of the table.

"Hey," Wells called down to them. "Have you seen Sasha?" They shook their heads, and exchanged a quick, confused glance.

"Where'd she go?" Clarke asked, starting to rise to her feet. "I'll go look for her."

"Never mind," Wells said quickly. He stood and hurried over to the next table, where Max was poring over something that looked like a blueprint. On any other day, he would have been excited to see an artifact like that in person, but at the moment, there was only room for one thought in his mind.

"Excuse me, Max? Did Sasha come back yet?"

Max's head shot up. "Come back from where?"

Wells opened his mouth to reply, then closed it again, not sure what to say. He was confused—didn't Max know Sasha was going to get food from their village? Hadn't she checked in with him before she left?

Max pushed back his chair and jumped to his feet, his whole body tensed. "Wells, where did she go?"

"I thought you knew," Wells replied, his voice a hoarse whisper. "She—she went back to the surface. To get more food."

"She *what*?" Max banged his fist on the table, making a number of people jump. He spun around and called out to everyone in the room. "Sasha left Mount Weather. Did anyone see her come back?" Dozens of eyes went wide, and everyone within earshot shook their heads, murmuring.

"God damn it," Max muttered under his breath before turning back to Wells. "I should have known she would try to fix this on her own. We were going to send out a group tonight, after dark. But she was worried people would be hungry before then."

"I'm so sorry, Max. I didn't realize—"

"It's not your fault," Max said curtly, clearly keen to end the conversation.

"Sir?" a man called from the doorway. "Everyone else is accounted for. She must have gone alone."

Max paled, and his face fell in a way that shot like an arrow through Wells's heart. But he composed himself just as quickly and began giving orders, putting a woman named Jane in charge while he went up to find Sasha. He strode purposefully toward the door. Heads turned as he made his way through the cafeteria, and a few people jumped up to follow him.

Just before he left the dining hall, Max turned back to Wells. "Stay here," he commanded. "It's not safe out there."

Wells sank onto a bench, too stunned to think for a moment. Clarke and Bellamy approached, but he didn't look up. "We're going to go see what we can do to help," Clarke said. Wells nodded, and they slipped out of the room.

After a moment, Wells raised his head and was surprised to find himself alone in the dining hall. Suddenly he couldn't sit still a moment longer, not while Sasha was in danger. Max had ordered him to stay inside Mount Weather, but there was no way he could just sit here and wait for Max's men to return. He didn't care what anyone had to say about it—he was going after her.

Wells jogged down the empty corridor. He could hear voices around the corner and the clatter of people arming themselves with bows, arrows, and spears. He ducked down another hallway and started to run up the steep, twisty stairs before anyone saw him.

A few minutes later, he stepped into the sunlight and blinked as his eyes adjusted. The woods around him were silent—unnaturally so. He studied the spaces between the trees, something Sasha had taught him to do. He saw nothing except more brush and foliage. He moved forward, toward the settlement as quietly as he could.

The village was ominously still. No smoke curled from the chimneys, no children ran across the yards. Wells stopped to make sure it was safe to go further. From his vantage point, he could see that it looked exactly as it had when the Earthborns left—as if they had simply put down their belongings and disappeared.

He was halfway down the sloping path when he heard a sound from the bushes off to his right. He froze, his heart beating a hard rhythm against his ribs. The sound came again, louder this time.

"Help," a shaky voice pleaded. "Somebody, please."

A jolt of cold fear sizzled through Wells's body, far worse than anything he'd felt during his terrible nightmares.

It was Sasha.

Wells dove into the brush in the direction of her voice.

"Sasha!" he called out. "It's me. I'm coming!" Wells thrashed through the trees, tripping over vines and roots as he made his way deeper into the knot of foliage.

None of the horrific images that had haunted him all

night could've prepared him for what it felt like to find her. She lay on her side on the ground, curled up and covered in blood. "*No*," he bellowed, the sound ripping through him like a knife. He flung himself on the ground next to her and grabbed her hand. Her stomach was stained a deep red. He raised the edge of her shirt and saw a deep wound in her abdomen.

"Sasha—I'm here. You're safe now. I'm going to get you back home, okay?"

She didn't answer. Her eyelids fluttered as she slipped in and out of consciousness. He picked her up carefully. Her head lolled to one side, bouncing as he ran back up the hill and toward the main entrance to Mount Weather.

Wells moved as quickly as he could, panting and ignoring the painful stitch in his side—and the risk of attack by Rhodes's men, who were certainly still in the vicinity. *Come and get me*, Wells wanted to scream. *Come and try to hurt me so I can rip you to shreds*.

Several meters out, he heard someone call his name. A troupe of Earthborns materialized from the woods around him. They had been on their way out to find Sasha.

"She's alive," Wells said to them, his voice desperate and strained. "But we need to get her back inside, fast."

The Earthborns formed a circle around him, jogging at his side with their weapons raised. They approached the rock face that concealed the heavy front door to the bunker. One of them flung it open, and Wells rushed inside.

Max stood just on the other side of the door. His face lit up with hope when he first saw Wells, then crumpled when his eyes fell on his daughter.

"No," Max whispered, reaching out for the wall to steady himself. "No, Sasha." He staggered forward and placed his hands on either side of her face. "Sasha, sweetheart . . ."

"She's going to be okay," Wells said. "We just need to get her to Clarke."

One of the Earthborn women sprinted ahead while Max helped Wells carry Sasha down the stairs. He felt as if he was moving through a dream or watching from above as he carried Sasha along the corridor. Light and sound seemed far away, at the end of a long tunnel. This couldn't be happening. This had to be one of Wells's nightmares. In just a moment, he'd sense Sasha smiling over him, her long hair tickling him awake as she whispered *good morning* into his ear.

"The old hospital's just around the corner," Max said, panting as they ran.

They turned a corner, and Max shoved the door open, holding it as Wells rushed inside and laid Sasha down on an operating table. While Max ran to turn on the lights, Wells gripped her hand. It was cold. Frantic, he lifted her eyelids—something he'd watched Clarke do a hundred times in the last few weeks. Her eyes rolled back in her head. Her breathing was shallow and rough.

"Sasha," Wells pleaded. "Sasha, please. Stay with us. Sasha—can you hear me?"

She gave a slight, weak nod, and Wells felt something inside his chest crack open, flooding his body with relief. "Oh, thank god."

Max ran over and grabbed hold of her other hand. "Just hang in there. Help is coming. Just hold on."

"We need to keep her conscious," Wells said, turning to the door, as if his eyes had the power to pull Clarke there faster. "Keep her talking."

"What happened?" Max asked, pushing her hair back from her pale, sweat-covered brow.

Sasha opened her mouth to speak, but no sound came out. Max leaned over and put his ear close to her lips. A moment later, he looked up at Wells. "Snipers," he said grimly. Sasha tried to speak again. This time they could both hear her.

"I was at the storeroom. I never saw them coming." Her voice was ragged.

Clarke sprinted into the room, her blond hair streaming behind her. A moment later, Bellamy ran in after her. Clarke crossed to the bed in two steps, reached for Sasha's wrist and checked her pulse. She didn't say anything, but Wells could read it in Clarke's eyes. He knew it was bad. Clarke lifted Sasha's shirt and exposed the deep wound in her gut.

"She's been shot," Clarke said. "And she's lost a lot of blood." Max clenched his teeth but said nothing. Clarke spun around and began pulling open drawers, riffling through them. She pulled out a vial and a syringe and quickly filled it. She injected the clear liquid into Sasha's arm. Sasha's whole body relaxed instantly, and her breathing evened out. Clarke examined Sasha's abdomen more closely. Wells loosened his grip on Sasha's hand. Max stood silently, his head hanging.

"She's comfortable now," Clarke said slowly as she turned to Max and Wells.

"So what's next?" Wells asked. "Are you going to try to remove the bullet? Or did it go all the way through?"

Clarke said nothing. She just stared at him, her eyes filling with tears.

"Let's go, Clarke," he snapped. "What's the plan? What do you need to fix her?"

"Wells . . ." She walked over from the other side of the table and placed her hand on his arm. "She's lost a lot of blood. I can't just—"

Wells jerked away, out of Clarke's grasp. "Then get more blood. Take mine." He rolled up his sleeve and placed his elbow on the table. "What are you waiting for? Go get a needle or whatever you need."

Clarke shut her eyes for a moment, then turned to Max. When she spoke, her voice was shaky. "Without life support equipment, Sasha wouldn't last more than a few minutes if I tried to operate on her. I think it's better . . . this way. She's resting comfortably, and you'll be able to spend some time together before . . ."

Max stared at her. Stared through her, really, his eyes wide and blank, as if his brain had cut the feed to protect him from the horror playing out in front of him. But then his expression shifted, and he locked eyes with Clarke. "Okay," he said, his voice so quiet, Wells might've just imagined it.

He leaned over to face Sasha, still holding her hand while he smoothed back her hair. "Sasha . . . can you hear me? I love you so much. More than anything."

"I . . . love . . . you," Sasha breathed, her eyes still closed. "I'm sorry."

"You have nothing to be sorry for." Max's voice cracked as he choked back a sob. "My brave girl."

"Wells . . ." Sasha called his name hoarsely. He ran over and grabbed her other hand, interlocking his fingers with hers.

"I'm right here. I'm not going anywhere."

They stayed just like that as the minutes went by. Clarke stood off to the side, at the ready in case Sasha needed more painkillers. Bellamy stood behind her, wrapping his arms around her. Wells held vigil on Sasha's right side, holding her hand and brushing her hair back from her forehead. Max held her other hand and leaned down to whisper in her ear. Tears streamed from his eyes onto her cheeks. Sasha's breathing slowed and became intermittent. Her body was shutting down, and they stood by as witnesses, powerless to stop it.

If Wells could've reached into his chest and ripped out his own heart to replace her fading one, he wouldn't have hesitated. That pain couldn't be any worse than what he was feeling right now. With each labored breath, Wells's own chest tightened, until he was sure he would black out. But he didn't. He stayed just where he was, his eyes locked on Sasha, taking in everything from her long, trembling lashes to the freckles he loved so much. The freckles he'd thought would be a part of his life forever, as constant as the stars.

He might've only known her for a few weeks, but his whole life had changed in that time. When he'd met her, he'd been lost and scared, pretending to be in control but really feeling like a fraud. She'd believed in him; she'd helped him become the leader he was always meant to be, and served as an example for him to follow—showing him what it really meant to be brave, selfless, and noble.

"I love you," he whispered, kissing her forehead, her eyelids, and finally her lips. He exhaled, wishing more than anything that he could pass his breath into her body. He would've gladly taken a thousand bullets if it meant Sasha could have escaped just this one. If it meant he could have spared Max this pain. And he knew he would never, ever forgive himself or the men who had done this to her.

Sasha let out one gasp, then her breathing stopped. Clarke broke away from Bellamy and ran over to start performing CPR while Max and Wells looked on in silent agony. After the longest few minutes of Wells's life, Clarke brought her head to Sasha's chest, held it there a moment, and looked up, tears streaming down her face.

"No," Wells moaned, unable to meet Clarke's face, unable to look at Max. It was over.

Someone—maybe Bellamy—put an arm around him, but Wells could barely feel it. All he could feel was the weight crushing his chest, as his rib cage caved in on itself. And then everything went black.

CHAPTER *20*

Glass

Luke was burning up with fever. Glass could tell just by looking at him. His eyes were glassy, and although his face was flushed, his lips were dry and gray. She racked her brain for all the things her mom used to do when she was sick as a little kid. She put a wet cloth on Luke's forehead. She uncovered him and took off his shirt, letting the cool air from the window wash over his sleeping body. She sat him up every couple of hours and tipped a cup of water to his lips, urging him to drink. But there was nothing she could do about the horrible wound on his leg.

The spear had cut Luke deeply. Glass had almost fainted when she dragged him inside, laid him out on the floor, and ripped open the leg of his pants to see it. Through the blood and dirt, she saw startlingly white bone.

For the first hour, she and Luke had taken turns trying to stop the bleeding by tightening a tourniquet around his upper thigh, but nothing had worked. Glass watched in horror as Luke grew pale and the wooden floor became slick with blood.

"I think I need to cauterize it," he said, clearly trying to keep his voice calm even though his eyes were large with fear and pain.

"What does that mean?" Glass asked, as she tossed a blood-stained bandage aside and reached for another strip of cloth.

"If I apply enough heat, it'll stop the bleeding and prevent infection." He nodded toward the glowing embers in the fireplace. "Can you add some more wood and get it going again?"

Glass hurried over and threw a few smaller pieces of kindling into the dying fire, holding her breath as she watched them ignite. "Now grab that metal thing," Luke said, pointing at the long, thin tool they'd found leaning against the fireplace the first night. "If you place it directly in the flame, it should get hot enough to do the trick."

Glass had said nothing, but watched in growing horror as the metal began to turn red. "Are you sure about this?" she said hesitantly.

Luke nodded. "Bring it over here. Just be careful not to touch it." Glass walked over and knelt down slowly next to Luke. He took a deep breath. "Now, on the count of three, I need you to press it against the wound."

Glass started to tremble, the room suddenly spinning around her. "Luke, I can't. I'm sorry."

He winced as a new wave of pain washed over him. "It's okay. Just give it to me."

"Oh God," Glass whispered as she passed Luke the still-glowing piece of metal and squeezed his other hand. His skin was somehow both cold and covered in sweat.

"Don't look," he said, gritting his teeth. A moment later, he screamed as a sickening sizzle filled her ears along with the smell of burning flesh. Sweat poured from his forehead, and his scream felt never-ending, but he didn't stop. With a final grunt, he threw the metal off to the side, where it clattered to the floor and rolled away.

For a little while, it seemed like the drastic move had worked. The wound stopped bleeding, and Luke was able to get a few hours of rest. But by the next morning, the fever set in. Now his entire leg was hot, red, and puffy. The infection was spreading. Periodically Luke would wake up for a moment, shudder in pain, and then lapse back into unconsciousness. Their only hope was making it back to camp and finding Clarke, but the odds of that were slimmer than Luke making a miraculous recovery. He couldn't stand, let alone walk for two days. And the Earthborns were still out there, watching them. She could sense their presence as strongly as she could feel the heat radiating off Luke's skin.

Glass had never felt this alone, not even during her long months in Confinement. At least there she saw her bunkmate or the guards, and someone brought her food. But here, with Luke unconscious and the constant threat of another attack hanging over her, Glass was both isolated and terrified. There was no one to call for help. Glass kept one eye on Luke, and one eye on the woods surrounding the cabin. She listened so hard her head hurt, straining to catch the slightest snapping of a single twig—anything that would warn her if they came back.

Glass stood by the front door, nervously scanning the leaves for anything out of place. The cool forest air washed over her face, taunting her with the memories of everything she and Luke had enjoyed together—the trees, the moonlight reflecting off the water—all the beauty that would become meaningless if Luke was taken from her. He stirred on the makeshift bed on the floor behind her. She ran across the room and grabbed his hand, stroking his hot forehead.

"Luke? Luke, can you hear me?"

His eyelids fluttered but didn't open. He moved his lips, but no sound came out. Glass squeezed his hand and bent down to whisper in his ear.

"It's going to be okay. *You're* going to be okay. I'm going to figure something out."

"I'm late for patrol," he said, twisting from side to side as if trying to get out of bed.

"No, you're not, you're fine." Glass placed her hand on his shoulder. Did he think he was back on the ship? "You have nothing to worry about."

Luke barely managed a nod before closing his eyes again. Within seconds, he was asleep. His grip slackened on Glass's hand, and she gently placed his arm down on the bed. She checked his leg. The redness had spread all the way down to his knee and up to his hip. She didn't know much about this kind of thing, but Glass had enough sense to know that if she didn't get him some help, Luke was going to die. They had to go. *Now.*

Glass sat down at the wooden kitchen table and tried to clear her head, trying to push away the fear that had been gnawing a hole through her gut for days. Fear was not going to get them out of here. She had to *think*. They had to get back to camp. That was their only shot at getting Luke the help he needed. But Glass would have to figure out how to transport Luke, who could barely walk even with her help, and evade the Earthborns at the same time. A spacewalk was suddenly looking simple compared to this. How could they possibly move fast enough to escape, with Luke in this condition?

Glass scanned the tiny cabin, searching for inspiration. The paralyzing grip of fear slowly began to release its hold on her, and her mind kicked into gear. Yes, if she could get him to the river . . . that would work . . . but how to move him? Her eyes fell on an odd device she and Luke had scratched their heads at when they first got there. It leaned upright against a wall in the corner, behind a broom and some other ancient-looking cleaning supplies. She crossed the room and dug it out, laying it down on the floor. It was as tall as she was, made of long wooden slats. It was almost a long plank, but at one end the slats all curved back on themselves. There was a rope tied there.

It reminded her of something she'd read about in tutorial once. Something kids used to ride in the snow on Earth. She racked her brain for the word. *Slide? Sloop?* Glass stepped on the slats with one foot, testing their strength. It was old, but it was solid. If she could get Luke onto it, she could pull him, but she'd have to make a few adjustments.

She stood up, grabbed a few items from around the room, and laid them out on the floor next to the . . . *sled!* It was a sled. She was sure of it. Now she just needed to make it work. She arranged and rearranged things into different configurations, testing them, then trying again. Glass shook her head grimly. If someone had told her six months—or even six weeks—ago that she'd be rigging a contraption out of junk she'd found in an abandoned cabin on Earth to carry her mortally wounded boyfriend through the woods, she'd have laughed in their face and asked if they'd gotten into the illegal moonshine they sold on Arcadia.

She stepped back and surveyed her handiwork. It was going to work. It *had* to work. Glass would use the rope to pull Luke along behind her. To keep him in place, she had cut a blanket into long strips that would secure him around the waist, arms, and good leg, all tied to the top of the sled.

It was pretty rudimentary, but with any luck, it would get them to the water. That was all she needed.

Glass crossed to Luke and gently roused him. "Luke," she whispered in his ear. "I'm going to move you, okay? We need to get back to camp." He didn't respond. Glass slid her hands under his arms, crossed her arms over his chest, and, with a grunt, eased him onto the floor. He flinched as his injured leg moved, but didn't wake up. She pulled him onto the sled and fastened the sheet around him. Glass squatted down, grabbed the rope and looped it around her hands, and rose to a standing position. She took a few steps forward, and Luke moved along the floor behind her. It had worked.

Glass grabbed Luke's gun—though she wasn't sure she had the nerve to use it—and lumbered toward the door. At the last second, she turned back and snatched a pack of matches off the table in case she'd need to start a fire during their journey. The weight behind her was awkward and threw her off-center, but she would have to get the hang of it. Without a backward glance, she stepped out of the cabin, dragging the sled behind her into the narrow clearing that circled the house.

Thwack! Glass spun her head around, searching for the source of the sound. *Thwack!* It came again.

She glanced at the forest. In the twilight, every shadow looked like it could be an enemy.

She lunged back toward the cabin, yanking Luke behind her. She caught movement out of the corner of her eye and felt something whiz by her ear.

Glass strained against the weight of the sled and heard Luke groan in pain. She yanked open the door and charged through it as an arrow smacked in the door frame, quivering where her head had been only a split second before.

The sled slid in after her, and Glass dropped the harness and slammed the door shut, just as two more arrows thudded into it. She leaned against the closed door, gripping the gun in her suddenly clammy hand. She looked around the cabin. Could she barricade the door? Would they break in through one of the windows?

She latched the door and tentatively lifted Luke's gun, steeling herself. If one of the Earthborns broke in through the window, could she fight them? Could she bring herself to fire a gun at another living person? Even if she did, there was clearly more than one of them. One girl who had never before fired a gun was no match for a group of murderous Earthborns.

From the sled, Luke groaned.

"It's going to be all right. I'll figure something out," she said, wincing at the lie. How could she escape a cabin that was surrounded by angry Earthborns?

She peered through the corner of a window. The graying light played tricks with the shadows, but there was movement out there. Figures darted between the trees, their hands gripping bows and axes.

Glass leaned against the door and closed her eyes. This was it. This time, they would finish off Luke and kill her too.

She listened for the sound of footsteps, the crash of windows, the feel of the door being smashed open behind her.

No sound came but the wind, and the rush of the river. They were expecting her to come out. Had they been outside the entire time, waiting for her to emerge so they could get a clean shot?

They had her cornered. There was nowhere to go, nothing to do but hope that they'd get tired of waiting and batter down the door or crash in through the windows. Her mind raced, searching for any way out.

Even if she was able to distract them long enough to get

away from the cabin without being riddled with arrows, what then?

Frantic, she cast her eyes around the room, desperate for something—anything—she could use as a distraction, to buy them some time. Nothing. She was about to let out a scream of frustration when she realized there was something in her hand. She'd been clutching it so tightly she'd almost forgotten about it. Glass uncurled her fingers, and there, squashed in her palm, were the matches she'd grabbed on her way out the door.

A desperate, foolish plan formed in her mind. If she couldn't outrun them to the river, she would need to find a way to escape that didn't call for running. Before she had time to think better of it, she set to work.

Glass crawled across the floor and sat under the window by the front door. She wrapped a strand of the ripped bed sheet around the end of a piece of firewood and struck a match. She lit the sheet, and a few seconds later, she was gripping a burning torch.

As the flame flickered and grew, Glass took a deep breath and counted down. "Three, two, one . . ." She jumped up and with a quick glance out the open window, aimed for the pile of dried firewood Luke had stacked up against the wall of the cabin before he'd gotten hurt.

She dropped back down to the floor and waited. There was

silence, and for a painful moment, she thought her plan had already failed. Then she heard it: a sharp crackling, followed by a soft whoosh as the pile of wood caught fire. The cabin began to glow as the flames caught on the brush and spread outward toward the woods—just as she'd hoped.

Glass turned to Luke. He hadn't moved. His breathing was shallow, and his brow twitched as he lay, barely conscious, by the fireplace. If Luke died, Glass would die too. She knew that as clearly as she knew her own name.

The sound of the flames was growing louder, and within a few minutes, the air in the cabin began to change. Glass cursed to herself when she realized the foolish thing she'd done—the house may have been made of stone, but that wouldn't stop the smoke from suffocating them if the fire encircled the whole place. A little bit of smoke was just starting to waft in through the open window, visible in the flickering light of the fire.

Glass moved closer to the door, getting ready for a quick exit. As the smoke began to fill the room, she pulled the blanket off of Luke and doused it with the last of their water. Outside, she could hear voices calling to one another across the clearing.

She knelt next to Luke and pulled the soaked blanket over both of them. The air grew warmer and she could see orange flickering against the window from under the edge of the blanket. Now the voices outside were laughing and cheering. Let them think they'd won. Let them think she was already dead. Perhaps they would be too shocked to chase her when she and Luke made their escape.

Luke shifted on the sled, a low moan escaping his lips.

"I'm sorry," she said. "I should have gotten you help sooner. We shouldn't have stayed so long."

The air was boiling now, so hot Glass could almost feel her skin melting and peeling away. The smoke was coming in through the window in thick billows, making it hard to see anything, hard to breathe. They huddled under the blanket, Glass trying to guess just how much longer they could survive before it was too late. If they waited too long, the flames would be around the whole house, and there would be no way to escape. They would suffocate if they stayed here in the smoke. Eyes stinging, Glass pushed herself off the floor and ran to the door. It was now or never.

Glass yanked open the door and peered out. Night had fallen outside, and the roaring flames were playing havoc with the shadows, casting flickering orange and black lights across the clearing and on the trees.

She grabbed the sled's rope, hunkered under the blanket, and charged through the door. She gasped as she passed from the furnace of the cabin into the cooler night air.

Luke moaned as she pulled him across the bumpy ground,

downhill toward the river. For several long seconds, she ran with only the crackling of the fire behind her.

She heard the first shouts as she reached the boat and started pushing it into the water. The firelight and smoke hadn't been quite enough to cover her escape.

"Luke," she said as she pulled him up. "You have to help me. Just for a moment."

His eyes twitched open, and she could feel his muscles straining to move. He stood on his one good leg, and she slipped under his arm. Together they stumbled forward, and she tried to slow his fall as he almost collapsed into the boat. She tossed the sled in after him and began pushing the boat down the slope into the water.

Arrows flew by, landing with a splash just ahead of her. She could hear the thud of feet running down the hill toward them as she threw her entire weight against the boat, shoving it out into the current.

At the last second, she leapt, nearly missing the boat as the water grabbed it and pulled it downstream.

She whipped her head around and saw shadows against the flaming cabin, rushing down the hill toward her. Glass lay down next to Luke as more arrows ricocheted off the sides of the metal boat.

They picked up speed as the surging of the river took control of their movement. She poked her head up and could see figures running along the shore, silhouetted against fire and moonlight. They hardly looked human.

She kept her head down as the river swept them around a curve, and the last arrows pinged off the boat. After a few tense moments of holding her breath, Glass sat up, grabbing the paddle and sticking it into the water, trying to propel the boat even faster than the current. When it finally seemed like they'd outdistanced the Earthborns, she reached out and tried to use the paddle to pull the boat back to the shore, but she couldn't get enough leverage. Her heart pounded as the boat continued to move swiftly down the river. She had no idea if they were headed in the right direction. She needed to use Luke's compass. If he'd been right about heading due north from the camp, then they needed to head south.

It took nearly another half hour for the river to narrow to the point that the thick brush slowed them down. Eventually, Glass was able to drop into the chilly water and yank the boat onto the shore. She pulled the compass out of her pack and set it on the ground, the way Luke had showed her. Thank goodness, they had been heading south. At least, southeast. It wouldn't be too difficult to get back on track, she hoped. And if she could actually move with Luke . . .

"One more time, Luke," she said. "I just need you to get up and walk with me one more time."

He groaned, but when she pulled him out of the hull of

the boat he cooperated, letting her help him to stand. He staggered a few feet through the shallow water before finally dropping on the bank.

Relieved of their weight, the boat rode higher in the water, and the brisk current pulled it away into the night. Working quickly and silently, Glass maneuvered Luke back onto the sled and took up the rope again.

Just hold on, Luke, she thought to herself as she threw her entire weight against the sled and broke into a run.

The sounds of the river faded as they made their way deeper into the woods, but Glass was too afraid to stop and look behind them. She had to keep moving. She had to find help for Luke, even if it was the last thing she ever did.

CHAPTER *21*

Wells

It was entirely his fault. All of it.

Wells slammed his fist into the rock wall, hard. Blood dripped down his knuckles, but he didn't feel any physical pain. All he felt was the weight of his own stupid, selfish mistakes piling higher and higher, threatening to topple down and crush him at any moment.

He never thought he could feel worse than he did after Clarke was arrested or after his mother died. But this was the lowest Wells had ever been. He spun around in the tiny room, looking for something else to kick or hit. There was just his narrow bed. The bed Sasha had slept in just hours ago. And now she was dead.

Wells fell onto the mattress and lay on his back. The ache in his chest was so strong and solid, he felt like he could pick it up and hold it in his hands. He covered his face with his arms. He just wanted to block out the light, turn off his brain, and push away everyone and everything. He wanted blankness. He wanted to drift in the deep and endless silence of space. If he were back on the ship, he wouldn't hesitate before wrenching open the airlock and hurtling himself into the void.

He would end it if he could. He would take himself out of the equation if he thought it would help everyone else. But he was too ashamed to leave everything behind, not when he'd made such a mess of things. But how could he possibly put things right? There was no smoothing things over between the Earthborns and Rhodes. There was no bringing Sasha back. There was no fixing Max's broken heart.

If only he had stopped himself before he set all of this in motion. If only he hadn't made the leak on the airlock worse, then the dropships wouldn't have had to leave so suddenly. They would have had more time to prepare the ships, and maybe they could have sent more people down. Instead, everyone who didn't fight his or her way onboard was up there dying as the oxygen dwindled.

If only he hadn't staged a fake attack to break Bellamy out of prison, maybe Rhodes and the others wouldn't have been so afraid of the aggressive faction of Earthborns. Maybe they wouldn't have been so quick to the violence that killed Sasha. And if he hadn't gotten involved with Sasha in the first place, maybe she could have gone on living a long, peaceful life without him.

Wells thought he would suffocate under the pressure of all these thoughts. His breath came in shallow gulps, and he felt clammy with panic. There was nowhere to go, nothing he could do, nothing worth saying. He was trapped.

Just as he thought he might run for the door and escape Mount Weather, he heard a familiar voice saying his name. He opened his eyes and saw Clarke outlined by the light from the hallway.

"Can I come in?" she asked.

Wells jerked upright, then scooted back and leaned against the wall, burying his head in his hands. Clarke lowered herself onto the bed next to him. They sat like that in silence for a few minutes.

"Wells, I wish there was something I could say," Clarke finally said.

"There's nothing," he said flatly.

She placed her hand on his arm. Wells flinched, and Clarke made like she was about to pull away but she increased the pressure with a squeeze. "I know. I've lost a lot of people too. I know the words don't make any difference."

Wells didn't meet Clarke's eyes, but he was glad she knew

better than to start babbling about how Sasha was in a better place. He'd had enough of that when his mother died. But at least then there'd been a part of him that had managed to believe it. He'd imagined his mom on Earth, her spirit returning to humanity's *real* home instead of being sentenced to spend eternity among the cold, unfeeling stars. But this was different. Sasha had already been where she belonged. Now she was nowhere, exiled from the world she'd loved far, far too soon.

"I'm so sorry, Wells," Clarke whispered. "Sasha was incredible. She was so smart, and strong . . . and noble. Just like you. You made an inspiring team."

"Noble?" The word tasted bitter in Wells's mouth. "Clarke, I'm a *murderer.*"

"A murderer? Wells, no. What happened to Sasha wasn't your fault. You know that, right?"

"It was absolutely my fault. One hundred percent." Wells rose from the bed and began pacing the room like a Confined prisoner counting down the hours to his execution.

"What are you talking about?" Clarke watched him, her eyes full of confusion and concern.

"I'm the reason all of this is happening. I'm the selfish bastard who leaves a trail of destruction behind him wherever he goes. Everyone up there"—he jabbed a finger skyward—"would be alive today if it weren't for me."

Clarke rose from the bed and took a few hesitant steps toward him. "Wells, you're exhausted. I think you should lie down for a few minutes. You'll feel better after you've had some rest."

She was right. He *was* exhausted, but it wasn't entirely from the strain of watching the girl he loved die in front of him. The effort of holding in his terrible secret was what had truly drained every last ounce of strength. He dropped back onto the bed. Clarke followed, and wrapped her arm around him.

He had nothing left to lose. He already despised himself. What did it matter if he made everyone else despise him as well? "There's something I haven't told you, Clarke."

Her whole body tensed, but she remained silent and waited for him to continue.

"I broke the airlock on Phoenix."

"What?" He wouldn't look at her, but he could hear the confusion and disbelief in her voice.

"It was already faulty, but I made it worse. So that the air would leak faster. So that you would get sent to Earth before your eighteenth birthday. They were going to kill you, Clarke. And I couldn't let that happen. Not after what I'd already done to you. I was the reason you were Confined in the first place."

Clarke still said nothing, so Wells went on, a strange, numbing combination of relief and horror spreading through his limbs as he voiced the words he'd feared ever saying out loud.

"I'm the reason they had to abandon the ship so fast, and the reason so many people got stuck up there, suffocating. I did that to them."

Clarke still hadn't spoken, so finally, Wells forced himself to look at her, bracing for the look of horror and loathing. But instead, she just looked sad and scared, her wide eyes making her appear younger, almost vulnerable.

"You did that . . . for *me*?"

Wells nodded slowly. "I had to. I overheard my father and Rhodes talking, so I knew the plan. They were either going to kill you or send you to Earth, and I sure as hell wasn't going to let it be option A."

To his surprise, when she spoke, there was no rancor in her voice. Just sadness. "I would've never wanted you to do that. I would've rather died than endanger so many lives."

"I know." He placed his head in his hands, his cheeks burning with shame. "It was insane and selfish. I knew I wouldn't be able to live with myself if you died, but I can't live with myself now, anyway." He let out a short, bitter laugh. "Of course, now I realize that the right thing to do would've been just to kill myself. If I'd thrown myself out of that airlock, it would've saved everyone a lot of pain and suffering."

"Wells, don't talk like that." Clarke had scooted back in order to face him, and was looking at him with dismay. "Yes, you made a mistake . . . a big one. But that doesn't negate all the incredible things you've done. Think of all the people you *saved*. If you hadn't messed with the airlock, every single one of us would've been executed instead of being sent to Earth. Not just me. Molly, Octavia, Eric. Even more, you're the reason we all survived once we got here."

"Hardly. You're the one who saved everyone's lives. I just chopped some firewood."

"You turned a wild, dangerous planet into our *home*. You made us see our potential, what we could achieve if we worked together. You inspired us, Wells. You bring out the best in everyone."

That's what he'd loved about Sasha, the way she'd made him want to be a better person, a better leader. He'd failed her—there was nothing Clarke could do to convince him otherwise—but that didn't mean he should stop trying. He owed her more than that.

"I . . . I just don't know what to do now," he said quietly.

"You could start by forgiving yourself. Just a little bit."

Wells had no idea how that even worked. He had spent his entire life in the right place at the right time, doing as he was told, doing as he was expected to do. He had always taken the high road, made the right choice, regardless of his own feelings. But at the most crucial moment of all, he'd faltered, and thousands of people had suffered. It was unforgivable.

Clarke knew him so well. It was as if he had spoken all

his thoughts out loud. "I know better than anyone that you don't like to show your emotions, Wells. But sometimes you have to. You need to take all these feelings and use them. Be *human*. It will make you an even better leader."

Wells took Clarke's hand and gripped it tightly. Before he could reply, a commotion rang out through the corridor. They both hopped to their feet and hurried out of the room, following a steady stream of people down the hall.

Max stood at the front of the large, cavernous space that'd become their center of operations. His face looked ravaged, and his shoulders stooped on his gaunt frame. The fire was gone from his eyes.

"We have visitors," he announced, beckoning toward someone out of sight. As he spoke, hundreds of heads shot around to see who had entered the bunker. "Don't worry—none of them are armed. We checked." Wells and Clarke let out a loud sigh of relief as they recognized the dozen or so members of the hundred filing inside. Eric and Felix led the pack.

"Did Rhodes send you?" Max asked. The entire room held its breath, waiting for their answer.

"No," Eric said, shaking his head, his voice as steady and calm as ever. "We came to join you. We want nothing to do with Rhodes or the other Colonists anymore."

Max eyed them shrewdly, his years of experience had

clearly sharpened his ability to assess people's character. "And why is that?"

Eric met his eyes without wavering. "They've completely taken over. It's not the home we built anymore. There's no discussion, no cooperation. Rhodes tells everyone what to do, and the guards make sure they do it. It's just like being back on the ship. The prison cabin they built for Bellamy is already full, and the guards beat one woman up so badly I'm not sure she's going to be able to walk again." He paused and turned to face the Earthborns, who were staring at him uneasily, then scanned the crowd until he spotted Wells. "Everything was so much better when you were in charge, Wells. You stood for something, something worth fighting for."

The grief that had lodged in Wells's chest loosened its grip, and a faint glimmer of hope flared up in him.

Max cleared his throat, and all eyes turned to him.

"You're welcome to stay with us, then. We'll help you get settled shortly. But first, do you have any insight into what Rhodes might be planning?"

"We do," Felix said, stepping forward. "That's why we came when we did. I volunteered to work with the guards, so I heard their discussions. They don't believe there are two separate groups of Earthborns. They think you're dangerous, and we couldn't get them to believe that you aren't. They think you're all working together."

"They're planning an attack," Eric interjected. "A big one. And they have more weapons than we realized at first. We discovered that they've been hoarding guns and ammo in a secret cache in the woods."

The room filled with whispers and anxious murmurs, but Max hardly flinched. His old bearing had returned, and some of the light had returned to his eyes. "Are you willing to fight with us?" he asked the newcomers.

Eric, Felix, and the others nodded vigorously. Gratitude and pride surged in Wells's chest.

"Very well, then. I think we may have an opportunity now that we have your support." He shook his head grimly. "We might've started this to help your friends, but it's clear this conflict was inevitable. It was just a matter of time before Rhodes drew us into a fight. Better we deal with it quickly, before"—he took a deep breath—"before even more people get hurt."

Bellamy ran over to Eric. "What about Octavia? Did she come with you? Is she okay?"

"She's fine, but she didn't come with us. It was a tough decision, but she felt she had to stay with the kids, especially now that things have gotten more and more dangerous." Eric's face softened, and he placed a hand on Bellamy's shoulder.

"Don't worry," Wells said. "Once we kick Rhodes's ass, we'll be able to bring them all here. Octavia, the kids, and anyone else who wants to join."

Bellamy nodded, the wistfulness in his eyes hardening into resolve. Wells could tell he was gearing up for a fight. They all were.

Max was already deep in conversation with his deputies, and it was clear they had already started discussing battle plans. He looked over at Wells, who averted his gaze, still unwilling to meet Max's eyes. Certainly, the last thing Max needed was a reminder of the boy who got his daughter killed. But then, to his surprise, Max called his name. "Come over here, Wells. We need you."

CHAPTER 22

Clarke

Clarke had been spending every free minute in the radio room, and today was no different. After their strategy meeting with Max, they had gone their separate ways to prepare for battle. Eric had told them that Rhodes was preparing his guards to attack just before dawn the next morning. That was eight hours from now.

They had all agreed it was best to wait for the Colonists to come to Mount Weather, where the Earthborns would have the advantage. They had their solid bunker, protected by the rock formations surrounding them on all sides. They also had intimate knowledge of the terrain, which Rhodes and his men did not. A group of Earthborns had already been dispatched into the woods, climbing high into the trees where they would be invisible to anyone on the ground. As soon as the advancing Colonists passed below them, the Earthborn fighters would drop down from the trees. The Vice Chancellor and his men would be trapped between the Earthborns outside and the ones waiting to attack from inside Mount Weather.

It was a shaky plan, at best, but it was all they had. They would have to rely on the element of surprise—and a lot of luck. While the others paced the hallways anxiously, waiting for the signal to get in position, Clarke sought the solace of the radio room. She could almost feel her parents there, and that gave her comfort—and hope.

The quiet also gave her a chance to try and process everything Wells had told her. Never in her wildest dreams, or most unsettling nightmares, would she have imagined Wells was capable of such a thing. He endangered the lives of every single person on the Colony, just to give her a fighting chance of seeing her eighteenth birthday. A wave of nausea crashed over her, nearly bringing Clarke to her knees. All those people—practically everyone she'd ever known—dead, because of her. Because of what Wells had done to save her. But then, God knew she was in no position to judge him. When Clarke had discovered that her parents were conducting radiation trials on unregistered children from the care center, she'd done nothing to stop them. More than anyone, Clarke knew what it was like to put the people you loved ahead of everything else. She'd spent so much of her life seeing the world as black-and-white, separating right from wrong as confidently as she sorted plant cells from animal cells during a biology exam. But the past year had been a brutal crash course in moral relativity.

Clarke fiddled with the dials and switches as these thoughts ran through her head. A loud, steady hiss filled the room, bouncing off the stone walls. She tried a new combination, and the hiss deepened in tone. Then a high-pitched whine kicked in. She sat forward in her chair. That was a sound she hadn't heard before. Gently, Clarke nudged the dial a hair further. The whine dropped out, and for a beat, there was just the sound of static. Clarke's heart sank.

Then she heard something deep in the hiss. It was so faint, nothing more than a whisper into the wind. It was unidentifiable, yet somehow oddly familiar at the same time. The sound grew louder, as if it were moving toward her. Clarke tilted her head toward the speaker, straining to listen. She wasn't sure what she had heard. Could it have been . . . ? She shook her head. She was probably imagining things. Was her desperation making her go nuts?

But the sound grew louder and clearer—and it was definitely a *voice*. She wasn't making this up. Goose bumps sprinkled her skin, and her heart began to pound in her chest. Clarke knew that voice.

It was her mom.

The words grew to full volume. "Radio check," her mom said in a neutral tone, as if she'd spoken those words a thousand times before. "Radio check. Alpha X-ray radio check."

Clarke closed her eyes and let her mother's voice wash over her, filling her with the most wonderful mix of relief and joy, like the sound of a heartbeat after a patient had gone into cardiac arrest. Her hands shook as she reached for the button that transmitted her voice across the airwaves.

"Mom?" Clarke called out, trembling. "Is—is that you?"

There was a long pause, and Clarke held her breath until her chest began to hurt.

"Clarke? *Clarke?*" There was no question: It was her mom. Then Clarke heard a man's voice calling out in the background. *Her dad.* It was true. They were alive. "Clarke, where are you?" her mom asked across the frequencies, with equal parts amazement and disbelief. "Are you on *Earth?*"

"Yes . . . I'm here. I'm—" A sob tore its way out of her throat as tears began to stream down her face.

"Clarke, what's wrong? Are you okay?"

She tried to tell her mother that she was fine, but nothing came out of her mouth except more sobs. Clarke released all the tears she'd been too numb to shed during her long, lonely months in Confinement when she'd believed she was truly alone in the universe. Her heart was so full of joy, her happiness was almost an ache, yet she couldn't stop crying.

"Clarke, oh God. What's going on? Where are you?"

She wiped her nose with the back of her hand and tried to take a breath. "I'm fine. I just can't believe I'm talking to you. They told me they floated you. I—I thought you were dead!" She thought of all the one-sided conversations she'd had with her parents over the past year and a half, imagining what they'd say when she told them about her trial, about Wells, and, most of all, about the wonders of Earth. For eighteen months, everything she'd thought, everything she'd told them, every prayer and every plea had been met with nothing but suffocating silence. And now the silence had lifted, releasing a weight she hadn't realized had been chained to her heart.

"It's okay, Clarke. We're here. We're alive. Where are you now?" Her father's voice was so solid, so reassuring.

"I'm in Mount Weather," she said, grinning as she wiped her nose on her sleeve. "Where are you?"

"Oh, Cl—" her mom began, but her words were cut off sharply as the high whine returned.

"No!" Clarke shouted. "No, no, no!" She swiped frantically at the dials, but she couldn't find the right frequency again. Her tears of joy turned to frustration as anxiety welled up in her chest. It felt like losing them all over again. "Damn it," she cried, smacking her hand against the console. She had to get the signal back.

Before she had a chance to try anything else, the door burst open, and a few of Max's men ran into the room.

"Clarke," one of them said. "They're here. Let's go."

"But it's too early," she said, startled. "How did they get here so fast?"

"We don't know, but we need to move into position."

Her head swam as she tried to process what this meant. Rhodes and his guards were preparing to attack Mount Weather. "But we're not ready—"

"We have to be ready," the man said. "Time to move."

Clarke jumped from her seat and wiped tears from her face, grateful that everyone else would be too preoccupied to ask why she was crying. Without a backward glance at the flashing lights and endless hiss and crackle of the radio, she ran from the room, ready to arm herself for battle.

CHAPTER 23

Bellamy

Bellamy's shoulder didn't hurt anymore. The adrenaline coursing through his body was better than any painkiller. He hopped from one foot to the other and shook out his hands, which were itching for a weapon. He couldn't decide what would be more satisfying—sending one of his perfectly aimed arrows right through Rhodes's throat or thrusting a spear into his chest.

The Earthborns were gathering in the cavernous hall that had become their command center. Many of the adults were arming themselves with knives, spears, and the odd bow, while others were preparing to lead the children and the elderly deeper into the fortress. Bellamy reached for a bow, his brow furrowing in concentration as he tested the string.

"Are you sure this is a good idea?" Clarke asked quietly. "You were *shot*, Bel. You have a long way to go before you're fully recovered."

"Save your breath, Griffin," he said as he began rooting around for arrows. "You know there's no way in hell I'm letting these people risk their lives for me while I sit around twiddling my thumbs."

"Just be careful." Her face was pale, and her eyes were red. In the few minutes they'd had together, preparing for the fight, she'd told him about speaking to her parents. But there was no time to celebrate that small miracle; they both had to focus their attention on the task at hand—making Vice Chancellor Rhodes regret he'd ever set foot on Earth.

"Careful is my middle name," he said, placing a few arrows that had passed his inspection to the side.

She smiled. "I believe you've also said the same thing about Danger and Victory."

"That's me. Bellamy Careful Danger Victory Blake."

"I'm jealous. I don't even have one middle name."

"Oh, I can think of a few that would suit you," Bellamy said, wrapping his arm around her waist. "Let's see, how about Clarke Know-It-All . . . Bossy . . ." She rolled her eyes and smacked him playfully on the chest. He smirked and pulled her closer, leaning down to whisper in her ear. ". . . Brilliant . . . Sexy Griffin."

"I'm not sure all that will fit on an office door, but I like it."

"Everybody ready?" Wells asked, striding toward them. His whole demeanor had changed. Although he was only wearing a faded, stained T-shirt, and ripped, slightly too-short pants, he moved like he was still wearing his officer's uniform. A few weeks ago, Wells's bearing might've irritated Bellamy, but right now, he felt grateful that his brother was so capable.

"I'm more than ready," Bellamy said, trying to psych everyone up. He reached over to bump fists with Felix, who was pale and shifting from side to side nervously. "I can't wait to kick some Colony-Guard ass." Bellamy shot Wells a devilish grin.

"I wish I had your confidence," Felix said.

"It's not confidence," Bellamy quipped. "It's arrogance. There's a big difference."

"Whatever it is, it's a good thing," said Wells to Bellamy's surprise. "We're going to need it."

At Max's nod, Wells stepped to the front of the room, which quickly fell silent, although the tension was so thick, the air practically buzzed with it.

"Friends," Max began, his tone grave. "We have news that there are about two dozen Colonists approaching Mount Weather. In just a moment, we will go to our appointed positions and prepare to fight. They have arrived much more quickly than we expected them to, but rest assured, we'll meet them with all our might. And remember: Our goal is not to inflict harm, but to prevent them from committing sense-less acts of violence against others. If we need to use strength to protect ourselves, then so be it. But that is not our purpose."

He turned to nod at Wells, who cleared his throat as he prepared to address the crowd. "As we expected, they're car-rying guns . . . lots of them, so be careful and don't take any unnecessary risks. But although they might have firearms, they're not infallible." He went on to explain a little about how the guards trained, the formations they used, and the tactics they were most likely to employ—it was a good thing they had insider information from Wells's days as an officer, Bellamy realized.

"The thing to remember," Max said, "is that we're not just fighting to protect these young people who've turned to us for help, we're fighting to protect our way of life. We've tried to reason with our new neighbors, but it's become increas-ingly clear that peace and cooperation is not their priority. If we don't deal with them now, there's no knowing what they'll try next time." He paused, scanning the room. "I've already lost my daughter . . . I couldn't bear to lose any of you." He took a breath, and a new fierceness crept into his voice. "Our people have struggled against enormous odds, but we have persevered. Others might've left Earth to burn, but we stayed behind and fought to keep it our home."

A few shouts rose up from the crowd, and Max smiled.

"This is our land, our *planet*, and now's the time to decide how much we're willing to risk to protect it."

Wells grinned and reached to shake Max's hand. The older man clasped it in his, then pulled Wells toward him and clapped him on the back.

"Is everyone ready?" Wells asked, turning back to the crowd.

A battle cry shook the rough stone walls as everyone raised their fists in the air and gathered up their spears, arrows, and knives. They headed for the exits, growing silent as they slipped outside and took their positions in the darkened woods just outside Mount Weather.

Clarke slung a bag full of medical supplies over her shoulder and reached for a long knife. "Where are you going?" Bellamy asked, his excitement giving way to cold fear.

She raised her chin and gave him her most determined stare. "People are going to get hurt out there. They need me."

Bellamy opened his mouth to protest but shut it when he realized how selfish that would be. Clarke was right. As the person with the most medical experience, it made perfect sense for her to be on the ground. "Just be really, really careful, okay?" he said. She nodded. "You promise?"

"I promise."

Bellamy put his hand under her chin and tipped her

face up to his. "Clarke, whatever happens, I just want you to know—"

She shook her head and cut him off with a kiss. "Don't," she said. "We're going to be fine."

He smiled at her. "You're getting the hang of this arrogance thing."

"I learned from the best."

He kissed her again, then grabbed his bow and started walking toward the stairs.

"Bellamy," Wells called, jogging over to him. "Listen, I know you're not going to like this, but we think it's best for everyone if you stay inside."

"What?" Bellamy narrowed his eyes. "You can't be serious. There's no way in hell I'm staying in here. I'm not afraid of Rhodes, or any of them. Just let them try to bring me down again."

"That's the thing. You're too much of a target. You'll endanger everyone around you. I know you're a great fighter, one of the best we have, but it's not worth the risk."

Bellamy stared at Wells, fighting the anger and indignation bubbling up from his stomach into his chest. What the hell was Wells thinking, trying to keep him out of the battle? As if dating the Earthborn leader's dead daughter somehow made him Max's second-in-command. But the vile thoughts taking shape in his brain disappeared as quickly as they'd arrived. Wells was right. This was about a lot more than Bellamy and his revenge. He needed to do what was best for the group, and in this case, it meant lying low.

He shot Clarke a rueful smile as he set his bow on the floor, then turned to Wells and held out his hand. "Be careful out there, man. And give Rhodes hell for me."

Wells grinned as he took Bellamy's hand and pulled him in for a hug. "I'll see you soon." Wells stepped back and glanced at Clarke.

She nodded at him, then turned to Bellamy. He wrapped his arms around her waist, held her close as she rested her cheek against his chest for a long moment while he kissed the top of her head. "I love you," he said as she pulled away.

"I love you too."

"Take care of her, Wells," Bellamy called as he watched them make their way toward the stairs. Wells turned to meet his eyes and nodded.

"And take care of him, Clarke," Bellamy said, a little softer this time. "Take care of each other."

A moment later, they were gone.

———

Bellamy wasn't sure how many miles he'd logged, pacing the hall, but it was impossible for him to stand still. He had to keep moving. The bunker was eerily silent. Fifteen minutes passed, then twenty. Bellamy couldn't take it. He slipped out of the room, ran up the circular stairs, and cracked open the door to Mount Weather. He stood in the shadows of the hallway, listening for a sign that the battle was about to begin.

Finally, a long, low whistle echoed across the hilltop, followed by three short chirps. Rhodes's men were close. Bellamy held his breath. Seconds later, the first shot rang out, then another, then too many to count. The night sky lit up with gunfire, and dozens of spears and arrows whizzed down from the trees in a blurred swoosh. Agonized cries and shouts rose up as if from the earth itself. Then, as if they were materializing from thin air, wounded men and women began stumbling out of the forest, into the clearing outside Mount Weather. Some were Colonists, others were Earthborns. All were covered in blood and writhing in pain. It was instant carnage, as bad as anything Bellamy had seen when the dropships crashed.

Without thinking, Bellamy bolted through the door. He snatched up a club from the hand of a fallen Earthborn and began swinging it wildly in every direction. He was doing some pretty good damage too, until three Earthborns swooped down on him, grabbing him by the arms and practically lifting him off his feet. They hauled him backward into the entrance to Mount Weather. Bellamy kicked and tried to break free. "Let me go," he yelled. "I want to fight!"

"You need to stay out of sight," one of the women

admonished, and Bellamy instantly felt remorseful—how had he let himself get carried away *again*?

He stopped struggling and began running toward the door. The Earthborns circled him for protection and ran alongside him. Just steps from the safety of Mount Weather's walls, a man to Bellamy's right let out a cry and fell to the ground. Bellamy froze and looked down in horror. Blood poured from the man's chest, but he raised his arm and gestured for Bellamy to keep moving. Bellamy did as he was told, leaping forward in a full sprint. It was just a few feet. He felt the attackers closing in from behind, practically breathing down his neck. He pushed his muscles harder than ever, his legs burning and his fists and elbows pumping up and down as he ran.

Before he could reach the safety of the bunker, though, everything suddenly went silent.

"Stop, Blake, or I'll shoot them all," a man barked from behind him. Bellamy came to a halt. Panting for breath, he turned to see a group of bloodied and bruised Colonists approaching, guns raised and pointed right at him. The two Earthborns guarding Bellamy stepped in front of him and raised their spears. Bellamy clenched and unclenched his fists. His heart pounded so hard, it shook his whole body.

A Colonist in a guard's uniform stepped to the front of the group. It was Burnett, Rhodes's second-in-command. His eyes lit up when he saw Bellamy.

"Step aside," Burnett commanded the two Earthborns standing between him and his prey.

"Not going to happen," one of the men replied, shifting his club from one shoulder to the other.

"What does this boy mean to you?" Burnett growled. "Why would you die to protect him?"

"To keep Earth from being overrun by assholes like you," the Earthborn said calmly. "Get out of here!" he called over his shoulder to Bellamy.

Bellamy backed slowly toward the door. More Colonists gathered behind Burnett, guns raised. Bellamy turned to run. He heard two sharp pops, then the dull thud as two bodies dropped to the ground. He gasped but stumbled forward. Just as he wrapped his fingers around the handle of the bunker door, a voice called after him.

"We have your sister."

Bellamy froze. His chest constricted, as if Burnett's words had formed a noose around his neck. "What are you going to do to her?" he asked as he turned around slowly, his voice strangled.

"For a boy so fixated on protecting his sister, it didn't take much for you to leave her behind, did it?"

"She had a life there," Bellamy said slowly, unsure if he was talking more to Burnett or to himself. "She was starting to know what it meant to be happy."

Burnett smirked. "And now she knows what it means to be under arrest."

White-hot anger surged through Bellamy's veins. "She hasn't done anything wrong."

"Don't worry. We haven't hurt her . . . yet. But I suggest you come along with me, quietly. Or else I won't be able to do anything to assure Ms. Blake's safety."

Bellamy winced at the image forming in his mind. Octavia shackled in the prison cabin, just like he'd been. Her tear-stained face gaunt and pale as she cried out for help, cried out for the brother who'd left her alone with the enemy after swearing to keep her safe.

"How do I know you're telling the truth?" Bellamy asked, stalling for time while he tried to figure out his next step.

Burnett raised an eyebrow, then turned and let out a shrill whistle. Moments later, he was answered by the stomp of boots and a muffled cry. Four guards appeared from behind the trees, dragging two figures between them. For the briefest moment, Bellamy was relieved to see that neither was Octavia.

But then a fresh wave of cold horror ran down his spine.

They had Clarke and Wells.

Each was flanked by two guards. Their hands were bound tightly behind their backs, and someone had placed gags over their mouths. Clarke's eyes were darting back and forth wildly, wide and blazing with fear and fury. Wells was thrashing from side to side, desperately trying to escape his captors' grip.

"So what I need you to do," Burnett said, "is come with us. Otherwise, you'll force us to do something we don't want to do." *Like hell you don't, you sadistic bastard*, Bellamy thought.

His eyes locked on Clarke's. They held each other's gaze for a long moment. She shook her head ever so slightly, and he knew what she meant. *Don't do it. Don't give yourself up for us.*

But it was too late. Rhodes and Burnett had won. There was no way Bellamy was going to put Clarke and Wells in any more danger. They'd already risked far too much for him.

"Let them go," Bellamy said as he dropped his bow and started walking, hands raised, toward Burnett. "I'll do whatever you want."

Burnett's men lunged forward and grabbed Bellamy by the elbows, then quickly restrained his hands.

"I think we'll take all of you," Burnett said.

The guards shoved Bellamy next to Clarke and Wells. He could feel the warmth of Clarke's body next to his, and he shifted his weight so their arms brushed together. Burnett signaled his men to move out, and they pushed Bellamy, Clarke, and Wells toward the path.

They walked single file, Bellamy behind Clarke and in front of Wells. Despite the awkwardness of walking with her hands bound, Clarke's chin was held high and her shoulders were thrown back. *She's fearless*, Bellamy thought, feeling a surge of admiration despite the grim circumstances. The weird thing was, Bellamy didn't feel afraid either. He'd done the right thing. No one else was going to die on his behalf, and if that meant his final hours were fast approaching, then so be it. He would rather face a thousand bullets that night than spend another day wondering who else would end up suffering because of him.

He craned his head back to look at the stars glittering in the patches between the leaves. The years he'd spent living in space were starting to feel like a dream. This was his home now. This was where he belonged.

"Hope you're enjoying the view," Burnett called from behind him. "Your execution is set for dawn."

This was where he was going to die.

CHAPTER 24

Glass

Nothing about Earth seemed beautiful anymore. Every mile of tree-covered land was simply another mile she'd have to cross in order to save Luke, who was growing weaker by the moment.

Maybe we should have just died up there, with the rest of the Colony, she thought grimly. *Maybe we never should have come here at all.* But no, she wouldn't allow them to die this way either: alone and terrified. Luke twitched in his sleep. She stood up, her legs shaky beneath her. Glass ran her hand down his stubbly cheek and touched his lips. The thought of his body shutting down made her chest seize with sadness. How could Earth just go on existing if Luke were gone? How could she? No. She couldn't just let him fade away out here in the woods. She owed him more than that.

With every meter, Glass grew more adept at traveling this way, but as her muscles grew sore and her mind grew tired, she worried more and more that she was moving in the wrong direction. The compass told her she was heading south, but nothing looked familiar. Had they passed this way at all?

By midday, Glass was soaked in sweat. Her back ached, and her limbs were shaky with exhaustion. She had no idea how much farther it would be to camp. She had to rest. She stopped, pulled the harness over her head and nudged the sled up against a tree. Luke grunted in pain and stirred. She knelt down to his side.

"Hey," she whispered, dropping a kiss on his forehead.

She could feel with her lips that he was still burning up. He'd had a fever for days. A wave of uncertainty crashed down on her again. How could she do this? How could she get him all the way back by herself? She was barely strong enough to lift him, let alone hold him up and fend off violent predators. If they were attacked again, she knew it would be the last time.

Glass stood with her hands on her hips and looked up at the sky. She exhaled slowly, trying to bring down her heart rate. She could do this. She *had* to do this. As she summoned her strength, her eyes ran down the trunk of the tree behind the sled. A few feet above her head, she saw something—an indentation paler than the ridged wood around it. Glass stood on her tiptoes and strained her neck to see. She squinted and pushed herself up as high as she could go. When she finally grasped what she was looking at, she let out a gasp of surprise, then laughed out loud right there in the forest, with no one but an unconscious Luke to hear her. In the middle of a landscape so wild and untouched it was as if people had never even walked the Earth, there was a message, carved into the bark by a human hand. She just could just make it out: *R* ♡ *S*.

It was as if a voice had reached out of the past to whisper to her, telling her everything would be all right. R and S had loved each other, right here under this tree, where Glass now fought for the boy she loved. Under other circumstances, she and Luke could have carved their initials just like them. But who were R and S, and how long ago had they sat here together? Were they young or old? First love, or old married couple? Maybe it was a couple from before the Cataclysm, who probably didn't survive. People who probably didn't know the extent of the horrors that awaited the human race. All they knew was that they loved each other enough to leave behind a symbol of their affection for generations to come. The sight of that long-forgotten emblem stirred something in Glass's chest. This couple could never have known that one day a girl from space would stumble upon their carving. Would it have mattered to them? Probably not. Their love was all they cared about. All they should have cared about.

Glass looked down at Luke, whose chest rose and fell in a steady rhythm. No matter how scared she was, no matter whether they made it back to camp or not, they were lucky to be alive right then, right there. That moment was all they had. If they wanted more, then she was going to have to fight for it—for both of them. She squatted down and slipped the rope over her shoulders again, a renewed energy coursing through her body.

They had to get back to safety. There was no way she was giving up now.

Glass pushed her way through a particularly thick copse of trees, then saw something that made her stomach flip. It was a lake. But could it be . . . ? Surely all lakes on Earth looked somewhat similar. Suddenly, in the distance, she saw it. The remains of the charred dropships.

Glass let out a whoop and would've jumped up and down if she hadn't been bone-tired. She was almost there. She couldn't be more than a few miles from the camp. But as she stared up the steep incline on the far side of the lake, her heart sank. It would take hours to drag Luke around the water and back up to camp. Would he even make it that long? If not, she could only hope that her own body would quickly succumb to grief. She'd rather lie with Luke, still and peaceful in the forest forever, than spend the rest of her life with an even heavier burden than the sled—the weight of a broken heart.

CHAPTER 25

Wells

Wells stumbled into camp behind Clarke and Bellamy. His hands were numb from the cuffs that bound them behind his back, and his face stung from the branches and thorns that had scratched him as they trekked through the woods.

They stood outside the prison cabin. One of the guards removed the fabric gags from their mouths. Wells moved his jaw in a slow circle and opened and shut his mouth a few times, trying to regain sensation.

"Wait here," the guard ordered. He scuttled inside while another man posted by the front door kept an eye on them. Wells, Bellamy, and Clarke all took the opportunity to look around. The camp sprawled out before them, and Wells could tell at a glance that it wasn't the same place they'd left behind just a few days before. One look at Bellamy and Clarke's wide eyes told him they saw it too.

Although it couldn't have been much later than eight or nine at night, the camp was ominously quiet, except for the sounds of footsteps on the dusty ground and logs clattering on the pile. Two kids carrying firewood toward the pit wore tense, pained expressions. A boy hauling a water bucket looked near tears. A group of adults sat silently together by the fire, shooting nervous glances at the trees. No one spoke. No one laughed or gave one another a hard time. No one smiled. It was as if all the energy and camaraderie—all the *life*—had been sucked from the very air.

A breeze swept through the trees, and a putrid smell wafted into Wells's nostrils. He suppressed his gag reflex, and he saw Clarke and Bellamy doing the same. Wells looked around and took a few steps toward the tree line. Sure enough, a rancid pile of animal skins, bones, and organs lay on the ground, covered in flies and slowly rotting. It was disgusting—and unsafe. Not only would the odor attract predatory animals, but the bacteria growing in that pile would be enough to sicken everyone in camp.

"What the hell . . ." Bellamy said hoarsely. At first, Wells assumed he was looking at the animals as well, but when he turned his head, he saw that Bellamy's eyes were fixed on something else in the distance. A group of the original hundred were hard at work on a new cabin; he could hear their low grunts as they struggled to place an enormous log at the top of the growing wall. A few adults stood to the side, holding torches to illuminate the site, suggesting that they were planning to work long into the night.

That wasn't remarkable in itself. With so many people crammed into the camp, it made sense to build new structures as quickly as possible. But then the moon slid out from behind a cloud, and Wells finally saw what had caught Bellamy's attention.

As the moonlight shined down on the half-completed cabin, it glinted on their friends' wrists, reflecting off something metallic. "*No*," Wells breathed, blinking rapidly, unable to believe his eyes.

Each of them had a thick metal band clasped tightly around one wrist.

"This is madness," Clarke said, a note of confusion in her voice, as if her scientist brain didn't trust the image being transmitted through her eyes.

When they'd been taken from their cells in the detention center, each member of the hundred had been fitted with a tracking device. Ostensibly, they were meant to transmit vital signs back to the Colony, to let the Council know whether Earth was indeed survivable, or if their test subjects were slowly succumbing to radiation poisoning. However, within their first few days on Earth, most of them had either removed the bracelets or purposely damaged them beyond repair.

"Do you think Rhodes brought them down to Earth with him?" Wells asked.

"He must have," Clarke said. "But *why*? It's not like he has the technology to actually track any of them."

Bellamy snorted. "I wouldn't be so sure. Who knows what he brought on that dropship with him?"

"So . . . they're prisoners again?" Clarke said, her voice disbelieving.

"So much for our 'contribution' and 'sacrifice'," Bellamy said, his voice thick with bitterness.

A few moments later, Wells, Bellamy, and Clarke were all yanked roughly into a line, standing shoulder to shoulder, with a guard behind each of them. Wells clenched his teeth as Vice Chancellor Rhodes approached, flanked by two armed guards of his own.

"Welcome back. I hope you three enjoyed your little holiday."

"I see you've been busy making my friends play dress up," Bellamy said with a sneer. "That's quite the collection of bracelets you brought with you."

Rhodes made a show of looking behind him. The kids

who'd been busy building the cabin had stopped what they were doing and were staring at the prisoners in wide-eyed horror. Molly lowered her hammer and took a few steps forward, staring at Wells. Even from a distance, he could tell it was taking all her self-control not to run to him. He shook his head slightly, warning her against it.

"Ah, yes," Rhodes said. "I do have a few extras, but it seems like a waste to give them to people who'll soon have nowhere to wear them."

"Really?" Bellamy managed one of his signature smirks. "Because I heard my trial is going to be the social event of the season."

"Trial?" Rhodes repeated. "I'm afraid you must be mistaken. There's not going to be a trial . . . for any of you. I've already found all three of you guilty. Your executions are scheduled for dawn." He made a show of looking up at the sky. "Though, that does seem like a rather long time to wait. If any of you are in a rush, I'd be happy to expedite the proceedings."

Wells's heart froze in his chest, like an animal that'd just caught sight of the hunter's drawn bow. What was Rhodes talking about? They hadn't done anything meriting *execution*.

But before he could say anything, Bellamy made a sound that was half-shout, half-moan. "What the hell are you talking about? They didn't do anything. I'm the one you wanted. *I'm* the one you need to kill."

"They aided and abetted a fugitive. The punishment for that is perfectly clear in the Gaia Doctrine."

"*Fuck* the Gaia Doctrine," Bellamy spat. "We're on Earth, in case you haven't noticed."

"I see no reason to abandon the guidelines that have allowed humanity to flourish for centuries just because we're on the ground."

Wells had never felt such raw, pure loathing for anyone, or anything, in his entire life. "That's not what my father would say, and you know it."

Rhodes narrowed his eyes. "Your father isn't here, Wells. And in case you were too busy seducing other little criminals"— he shot a glance at Clarke—"to pay attention during your civics tutorial, the Chancellor's *son* doesn't factor into the chain of command. I'm in charge, and I've sentenced the three of you to die by firing squad at first light."

Wells heard Clarke gasp next to him, and his whole body went numb. He waited for another surge of fear or anger to kick in, but neither came. Perhaps there was a part of him that had expected this to happen. Perhaps there was a part of him that knew he deserved it. Even if Rhodes had no idea what Wells had done back on the ship, Wells was the reason their friends, their neighbors, were all slowly dying of oxygen deprivation. At least this way, he'd never have to face what he did. He wouldn't have to look up every night, trying to picture the ship that would soon be filled with silent, still bodies.

"Oh my god, *Bellamy*!" The sound of Octavia's voice pulled Wells back. She was running toward them, her face streaked with dirt and tears. Two guards stepped in front of her, blocking her path and holding her back. She fought against them but couldn't get through. Bellamy called her name and lunged toward her, but a guard jabbed a gun to his ribs and he keeled over. "Stop it," Octavia sobbed. "Let them go, *please*."

"It's okay, O," Bellamy said hoarsely, struggling to catch his breath. "I'm okay."

"*No*. I'm not going to let them do this to you."

Other people had begun to gather around them. Lila walked up next to Octavia, and for a moment, Wells thought she was going to pull her away, but instead she put her arm around the younger girl and glared at the guards defiantly. She was joined by Antonio, Dmitri, then Tamsin and others. Even *Graham* came over to stand among them. Soon, there were nearly fifty people standing in a large semicircle around the prison cabin.

"Everyone, back up," Rhodes commanded. When no one moved, he signaled to the guards who stepped menacingly toward the crowd. "I said *move*."

But no one retreated. Not even when the guards raised

their guns to their shoulders, half of them aiming at the prisoners, half out into the crowd. Some of the younger ones looked nervous, but most of them were staring at Wells, Bellamy, and Clarke with a mixture of rebellion and something else. Something like hope.

No matter how this ended, they needed to see how a real leader bore defeat. Wells would be honored to sacrifice himself if it meant no one else got hurt, and he certainly wasn't going to face death like a coward. Wells turned back to Rhodes, raised his chin, and fixed the hateful man with his stare.

Bellamy moved even closer to Wells and stood shoulder to shoulder with him. Wells could tell by the set of Bellamy's jaw that he was thinking the same thing. Clarke moved next to Bellamy, and the three of them stared down the Vice Chancellor together. Wells pushed away an image of the three of them lying bloodied on the ground, taking their last breaths in unison. Bellamy and Clarke both looked at him. Bellamy's muscles were tensed, his body charged with energy. He was the embodiment of a resolve and strength Wells had never seen before. Clarke's eyes were practically alight with emotion. They were filled with a fierceness and determination that stunned him.

"Okay, get moving," a guard said. Someone reached from behind and tied a blindfold around him. Guards grabbed on to Wells's arm and began to drag him away.

"Where are you taking me?" Wells grunted, digging his heels into the ground. With the blindfold covering his eyes, he focused as hard as he could on what he could hear, but the grunts and shuffling sounds told him nothing about what was happening to Clarke or Bellamy.

Wells struggled against his captors, but there was nothing he could do. He gritted his teeth and fought against the panic flooding his body. At least the last thing he'd seen were Clarke's and Bellamy's brave faces—that would be enough to get him through the next few hours. Wells knew he'd set sight on Earth for the last time.

By the time they removed the blindfold, there would be a bullet in his brain.

CHAPTER 26

Bellamy

There was no way to know if Rhodes had waited until dawn to send for them. With the blindfold on, Bellamy couldn't tell if the sun had risen, though by the scent of dew clinging to the grass, his guess was that it was still dark out. Apparently, Bellamy had already seen his last sunrise. By the time the sky turned pink, he would be dead. All three of them would.

Bellamy had spent a hellish, agonizing night straining his ears for any sign of Clarke, who'd been locked away somewhere else. He wasn't sure what would be worse: listening to her scream in pain or cry out in despair, or hearing nothing but silence and wondering whether she was already gone.

The quiet had turned out to be unbearable, as Bellamy's

brain filled it with horrific sounds of its own: Clarke sobbing as she felt her last hours slip away, knowing that she'd never set eyes on her parents again. The sound of a gunshot ripping through the silence, tearing apart Bellamy's heart.

With a guard on either side of him, Bellamy was marched to what he assumed was the center of the clearing and pushed up with his back against a tree. A tiny, twisted part of him almost had to laugh. After all the near misses he'd had in his life, all the rules he'd broken, this was how it was going to end. He should have guessed it'd be something dramatic, like a public execution on a dangerous planet. Nothing boring for him. His only regret was that Octavia would have to see this. It was hard enough to think she'd have to go on without him, but she had proven her grit in the last few weeks. He knew deep down she could take care of herself now. No, mostly it was that she would have to watch. Bellamy could hear the guards moving through the camp, dragging everyone— adults and kids—out of their cabins to witness what Rhodes probably viewed as the most momentous event on Earth in three hundred years. The moment order would be restored to the wild, untamed planet.

It was monstrous. No one should have to see this, his sister least of all. He only hoped that his unbowed head would make his sister proud of him. He wanted to show her how to live, even after he was gone.

Bellamy wished he could reach out and grab Clarke's hand. Why hadn't they brought her out yet? Had something happened? Or was she silent, her heart in her throat as she struggled against the ropes? He couldn't believe this beautiful, brilliant girl was about to be executed. It was inconceivable to think that someone so full of life, whose green eyes lit up in wonder every time she spotted a new plant, who went days without sleeping in order to care for her patients, was about to be shut off like a piece of machinery.

"Clarke!" he shouted, unable to contain himself any longer. "Where are you?" All he could hear was the anxious whispering of the crowd. *"Clarke!"* he screamed again, his voice echoing throughout the clearing, but not loud enough to reach her if she'd already . . .

"Calm down, Mr. Blake," Rhodes commanded, as if Bellamy were an overexcited child instead of a condemned prisoner moments away from death. "I've decided to show your friends mercy. Neither Officer Jaha nor Ms. Griffin is going to die today."

A sliver of hope pierced the dread that had been building in his chest, allowing him to take his first real breath since leaving the cabin. "Prove it to me," he said hoarsely. "Let me see them."

Rhodes must've nodded, because a moment later, someone was fumbling with Bellamy's blindfold.

He blinked as the world came back into focus. A line of guards stood about ten meters in front of him. The entire camp was gathered behind them, with Wells, Octavia, and Clarke in the front. *They're still alive.* Relief poured through him. That was all that mattered. He didn't care what happened to him anymore as long as they were safe.

Wells and Clarke still had their hands bound, but Octavia was struggling against the guards holding her. "Bellamy!" she shrieked.

He met her eyes and shook his head. *No*, he communicated silently with a sad smile. There was nothing she could do now. She stared at him, her big blue eyes filled with panic and tears.

I love you, he mouthed. *It's going to be okay.*

Through her sobs, Octavia managed to force a smile. "I love you. I love you . . ." But then her face crumpled, and she turned away. Graham said something to the guard, and he released Octavia's arms, letting Graham hold on to her instead. But even from a distance, it was clear he was being gentle. He even wrapped his arm around her, shielding her from the horror that was about to take place before her eyes.

"Guards, at the ready!" Rhodes shouted.

Bellamy turned to Clarke. Unlike his sister, she'd refused to look away and was staring at Bellamy so intensely, for a flickering moment, he felt the rest of the world melt away. It was only him and Clarke, just like it'd been when they first kissed or that magical night in the woods when Bellamy had felt that Earth was far closer to the heavens than the Colony had ever been.

Just look at me, he could feel her saying to him. *Just look at me, and it'll all be okay.*

Sweat was pouring down his face, but he didn't look away from her. Not even when the guards cocked their guns, and his heart began beating so fast, he was sure it'd explode before the first bullet.

Just look at me.

He tilted his chin higher and clenched his fists, inhaling sharply through his nose. It would happen any second now. He tried to slow down time for a moment. He deepened his breathing and willed his heart rate into a steadier rhythm. He inhaled the scents of camp and Earth: cold ashes, wet dirt, crushed leaves, and *air*—the crisp, clean, delicious scent of the very air they were breathing at that moment. He'd had the chance to be here, and that was enough.

Just look at me.

Several shots rang out across the clearing, abrupt and loud. Bellamy realized a few things all at once: He wasn't in any pain, he hadn't felt a blow, and the sound had come from behind them, not in front of them. It wasn't Rhodes's men who had fired—someone was firing on them.

Then he saw them—a swarming band of aggressive Earthborns fanning out through the camp, swinging clubs and raising guns to fire at the Colonists. The entire place had erupted into chaos. No one was watching him anymore. Except for the high-tech bands around his wrists, he was free to run. Bellamy looked around frantically, hoping for a break. He found it: Rhodes's right-hand man, Burnett, lay dead nearby. Bellamy wasn't one to waste an opportunity—plus there was nothing he could do to help the guy. He dropped to his knees and turned his back to the body, blindly fumbling in Burnett's pocket.

"Clarke, Wells—keys!" he yelled. They raced over. Wells and Clarke stood back-to-back and Bellamy unlocked her restraints. After he and Wells were freed as well, they bolted toward the supply cabin, where they knew they could find weapons.

Once they had armed themselves as best they could—Bellamy with a bow and arrow, Wells with an ax, and Clarke with a spear—they headed into the fray, moving in a circle with their backs to each other. It was a brutal, dirty battle. All around them, the hundred and the Colonists fought side by side. Barely taking the time to breathe, Bellamy aimed and shot, again and again. He was grimly satisfied to see his arrows finding their marks as a few Earthborns screamed and collapsed to the ground at the edges of the clearing. Bellamy's arms began to burn from exertion, but he was driven by a desperate, almost primal energy.

"You good?" he shouted to Wells over the din.

"Good," Wells grunted as he clubbed an Earthborn over the head with a sickening *crack*. "You?"

Before Bellamy could respond, an Earthborn with maniacal eyes lurched at him. The man let out a cackling yelp as he swung an ax high in the air, aimed right at Bellamy's head. Bellamy sidestepped just as the blade came down. He felt a breeze as it whisked by his cheek. The Earthborn growled in frustration. Flush with renewed energy, Bellamy dropped into a low, defensive crouch, bouncing on the balls of his feet, ready for round two. His opponent raised the ax again and took a few staggering steps forward. Nostrils flaring and adrenaline coursing through him, Bellamy forced himself to stand still and let the man approach. *Wait*, he told himself. *Just wait.* When the Earthborn was close enough that Bellamy could smell the sweat on him and the ax had just begun its descent toward Bellamy's head again, Bellamy dropped to the ground and rolled out of range. The Earthborn screamed in rage.

Bellamy waited again, letting his enemy tire himself out.

As the man got close, Bellamy squatted down low, pulled one knee into his chest, and, with all his strength, kicked the Earthborn square on the side of his kneecap. The man's leg splintered under him, and he dropped to the ground like he'd been shot.

Suddenly what felt like a thousand-pound weight landed on Bellamy's shoulders, almost knocking him to the ground. He stumbled and righted himself as forceful hands closed around his neck. Frantic, he gasped for air but got none. Bellamy reached behind him to pull off his new attacker. He got a handful of hair, and he pulled it with all his strength, ripping some of it out at the roots. The man's grip loosened just enough. His heart pounding and his chest hurting from lack of oxygen, Bellamy seized his chance: He bent forward, doubling over and flipping the Earthborn over his head and onto the ground. The man slammed into the dirt with a thud. Bellamy took a step backward, reached for his bow, and lined up an arrow, all in one smooth motion. Just as the man staggered to his feet, a nasty gleam in his eye, Bellamy let the arrow fly into his chest.

Bellamy didn't stick around to watch the outcome. He turned back to see if Clarke and Wells were okay. In the heat of the moment, they had somehow all gotten separated. As he turned to look, someone slammed into his shoulder, and he lurched sideways. Struggling to regain his balance, Bellamy stepped backward, and his foot landed on something solid but soft. It was a person. He spun around and pointed a tightly strung arrow at the ground.

It was Vice Chancellor Rhodes.

Rhodes was alive and conscious but badly injured; there was blood coming from somewhere on his head, and his face and shirt were drenched in red. He was doubled over in pain, gagging and coughing. He couldn't speak, but he looked up and locked eyes with Bellamy. There was a pathetic, pleading look in them. The man led like a coward, and he lost like a coward too.

Bellamy's whole body relaxed. With the toe of one boot, he pushed the Vice Chancellor's shoulder back so he was lying flat on the ground. Bellamy placed his foot firmly in the center of Rhodes's chest, pinning him down. It felt good to see him trapped like the rodent he was.

Bellamy had a choice to make: He could either finish him off with one swift arrow to the heart, or he could let the bastard rot right here on the battlefield. His injuries looked bad enough to kill him. No one would argue that Rhodes deserved a better end. A powerful, satisfied feeling coursed through Bellamy, but something else awoke in him too. It wasn't an emotion he was used to, but he recognized it right away: It was pity. Bellamy studied Rhodes's dirty and bloodied face. His hands were clasped together, begging. Conflicting emotions surged through Bellamy—his desire for vengeance, and the deep-seated knowledge that he didn't want to watch anyone die again. His brain was already full of memories he'd never be able to shake. Rhodes didn't deserve a place among them.

Bellamy sighed and dropped his arms to his sides, letting the arrow fall away from the bow. He couldn't do it. He couldn't fire the shot, and he couldn't turn his back on a broken man, leaving him to die here. He sure as hell hoped he wasn't going to regret this later. Bellamy bent down and extended one hand. Rhodes just stared at it, unsure if Bellamy was toying with him.

"Let's go before I change my mind," Bellamy growled.

Rhodes reached up with a shaky hand, and Bellamy bent down and hauled him up, half carrying him back down into camp.

CHAPTER 27

Wells

Wells lost track of Bellamy in the chaos. He had no idea how many Earthborns he had fended off. His hands were blistered and raw from gripping and swinging the ax, and his muscles ached with fatigue. Wells found himself standing momentarily alone with no one charging or grabbing him—a respite in the sea of struggle. All around him, people fought for their lives, while others lay on the ground, wounded or dead. Wells couldn't tell who had the upper hand, the Earthborns or his comrades, but he feared it was the enemy. The Colonists and the hundred looked like they were getting beaten, badly. He needed to get a better vantage point.

No one seemed to notice as he slipped away from the scrum, leaping over bodies and rubble, and headed for the edge of the clearing. He moved a few meters into the woods and circled toward the side of the camp, where he knew he could be less visible and get a higher sight line. He could still hear the cries and moans of injured people as he ran through the thick foliage.

Wells emerged from the forest near the prison cabin. He quickly scaled the side and perched atop the building, scanning the battleground. He was shocked by what he saw. From the middle of the fight, it felt like total mayhem, but the Earthborns had clearly been strategic about their attack. They had destroyed nearly every vital element of the camp: several of their food stores, all the extra ammunition. Yet the dormitories, dining hall, and prison were intact. There was no way they could have just guessed which buildings' destruction would cripple the Colonists the most. They had to have known the purpose of each.

Wells struggled to figure out how. Spying, maybe, but the Colonists had routinely swept the woods around camp and hadn't caught anyone yet. Just then, a small group of Earthborns stormed through the center of camp, their stolen guns raised high. Wells gasped in shock and horror when he saw who led them: *Kendall.*

She was no longer wearing the clothes of a Colonist, and

in a sick flash, Wells had all his worst suspicions confirmed. Kendall was an Earthborn.

Everything made sense. Her forced Phoenician accent, the way her stories never quite added up, her insistence on following Wells around. She'd been *spying* on them all along.

Wells could have kicked himself for not acting on his hunch. He had known in his gut that something was wrong, but he hadn't done anything about it. He had backed down when Rhodes told him to. And that's what she had relied on. Kendall had known that the arrival of more dropships, more people—grown-ups—would weaken the Colonists' community, not strengthen it. That's what she had taken advantage of.

He *was* completely useless as a leader. What had he been thinking, pretending like he had what it took to inspire, to keep the others safe? No matter what he did or where he went, people suffered.

Wells heard a scrabbling sound in the cabin beneath him. *The Earthborns had invaded the prison, and he was the only Colonist on this side of camp.* He hefted his ax over his shoulder and prepared to face them. He might not be the leader his people deserved, but he could still kill a few Earthborns for them.

He would wait until they came outside, then attack from above. He squatted down and tried not to move, for fear of making any sound.

Two small figures scurried out of the cabin into the shadows below him, a small boy and girl. Wells recognized the boy—it was Leo, one of the kids Octavia had been caring for. What was he doing on his own? Why hadn't Rhodes assigned anyone to look after the parentless children after dragging Octavia away to witness her brother's execution?

They were both trembling, tears running down their cheeks. "Hey," Wells whispered loudly. Their heads shot up to look at him, and the boy let out a scared squeal. "It's okay— it's just me. Watch out. I'm coming down."

Wells hopped onto the ground next to them. "Are you over here alone?" Wells asked. The girl shook her head. Wells turned; six more older kids emerged from the cabin, including Molly and the other younger members of the hundred. Their faces were dirty and bloodied; their shoulders slumped with fear and exhaustion. They stood silently, expectantly, watching him. Another handful of them began to step quietly out of the trees behind the cabin, where they had been hiding, and then another followed, until almost all the members of the original hundred stood before him.

Wells looked at each of their faces, these teenagers who up until a few weeks ago had just been normal young people locked up for some trumped up infraction.

They had been taken from their families, thrown in a cell, and, for all they could tell, forgotten. Now they were on a planet far from anyone they once knew and loved—people who were all dead by now. All they had was each other.

Rhodes didn't understand what it meant to be a community. He'd never be able to appreciate what the hundred had created during their short time on Earth, the foundations they'd laid for a better future. They weren't perfect—Wells knew that better than anyone—but they had what it took to turn the planet into a real home. Maybe now wasn't the time for him to stop trying. Maybe now was the time to accept the mistakes he made and move forward, learning from them. He'd never make up for what he did on the Colony, or the pain he'd caused Max and Sasha, but that didn't mean he had to give up.

Slowly a plan formed in Wells's mind. All the time spent talking through tactics with Max at Mount Weather had brought back everything he'd learned in his strategy classes. Their plan at Mount Weather had been a good one—to surprise the enemy from behind and take advantage of the attackers' position. There had just been extenuating circumstances—Rhodes had had the upper hand, with hostages back at camp. Well, not this time. Wells knew what they had to do. He just couldn't do it alone.

A renewed fire coursed through Wells. After all the hundred had faced, after all they had worked for, he wasn't going to let Kendall and her vicious accomplices take them down. No way.

"Listen up!" he yelled. Dozens of eyes locked on him, filled with a desperate longing for direction. "I know you're tired, and I know you're scared," he began. "I know there are more of them than there are of us. They have more weapons. But we have each other—and we aren't going to let them win."

Bellamy appeared at the back of the crowd. He looked wiped out, but Wells was glad to see that he was all right. They nodded at each other, and Wells continued. "They're coming at us from the north, and they're pushing us back against the tree line that way." Wells gestured with his ax. "They're busy with Rhodes's guys right now. You"—he signaled to one of the older boys—"stay behind to guard these younger kids. The rest of us will spread out into the woods and circle around to the north. We can attack them from behind. Who's with me?"

For a second, they all just stared at him. Wells wasn't sure he had read them right. Then a hand shot up, then another, then a dozen more. They pushed their shoulders back, raised their chins, and planted their feet firmly on the ground. Bellamy stood at the back, smiling grimly.

"Let's do it!" someone shouted from the small crowd. A rousing cheer went up, and Wells, for the first time since Sasha's death, didn't feel panic in the face of responsibility. He felt exhilaration.

"Okay. On my count. Three . . . two . . . *one!*"

At first the plan seemed to work: The hundred startled

the Earthborns with the attack from behind, pushing them toward Rhodes's men, who kept up their defense on the opposite flank. But Wells soon lost track of what was happening around him as he struggled to stay alive. Two Earthborns approached Wells at once, each wielding a spear. Wells feinted with the ax in his hand, pretending to swing to the right. As they both reacted in that direction, he turned in a circle and swung the ax from the left, hacking one Earthborn's spear into two pieces. The other stepped forward, and Wells sank the ax blade deep into his spear. It splintered into shards on the ground, and the two disarmed Earthborns scurried off.

Wells allowed himself a moment of satisfaction. During officer training, he'd worked hard in his Earth-combat conditioning classes, and it was paying off now. But just as a gratified smile flickered across his face, he felt an arm wrap tightly around his neck.

Wells tried to jab his elbows into his opponent, but he couldn't get enough leverage. The man's arm tightened, making it impossible for Wells to breathe. He couldn't even gasp—there was no way for air to get in or out. His lungs began to burn as his head spun.

No, Wells thought, wanting to scream but unable to make a sound. This wasn't what was supposed to happen. This wasn't how it was meant to end.

The Earthborn's arm tightened even further. Wells saw flashes of light in front of him, then patches of black as everything grew blurry.

Suddenly, the pressure released, and Wells fell to the ground with a gasp. For a long moment, all he could do was wheeze as his lungs became reacquainted with the air, clawing at it greedily. He rose up onto his knees and looked around. An enormous Earthborn was lying on his side, his hand clutched around the shaft of an arrow embedded in his arm.

Wells turned in the direction the arrow had come from. Bellamy stood a few meters away, a twinkle in his eye. He nodded at Wells, who just grinned back.

"Thanks!" Wells shouted.

"No problem," Bellamy called back.

Wells turned back in the direction of camp. For a moment, his whole body seized with panic: From where he stood in the woods, he couldn't see a single other member of the hundred still fighting near him. He swore under his breath and gathered his last ounce of energy before barreling back out into the clearing, Bellamy close behind him.

What he saw stopped him in his tracks. The hundred and the Colonists who could still stand were gathered together in a group, their chests heaving as they caught their breath. The few remaining guards seemed to have captured someone of importance—a large Earthborn man with a wounded leg, who was being held at gunpoint. Several other Colonists were speaking animatedly with a small group of Earthborns, seemingly negotiating terms, as the rest of the Earthborns sullenly surrendered their weapons and slowly backed away.

Wells couldn't believe it. It had worked! They were negotiating a surrender! Filled with new energy, he and Bellamy raced over to where the remainder of the hundred were standing. Sure, they were exhausted and injured, but they were victorious. Together, they sent up an eardrum-rattling cheer that seemed to echo up to the sky and back.

"Nice work! " Bellamy shouted over the celebratory din.

"You didn't do too badly either . . . for a Waldenite," Wells yelled back with a grin.

The assembled group danced around the clearing, hugging and cheering, until a cry rose above the noise.

"They're back!" someone screamed.

Wells and Bellamy spun around to find a group of strangers stumbling out of the woods and into camp. They raised their weapons and stood their ground. Something about these new arrivals, though, was different. Wells quickly took in their clothes, their demeanor, their confused expressions. These weren't Earthborns. These were . . . more Colonists?

The group stopped on the edge of the clearing. A woman stepped forward.

"We found you," she said, breathing heavily, her voice weak.

She looked vaguely familiar to Wells. He struggled to place her, and then it came to him: She had worked in his father's administration, in an office down the hall. They must have been on another dropship—one of the few that they figured must have veered off course.

"Please, do you have anything to eat?" she asked. Wells hadn't noticed at first how gaunt she and the others looked.

"It's okay," Wells said to the group. "They're from the Colony. Someone, please, get them some food and water."

A couple of kids scurried off.

Wells stepped forward. He felt hundreds of eyes on his back. "Where are you coming from?" he asked.

"Our dropship landed miles from here, way beyond the far side of the lake. We spent some time getting our bearings and recovering from our injuries. Then it took us several days to get to you. We followed the smoke from your campfires."

"How many of you are there?"

"We lost a few. But we started out as one hundred and fifteen."

Wells cast his gaze over the large group assembled behind her. Still more people emerged from the woods.

"Were you the last ship to launch from the Colony?"

The woman nodded.

Wells felt a question forming on his lips, but he wasn't

sure he had the courage to ask it. He wasn't sure he really wanted the answer.

"My father—" he began.

The woman's expression softened. She knew who he was—and who he was asking about. "I'm sorry," she said, her soft words still landing like a punch in the gut. She hesitated, as if unsure how much to share. "He was still in a coma when we launched. There were no more dropships available. The oxygen supply was essentially gone, and the ship—well, the ship was . . . it was breaking apart. There were five or six hours left, at most."

A silent scream of grief and guilt surged up in Wells, but he held it in. If he let himself feel the full weight of his loss at once, he would surely break into pieces. His whole body began to shake. The image of his father slowly suffocating made Wells gasp for air, as if the Earthborn's hands were still wrapped around his neck.

Wells staggered and almost lost his balance, then felt someone at his side, steadying him. It was Bellamy.

"Wells," Bellamy said. "I'm so sorry, man." His face was full of sympathy and something else . . . pain?

Wells nodded. In his own grief, he had forgotten that Bellamy had lost his father too—lost him before he ever even met him. In fact, every single Colonist on the planet had lost someone—lots of people. All the family, neighbors, and friends they'd left behind had already perished, destined to sleep forever in a giant, silent ship orbiting Earth. The Colony had turned into a tomb.

"It's a shame you never got to know him," Wells said, fighting to keep his voice even. Although he'd tried to prepare for the worst, he'd never been quite able to accept the fact that he'd never see his father step off a dropship, his face a mixture of surprise and delight as he saw the wonders of Earth, and how much his son had accomplished. He'd never join Wells around the campfire, listening to the happy chatter, and tell Wells that he was proud of him.

A curious look came over Bellamy, and he smiled. "You know what, though? I think I kind of did get to know him."

"What are you talking about?" Wells asked, racking his brain for a memory of when his father would've been able to spend real time with Bellamy.

"From what I've heard, he was incredibly smart, hard working, and deeply committed to helping others . . . kind of like someone else I know."

Wells stared at him for a moment, then sighed. "If you're talking about me, you've got the wrong idea. I'm nothing like my father."

"That's not what Clarke told me. She said that you have all your father's best qualities—his strength, his honor—but that you have your mother's kindness and humor." Bellamy paused and looked thoughtful. "I've never heard you say anything funny, of course, but I figured I'd take Clarke's word for it."

To his surprise, Wells let out a small laugh before Bellamy's face grew serious again. "Listen, I know you've suffered in ways I can't really understand. No one should have to go through anything like this. But you're not alone, okay? Not only do you have a hundred people who think you're a hero, maybe more than that actually, but whatever, we'll count later. What I mean is that you don't just have friends, you have a family. I'm proud to have you as a brother."

Bellamy was right. The pain of losing Sasha and his father and countless friends on the battlefield today would never go away, but Earth was still his home, where he belonged. The sorrow in his heart seemed to lift a little as he and Bellamy hugged and slapped each other on the back.

Earth was where his family lived.

CHAPTER 28

Bellamy

Bellamy paused in front of the door to the hospital cabin. Apparently, the Vice Chancellor wanted to talk to him, but Bellamy wasn't exactly in the mood for a chat. He was exhausted from the previous day's battle and its grisly aftermath. He and Wells had already buried several Earthborns, then set about collecting the blood-stained weapons they'd left behind. The camp would be having a burial ceremony for the Colonists and kids who had died in the attacks, later that day. Thank god, Octavia was okay, but not all of the hundred had been so lucky.

Yet despite the terrifying attack and the devastating losses of several of their people, the mood in the camp was still brighter than it'd been when Bellamy, Wells, and Clarke had been marched in two nights earlier. People were laughing again, and the new Colonists were asking the hundred for help and advice, no longer wary of angering Rhodes.

Part of Bellamy wanted to turn around and find Octavia, who'd organized a game of hide-and-seek for the younger kids. It was hard to let her out of his sight after everything they'd just gone through. But, after a moment, his curiosity got the better of him, and he stepped inside.

The cabin was full of injured Colonists and kids, but Clarke's usual efficiency and rapport with her patients kept the mood from being too grim. Thankfully, it seemed that most of her patients were going to make quick recoveries.

Bellamy walked toward the back where a long white sheet had been nailed into the ceiling and hung down to the floor like a curtain, giving the Vice Chancellor a tiny bit of privacy. In his head, he ran through everything Rhodes could possibly say to him, planning his response. If the man so much as threatened him or Octavia, there was no telling what he'd do to him. He didn't care if he was injured and helpless in a hospital bed.

Bellamy nodded at the guard positioned in front of the divider, then stepped around and stared at the man lying in the bed behind it.

Rhodes looked diminished. It wasn't just his exhausted body or the bandages encasing most of his arms and torso. It was something in his face. He didn't just look beaten—he looked broken.

Rhodes propped himself up on one elbow with some effort. Bellamy briefly considered reaching out to help but then thought better of it. He'd done enough for this creep already.

"Hello, Bellamy."

"How are you feeling?" Bellamy asked, more out of habit than from any actual concern. That's generally what you said when facing a dude covered in bandages.

"Clarke and Dr. Lahiri say that I'll make a full recovery."

"Great," Bellamy said, shifting his weight from side to side. This was ridiculous. What the hell was he doing here?

"I asked you to come because I wanted to thank you."

"Forget about it," Bellamy said with a shrug. He had saved Rhodes's life for himself, not because he thought this particular power-hungry madman deserved to live. He didn't particularly fancy a long heart-to-heart.

Rhodes paused and contemplated the empty space over Bellamy's shoulder for a long moment.

"I was reluctant to accept the idea that the original hundred —yourself included—knew more about living on Earth than I did. After all, I had been planning for this journey my entire

life, and you"—Rhodes fixed Bellamy with a hard stare—
"were nothing more than a bunch of juvenile delinquents.
You were stupid enough to get yourselves into trouble on the
Colony, so why should I assume you were smart enough to
survive down here?"

Bellamy flinched and balled his hands into fists, but kept
his expression neutral. He heard Clarke's and Wells's voices
in his head, imploring him to stay calm, no matter what
Rhodes had to say.

"But you were," Rhodes went on. "You not only survived
on Earth, you thrived. And it has come to my attention that
surviving on Earth is hard enough." He glanced down at his
many wounds. "To really *live*, well, that requires something
more than intelligence. That requires will."

Bellamy stared at the Vice Chancellor, wondering if he'd
heard correctly. Had Rhodes just praised him and the rest
of the hundred? Perhaps his head injuries were worse than
Clarke had realized.

He could tell that Rhodes was waiting for him to say
something.

"I'm glad you see it that way," Bellamy said slowly, pray-
ing that Clarke would come in to check in on her patient.
Or anyone, really. He didn't want to be alone with the Vice
Chancellor for another second.

"I hereby pardon you for the crime of kidnapping and the involuntary murder of Chancellor Jaha."

Bellamy tried to keep the scorn out of his face as he nodded. "Thank you," Bellamy said. He'd sort of just assumed that was the case, given the fact that he'd saved Rhodes's life.

As if reading his thoughts, Rhodes continued. "That's not all. Effective immediately, I'm instating a new Advisory Council. Wells was right. The Gaia Doctrine has no place on Earth. We need a new system, a better one. I'm going to suggest that we nominate people this evening. Perhaps . . ." He grimaced as a new wave of pain washed over him. "Perhaps that's something you would consider being a part of?"

Bellamy blinked a few times, trying to process what he had just heard. If he wasn't mistaken, and he hadn't accidentally eaten a hallucinogenic berry out in the woods, then Vice Chancellor Rhodes, the most corrupt leader the Colony had ever known, had just pardoned him *and* suggested he get into politics.

Bellamy couldn't help it: He laughed out loud.

"Seriously?"

"Seriously."

Bellamy couldn't wait to go tell Octavia so they could laugh about it. Unless she didn't think it was funny. Maybe O would actually *want* him on the Council. Hell, crazier things had happened over the past few weeks. Why couldn't Bellamy try his hand at running things for a while? There was just one person he needed to check with first.

With a smile and a nod, he turned and went to find Clarke.

CHAPTER 29

Glass

Every muscle in Glass's body felt like it was on fire. Her shoulders were rubbed raw from the rope. Her calves and thighs vibrated with exhaustion and threatened to give out any second.

When she saw the corner of a wooden building peeking out through the trees, she let out a loud sob of relief. They had actually made it back to camp. Luke had stirred once or twice on their journey from the abandoned cabin. She'd stopped a few times to give him water and make sure he was still alive, anxiously holding her breath each time.

Glass stumbled through the trees and into the clearing. It was as she feared—the sounds of gunshots and the smoke that had stained the sky early this morning must have been coming from here. The entire camp looked like a war zone. Broken spears, bullet casings, ripped clothing, and pools of blood littered the ground. Some of the cabins were totally destroyed. Others looked as if someone had tried to set them on fire. Shell-shocked Colonists milled about, but she didn't recognize anyone. It was if she had returned to an entirely different place, and she felt a cold shot of fear. What had happened to her friends? Where was Wells?

Then the sound of a familiar voice sent a wave of joy through her.

"Glass?" Clarke called from the doorway of the hospital cabin. "Is that you? Oh, no—is that Luke?" Clarke ran to them. Wells popped his head out of the doorway and bolted after her.

Glass freed herself from the sled. Clarke dropped to her knees and began examining Luke.

"Glass!" Wells shouted as he reached her side and threw his arms around her. "Thank god you're back. Are you okay?"

Glass nodded, but then all the terror and loneliness and exhaustion crashed down on her at once. Now that they were safe, she finally allowed herself to feel everything she'd been holding at bay for days. Tears welled up in her eyes and spilled down her cheeks. Wells put his arms around her and held her while she sobbed.

"What happened to him?" Wells asked after a moment.

Glass sniffed and wiped her face with her hands. "We were in an abandoned cabin way out in the woods. It seemed safe. But then they"—her eyes filled with tears again at the memory—"attacked us. The Earthborns. Not Sasha's people, the other ones." A deeply pained look crossed Wells's face, but Glass knew now wasn't the time to ask what had happened.

"Luke went out to chase them off, but they hit him with a spear. I did the best I could, but I didn't have any way to stitch up the wound, and when I tried to bring him here, they attacked us again."

Wells swore under his breath. "Glass, I'm so sorry you had to face all that on your own."

"It's okay. We made it back alive, right?" Glass managed a smile through her tears.

"Let's get Luke inside," Clarke said firmly. Clarke and Wells quickly but gently lifted Luke, still on the sled, and raced into the hospital, Glass following closely behind. They entered the crowded room. Glass couldn't believe how many people were injured.

"What happened here?" she asked, astonished.

"Same thing that happened to you," Wells said grimly, "only bigger."

Glass raised her eyebrows, a million unasked questions on her lips. Wells could practically read her mind. "But don't worry. Things are changing for the better here. Rhodes is loosening his iron fist, finally. We're voting a new Advisory Council in tonight."

A tall, gray-haired man Glass had seen around Phoenix limped toward them. He nodded in her direction, then conferred quietly with Clarke. They spoke in somber tones, examining Luke's leg closely and listening to his pulse, heartbeat, and breathing. Clarke filled a syringe from a small glass vial and injected something into Luke's shoulder. Then she began to clean his wound and suture it up. He flinched in his sleep but didn't wake.

Glass stood by helplessly. She had been so focused on getting Luke back to camp that she hadn't allowed herself to think about what they might tell her once they got there. Clarke and the older man stepped over to her. She tried to read their faces for some kind of hint, but they were both totally impassive.

"Glass, this is Dr. Lahiri," Clarke began. "I trained under him on the Colony. He's an excellent doctor."

"Nice to meet you, Glass." Dr. Lahiri extended a hand, and Glass shook it numbly. She was torn between her need to know Luke's condition and her desperate wish not to hear any bad news. She swallowed and willed herself to remain calm, no matter what they said.

"You're very fortunate," Dr. Lahiri said with a smile. Glass let out a long sigh of relief. "He's going to be fine. But if you hadn't gotten him back when you did, he would have lost the leg. Or worse." Dr. Lahiri put a steadying hand on her shoulder. "You saved him, Glass. You should be very proud of what you did for him."

"It's going to be okay," Clarke said, pulling her into a hug. "We've given him a high dose of antibiotics, and we will monitor him carefully. He's a strong guy. And he's lucky to have you."

"I think it's the other way around," Glass said through her tears.

"Do you want to sit with him?" Clarke asked. "I can have someone bring you some food." Glass nodded and collapsed onto the bed beside Luke. She curled up next to him, her hand on his chest, feeling his heart beat under her palm. She listened to his soft breathing, steadier now.

For those few days in the cabin, she had thought all she needed in the world was Luke. She loved their little hideaway, their secret life, where no one bothered them and they could be alone all day long. But now, after she'd come so close to losing him and had tested herself in ways she didn't even know were possible, she felt different. Surrounded by these people who worked so hard and cared so much, Glass knew that she and Luke needed more than just each other. They needed their community. They were home.

CHAPTER *30*

Clarke

They walked in silence. The only sound was the crunch of leaves under their boots and the rustle of the wind in the trees. The leaves had all brightened into vibrant yellows, velvety oranges, and deep reds. If she didn't need to keep her eyes on the ground in front of her, Clarke could have gazed upward all day. Shafts of sunlight beamed down through the trees, showering Clarke, Bellamy, and Wells in a golden glow. The air was much colder than it had been just days ago, and it smelled spicy and rich.

Clarke shivered, wishing she had another jacket. They were stockpiling the pelts of every animal Bellamy and the other hunters brought back, but their collection was still small. It'd be a long time until they had enough fur for everyone.

Without a word, Bellamy wrapped his arm around her, holding her close as they continued through the woods. Max had sent word that Sasha's funeral would be held tomorrow, and they were on their way to Mount Weather.

Wells was walking a bit ahead of them, but Clarke knew better than to call out to him. With all the chaos and excitement of the past few days, Wells had barely had any time to process his losses, and he was clearly grateful for the chance to be alone with his thoughts. Yet that didn't stop her heart from aching for him as she watched him tilt his head back and scan the trees, as if expecting Sasha to drop down from one at any moment. Or perhaps he was taking in the sight of the brightly colored leaves, trying to accept the fact that he'd never get to comment on their beauty to Sasha, never see them float down and land in her dark hair. That was the worst part about losing someone—finding a place to store all the thoughts and feelings you'd otherwise share with them. When Clarke had believed her parents were dead, there'd been times when she was sure her heart would burst from trying to contain it all.

As they got closer to Mount Weather, however, Clarke jogged ahead to catch up to Wells. She slipped her hand into his. There were no words Clarke could offer to lessen Wells's pain. She just wanted to remind him that he didn't have to go through this alone. They were in it together.

They reached the Earthborns' village just before nightfall. Max opened his door on the first knock, as if he'd known it was them. His cabin was heartbreakingly neat. All the machine parts and half-finished devices that had littered his table had been cleared away and replaced with countless dishes of food. "Please, help yourself," Max said, gesturing toward the table. None of them felt much like eating, but they sat down with Max and told him what had happened since they'd left Mount Weather. He'd learned about the attack but hadn't heard about the Vice Chancellor calling a vote for a new Council.

"So, *you're* on the Council?" he said to Bellamy, smiling for the first time that evening.

Bellamy nodded, his face reddening slightly with embarrassment and pride. "Yeah, trust me, I was as surprised as you were when they voted me in, but hey, I'm just giving the people what they want."

"Wells was voted in as well," Clarke said. "Actually, he was elected first, way before Bellamy." She smiled from one to the other. Bellamy returned hers. Wells didn't.

"I'm very glad to hear that," Max said, placing his hand on Wells's shoulder. "Your people are lucky to have such a fine young leader. I know you're going to do your father proud, Wells. You're going to make all of us proud."

"Thank you," Wells said, meeting Max's eyes for the first time.

As they helped Max clear the few dishes they used, he told them the plan for tomorrow. "It's our custom to bury our dead at sunrise," he said. "We believe that dawn is the time of renewal. Endings and beginnings are inseparable, like the moment before dawn and the moment after."

"That's beautiful," Clarke said softly.

"After the Cataclysm," Max went on, "our ancestors suddenly had to struggle with the idea that light doesn't always follow dark. That one day, the sun really might not come up again. That's where the tradition started. It's gratitude, really, that the sun came up for one more day."

"I bet Sasha liked that idea," Wells said with a smile that didn't quite reach his eyes. Something in his face had changed, Clarke thought, as she studied him in the flickering candlelight. There was something harder in it, but wiser too. "Max, do you mind if I spend the night in the tree house?" Wells asked.

"Not at all. Though it'll be pretty cold out there."

"I'll be fine. I'll see you all in the morning."

"I'll walk you," Clarke said, rising to her feet. "I want to go check the radio room one more time, if that's okay."

Max nodded. "Of course."

Bellamy stayed behind to keep Max company, and both Clarke and Wells stepped into the night.

"Are you sure you're going to be okay out here by yourself all night?" Clarke asked as they approached the tree house.

Wells gave her a look she couldn't quite read, a mix of sadness and amusement. "I won't be by myself," he said quietly. "Not really."

Clarke didn't have to ask him what he meant. She squeezed his arm, then gave him a quick kiss on the cheek and left him with his memories.

She walked quickly to the Mount Weather entrance and disappeared down into the bunker, back to the spot that had become so familiar to her. She fiddled with the radio dials, her fingers working from muscle memory. She moved through the standard combinations she liked to try, starting with the one that had worked the day she heard her mother's voice. Her desire to hear it again was physical, a craving.

An hour passed with no results. Clarke wasn't even sure anymore whether the hiss and crackle of the radio were in her head or coming through the speaker. Her back ached from leaning over the console, and her head had started to throb. Bellamy was probably going to come looking for her any moment.

She stood up and stretched her arms over her head, then leaned from side to side and shook out her wrists. She knew she should shut down the system, but she wasn't quite ready. *One more time*, she told herself. *Just one.* Clarke sat back down and began to adjust the dials.

She was so focused on listening to the tonal shifts in the static that she almost didn't notice the clomping of footsteps in the hall until they were right outside the door. They were quick and heavy. *It must be later than I thought.*

Clarke spun around on her seat and looked out the door. "Bellamy?" she called. "Is that you? Max?"

There was silence in the hall as whoever was out there paused. Clarke rose from her chair, the hair on the back of her neck standing on end. Surely Bellamy knew better than to play a trick on her at a time like this, after all they'd just been through. Could the violent Earthborns have returned?

Two figures stepped into the room, one right behind the other. Before she knew what was happening, Clarke had been enveloped in two sets of arms, and she was crying tears of joy.

It wasn't Bellamy.

It was her parents.

———

The next morning, Clarke, Wells, and Bellamy stood side-by-side on a bluff overlooking a river, shivering in the cool darkness. Row after row of stones jutted from the ground, the names carved on them unreadable at this early hour. Max stood at the head of an empty grave, staring silently down into it. Sasha's body rested nearby, wrapped tightly in a shroud the color of the dirt that would soon envelop her.

Clarke had spent all night talking to her parents, if talking was really the right word to describe the stream of words, sobs, and laughter that had poured out for hours after their reunion. Her parents were both much thinner than they had been the last time she saw them, and there was a lot of gray in her father's new beard, but other than that they looked exactly the same.

When she'd finally managed to stop crying, Clarke's mom had unleashed a series of questions, asking about everything that had happened during Clarke's trial, her Confinement, and then her trip to Earth. But her father had barely managed a word. All he could do was smile and stare at Clarke, holding her hand as if afraid that she would vanish into the air at any moment.

She told them about being dragged from her cell, about the violent crash, about Thalia and Wells and Bellamy and Sasha. As Clarke spoke, she felt herself growing lighter. It was like she'd been carrying two sets of memories with her for a more than a year—the memory of what really happened and how she'd imagined her parents would react. And now, every time her father smiled or her mother gasped, more of that weight broke off. Clarke was desperate to hear about her parents' time on Earth, but by the time her mother had finished questioning her, it was nearly dawn.

They decided that it was best for her parents to stay

behind at Mount Weather rather than make a sudden appearance at Sasha's funeral. Although they'd gotten on well with the Earthborns, the memory of the first Colonists' betrayal was still too fresh.

Standing between Bellamy and Wells, Clarke felt a strange mix of elation and sorrow. That seemed to be how things worked on Earth. There was too much happening, too much to process ever to feel one emotion at a time.

She turned to the side to look at Wells, wondering if he felt the same way, or if his grief were all consuming.

The sun cracked the horizon line, sending orange and pink scouts racing ahead of it into the sky, as Max laid his only child to rest. In a hoarse voice that made Clarke's chest ache, he shared some of his favorite memories of Sasha, some of which prompted chuckles from the assembled Earthborns, while others left hundreds of eyes glistening with tears.

As he wiped a tear away from his own eye, Max gestured to Wells and asked if he wanted to say anything. He nodded, let go of Clarke's hand, and stepped forward to speak.

"The connection we feel to other people isn't bound by geography or space," Wells began. Although Clarke could see him trembling, his voice was strong and clear. "Sasha and I grew up in two different worlds, each of us wondering and dreaming about what was out there. I watched from above, never knowing for sure whether humans had survived here on Earth. I didn't know if we'd ever set foot on this planet again or if it would happen in my lifetime. And she looked up"—he pointed at the fading stars, still faintly visible in the dark blue sky—"and wondered if there was anyone up there. Had anyone survived the voyage into space? Had people managed to stay alive up there all these hundreds of years? For both of us, getting answers to our questions seemed so unlikely. But a million tiny forces moved us toward each other, and we got our answers. We found each other, even if it was just for a moment." Wells took a deep breath and exhaled slowly. "Sasha was my answer."

Clarke shivered, though this time, it wasn't from the cold. Wells had said it perfectly. Everything about their time on Earth had been so unlikely, so astonishing. And yet these months were more real to her than all the years she'd spent on the Colony. Clarke could barely remember what mornings were like without crisp air, dewy grass, and birdsong. She could no longer imagine working long hours under the medical center's fluorescent bulbs instead of helping her patients heal in the sunlight, like their bodies were designed to do.

She tried to picture what her future would have been like if none of this had ever happened—if she hadn't told Wells about her parents' experiments, if he hadn't reported them to his father, if she hadn't been Confined, if Wells hadn't loosened the airlock, if the hundred had never come to Earth—but the scene just dissolved into blackness. There was nothing there but the past. This was her life now.

Clarke watched as a few of Sasha's friends lifted her body and gently laid her into the ground. She whispered a silent good-bye to the girl who helped make Earth their home, who'd brought Wells back to life when he'd been stuck in darkness. He would be okay, Clarke told herself, as she watched him join the Earthborns in throwing handfuls of dirt into the grave. If she'd learned anything on Earth, it was that Wells was stronger than he realized. They all were.

Bellamy took Clarke's hand, then leaned in and whispered, "Should we go check on your parents?"

She turned to him and tilted her head to the side. "Don't you think it's a little early to be meeting my parents?" she teased. "After all, we've been dating less than a month."

"A month in Earth time is like, ten years in space time, don't you think?"

Clarke nodded. "You're right. And I suppose that means that I can't get mad at you if you decide to call it off after a few months, because that's really a few decades."

Bellamy wrapped his arm around her waist and drew her close. "I want to spend eons with you, Clarke Griffin."

She rose onto her toes and kissed his cheek. "Glad to hear it, because there's no going back now. We're here for good."

As she said the words, a strange sense of peace enveloped her, momentarily softening the pain of the day. It was true. After spending three centuries desperately trying to get back to Earth, they'd made it. They were finally home.

ACKNOWLEDGEMENTS

I am immeasurably grateful to the tremendously talented team at Alloy. Josh, your creative instincts are even more on target than your golf swing, and it's a pleasure to watch your brain in action. Sara, your intelligence and kindness create an environment where stories can flourish, and make me feel so very much at home. Les, thank you for believing in this project and using your special brand of magic to help it take flight.

Huge space hugs to Heather David, whose creativity and tenacity resulted in one of the best days of my life. And thank you to Romy Golan and Liz Dresner for turning my jumble of words into a gorgeous book.

I remain in awe of Joelle Hobeika, who dazzles me with her talent, storytelling prowess, and ability to make everything more fun. The same goes for Annie Stone, the smartest, most confidence-inspiring editor a writer could ask for.

A million thanks to the incredible team at Little, Brown for their hard work, creativity, and publishing acumen. And a special thank-you to my lovely editor Pam Gruber, whose sharp vision for the series kept us on course, and to my fabulous publicist, Hallie Patterson.

I also feel incredibly lucky to be working with Hodder & Stoughton, who've blown me away with their dedication and enthusiasm for The 100. In particular, thank you to Kate Howard, Emily Kitchin, and Becca Mundy for making a home for me (and a hundred teen space delinquents) across the pond.

As always, thank you to my wonderful, hilarious, supportive friends. I owe every single one of you a drink at Puck Fair/the Red Bar/Jack the Horse/Henry Public/Café Luxxe/Father's Office/Freud and all the other places I showed up to half asleep during various phases of writing lockdown. A special medal of meritorious service goes to Gavin Brown, who went above and beyond to keep this story "afloat."

I am also hugely indebted to Jennifer Shotz, whose talent and imagination shaped this story in countless ways.

Thank you to my family, especially my amazing,

inspirational, endlessly supportive parents, Sam and Marcia, who turned me into a writer. You are forgiven.

And last but not least, a very special thank-you to my readers whose enthusiasm makes me feel like the luckiest girl on Earth. #Bellarke forever.

Enjoyed this book?
Want more?

Head over to

CHAPteR 5

for extra author content,
exclusives, competitions – and lots
and lots of book talk!

Our motto is
'Proud to be bookish',
because, well, we are ☺

See you there . . .

 Chapter5Books 🐦 @Chapter5Books